If I
should die

Note for Librarians: a cataloguing record for this book that includes Dewey Decimal Classification and US Library of Congress numbers is available from the Library and Archives of Canada. The complete cataloguing record can be obtained from their online database at:
www.collectionscanada.ca/amicus/index-e.html
ISBN 1-4120-5254-8

TRAFFORD

Offices in Canada, USA, Ireland, UK and Spain
This book was published *on-demand* in cooperation with Trafford Publishing. On-demand publishing is a unique process and service of making a book available for retail sale to the public taking advantage of on-demand manufacturing and Internet marketing. On-demand publishing includes promotions, retail sales, manufacturing, order fulfilment, accounting and collecting royalties on behalf of the author.

Book sales for North America and international:
Trafford Publishing, 6E–2333 Government St.,
Victoria, BC v8t 4p4 CANADA
phone 250 383 6864 (toll-free 1 888 232 4444)
fax 250 383 6804; email to orders@trafford.com

Book sales in Europe:
Trafford Publishing (uk) Ltd., Enterprise House, Wistaston Road Business Centre, Wistaston Road, Crewe, Cheshire cw2 7rp UNITED KINGDOM
phone 01270 251 396 (local rate 0845 230 9601)
facsimile 01270 254 983; orders.uk@trafford.com

Order online at:
www.trafford.com/robots/05-0149.html

10 9 8 7 6 5 4 3 2 1

If I
should die

Tom Hampshire

"If I should die, think only this of me:
That there's some corner of a foreign field
that is forever England ... "

The Soldier
Rupert Brook

Tom Hampshire was born in Hampshire, England, where he spent his early years.

After completing his education he served for six years in the Fleet Air Arm branch of the Royal Navy. Leaving the service he made his living for several years as an artist before moving to Southern Africa, where he worked as an engineer on various mines in South Africa, Zambia and Namibia, finally settling in what was then Rhodesia. During the Rhodesian conflict he joined the reserve branch of the security forces where he served on border patrol and in the Marine Division. It was there that he acquired much of the material for his first book *If I should die*.

The war being lost, depending on which side you were on, he and a friend bought a thirty-foot boat in England and sailed around the world for four years; a trip bedevilled by pirates and hurricanes. They were finally shipwrecked off the coast of New Zealand and had to work there for a year to repair the boat.

They carried on to Australia where Tom's partner left him to return home. Tom continued on his own to South Africa and eventually back to Australia where he became an Australian citizen.

His latest adventure was to walk from John O'Groats, in the north of Scotland to Land's End in the south of England, a distance of 1440km, which took him forty-six days to complete. Tom has now retired to Lake Macquarie where he enjoys writing, painting and walking.

CHAPTER ONE

The place was a few miles east of the Nyanga Mountains, where the Pangwe valley is halved by the Pangwe River, which meanders between the hills and in so doing provides a borderline between Nyanga and Mozambique. It was hot, very hot, and the day promised worse to come. However the heat did not provide the main discomfort for the five men who walked slowly through the dense bush. Heads ranging continuously and feet placed carefully to avoid dry twigs that could snap and give warning to their ever-present enemy. No! It was the Mopani flies that flew into eyes, nostrils and ears, irritating, tormenting and above all distracting, that drove the men mad. They seemed to sense that the men were committed to a slow, steady movement, and basked in the immunity from a sharp slap that might catch the attention of a watchful enemy. They gathered in gyrating clusters around each head, drowning occasionally in the liquid corner of an eye or getting trapped in the moist nostril hair; flicking across eyes, distracting attention in spite of tense muscles and screaming nerves keyed up for instant reaction to danger. Each man cursed silently within himself as he moved forward. Guns were cocked and safety catches off. They watched from the sides of their eyes for any slight telltale movement of grass or tree that might herald the opening gambit of an ambush.

The men walked in a patrol 'box' formation, a kind of trapezium shape; with the right-hand lead scout a few metres ahead of the left-hand lead scout. The right-hand 'tail-end Charlie' walked thirty metres behind the lead scout and inside of his line of advance. In the centre was the 'stick' leader. This ensured the best possible chance of missing their buddies when they swung around to fire instinctively in answer to attack from any quarter.

The right-hand lead scout eased the camouflaged band away from the dial of his watch, taking care not to reflect the sun's rays, and quickly checked the time. Another sixteen minutes before everyone shifted around one position clockwise, thus relieving him of the worst position in the box, the position that usually got fired upon first.

1

A rocky hillock appeared palely through the trees to the left. The stick leader whispered just loud enough for his men to hear. "Watch that gomo!" The two left flankers moved their guns slowly and let them range over the rocks. But it was the right-hand scout who saw the movement first. He threw himself flat yelling. "Action left!" as he opened up, 'double tapping' to keep the terrorists' heads down and to give the rest of the stick a chance to get into cover.

John had the left rear position; he was eighteen years old and had to have an affidavit signed by his father before the army authorities would let him out on patrol. His father, himself a police reservist often out in the bush, realising the necessity for maximum effort against the overwhelming odds, reluctantly agreed. This was his first patrol and the Mopani flies had succeeded in their deadly task of diverting his concentration. Even as he paused as the warning sank in a bullet from the ubiquitous Russian manufactured AK hit him just below his right nipple and hurled him backwards to the ground, where he was partially hidden from view by rocks and shrub.

The rest of the patrol were laying down a carefully controlled blanket of FN fire, trying to find targets among the shifting shadows that flitted between the rocks above them. The sergeant, an old campaigner at thirty-two, called for a skirmish line and they ran up one at a time forming a straight line facing the Gomo.

"Up right flank. Fire!" The two men on the right ran forward five paces, dropped to the ground and proceeded to fire as the sergeant called the left flank forward.

"Up left flank! Up right flank! Prepare for final assault!" Two men fired whilst the other two changed magazines. Then-

"Final assault! Go!"

The four men rose as one and at a steady pace clambered up the hill checking each rocky cover as they reached it.

John Kelso, aged twenty-three years, should have been at a university following his father's footsteps. But he discovered, as did a lot of other men between the ages of eighteen and thirty-eight years that the country needed soldiers more than lawyers, accountants or business executives. He, like the sergeant, was already a seasoned fighter of many patrols and the sole survivor of two such ambushes. His swift reactions and total commitment to killing terrorists had saved his life on many occasions. Hearing a scuffle behind a rock and a voice calling, "don't shoot baas," another man might have had some doubts and given the benefit of compassion. Not so Kelso. He threw himself forward, twisting to fire. He saw the black man, a smile on his face, in the act of throwing his gun away. Blood streaked his face from the ricocheting bullet that had knocked him out. He started to speak as Kelso shot him low down in the belly, then twice more in a line up his body, like buttons on a cardigan. "That's for Johnny, you bastard," he muttered and brought his rifle butt down on the bloody forehead, smashing the bone level with the ears. He wiped the butt free of hair and blood on the man's shirt then without remorse or emotion continued up the hill.

The patrol reached the top in time to see the tail end of the gang disappearing amongst the trees and rocks half a kilometre away. They fired a few rounds after them and had the pleasure of seeing one more drop, and then the stick fanned out and carried out a three hundred and sixty degree scout around the ambush site.

"Barry!" Called the sergeant. Barry McEvoy came running. "Go back and see if you can do anything for Johnny". McEvoy scrambled away, the occasional bark of a rifle in his ears as the wounded were finished off. The time for taking prisoners for future politicians to release was long since past.

The cicadas shocked into silence by the ear-splitting pandemonium broke out once again into their endless, monotonous clicking. The mopani flies returned in their hordes to cover both the living and the dead and Africa closed its ranks.

Barry McEvoy slithered his way down the last few metres of the hill, arriving at the bottom with a shower of stones bouncing at his heels. He moved quickly to where he had last seen Johnny and finally found him half concealed behind a rock. He was lying on his back and blood covered most of the right side of his shirt and trickled thickly into the dust. He seemed to be unconscious but he opened his eyes as Barry started to undo his shirt buttons.

"I've had it, Barry!"

"Nonsense, laddie! We'll have you back at base camp in no time at all".

"But I can't breath!" He struggled for air as blood filled his lung cavity. He tried to cough but a spasm of pain threatened to

3

overwhelm him. Barry, realising that the boy was choking in his own blood, carefully raised his shoulders and rested them against a rock. Johnny cried out in pain but his breathing seemed easier.

As he pulled the shirt away from the wound Barry thought 'Christ! How did I get this bloody job?' He was not a medic and had only the same basic training as the others, which consisted of several two-hour lectures. But because he carried the medical kit for the stick he was referred to as 'Doc' on these occasions and was shown the deference and respect afforded a fully trained G.P. The wound was clean and round. Bubbles of blood frothed around the hole as air was sucked in and out as Johnny breathed. But Barry knew from past experience that this was the least of the trouble. It was always the hole the bullet made as it left the body that was fearful.

Opening his pack he withdrew the medical satchel and reaching in pulled out a packet of Tampax, one of which he halved with the sterilised scissors. Trying to make light of the situation he grinned at the boy. "We must be the only army in the whole world that goes into battle with Tampax and Nylon tights!" Johnny did not seem to hear. Barry wet the end of the tampon by dipping it into the blood and carefully plugged the wound. Johnny opened his mouth to scream but fell into a faint before a sound came. Blood welled up into his mouth and trickled down his chin.

Working quickly whilst his patient was mercifully unconscious Barry pushed the plug in and covered it with a sheet of polythene, then taped the lot in place with Elastoplast. Moving behind he slipped the shirt over the boy's head and removed it. The wound at the back was fearful, as he knew it would be. He stripped the covers off three more Tampax and packed them into the wound, picking out pieces of splintered bone as he did so and casting them away. Hearing a noise behind him he turned reaching for his FN but it was only the rest of the patrol returning.

"How is he, Doc?" asked the sergeant. McEvoy smiled inwardly to himself at the acknowledgment of his medical incompetence. He glanced quickly at Johnny, still unconscious, and shook his head.

"He'll be fine!" He said his looks belying his words. "You'd better get on to base and get a chopper here as soon as possible. He needs expert attention.

Without a word Frank Stevens who carried the radio walked over and sat down with his back to the sergeant, not bothering to remove the set. The sergeant extended the ribbon aerial as far as it would go and fiddled with the knobs for a few moments. Then reaching into the bulky pocket of his trousers he removed a map and a list of daily codes. Spreading them out he set about coding his message together with grid references. A few minutes later, having coded everything to his satisfaction, he picked up the handset.

"Echo Charlie One! Echo Charlie One! This is Sierra Papa One Five. Do you read me? Over!"

He waited a few moments then repeated the call. There was a crackling of static, then a voice answered.

"Sierra Papa One Five! This is Echo Charlie One. Receiving you strength three. Over!"

"Echo Charlie One! I have a message. Are you ready to receive? Over!"

"Sierra Papa One Five! Go!"

"Echo Charlie One! Shackles on!" Then in the current shackle code the sergeant gave his report and position, requesting a helicopter and a medic to evacuate the wounded man.

"Message received! Wilco! Out!"

Johnny opened his eyes. The sergeant ruffled his hair and told him he had called for a chopper.

"You'll be in base hospital before you know it. Okay? Take it easy son!"

"Can I have a drink, Barry?"

"He's not supposed to drink, is he?" asked Frank.

"That's only for stomach wounds, he can have a sip!" Said McEvoy reaching for his bottle.

"Use his!" said the sergeant. "You may need yours later."

Barry slipped his bottle back and reached for Johnny's, wondering as he often did how the sergeant remembered all the details from the army manual. 'I suppose that's why he's a sergeant', he thought.

The sergeant turned to Kelso. "John! Find the nearest spot around here where a chopper can set down and make sure it's clear". Kelso got up from where he was sprawled in the shade of a tree and moved off. He had seen a clearing about a hundred metres away, small by ordinary standards but big enough for army helicopter pilots, who were used to setting down in virtually impossible places. He found the spot and removing a panga from his pack set to work to clear away the few shrubs from the area.

It was nearly an hour before the chopper arrived, in that time Johnny had gone into delayed shock. His skin was clammy and his breathing was rapid and shallow. Sitting up of course did not help the situation. McEvoy reached into his pack and removed a sterile saline transfusion set and after the second attempt managed to push the cannula up into the vein, which had collapsed. Then he removed the needle leaving the plastic sheath in place. He watched the blood seep up the hollow tube and plugged in the drip set, adjusting the flow to a fairly fast rate. He hooked the bag onto a suitable projection, then taking plaster strips he strapped the tube to the boy's wrist.

The sergeant watched making no comment. Frank Stevens in the meantime had cut two poles about five centimetres in diameter and two metres long, and using a few lengths of bandages had made a passable stretcher onto which they carefully laid the boy. Barry walked beside him holding him in a sitting position and carrying the 'drip', as the sergeant and Stevens carried Johnny to the cleared site.

As the helicopter approached the sergeant and Kelso removed their forage caps and turning them inside out replaced them on their heads, showing the orange 'dayglow' pads sewn into the lining. These were intended to catch the pilot's eye. But the sergeant, ever doubtful as to their efficiency, opened his map and waved it from side to side. It was this indeed that caught the pilot's attention first. Swinging the chopper around in a tight circle the pilot, with no apparent difficulty, landed on the minute patch. The rotor blades clearing the surrounding trees by a mere six metres.

The sergeant ran towards the helicopter, swinging around to approach at the seven o'clock position. The pilot handed him a package. "New orders from base command," he yelled above the clatter of the engine. "And that's your replacement!" He added, jerking his thumb to the rear. The sergeant stuffed the package into his pocket and signalled the replacement to climb out, reaching in to haul out his pack.

"Get your wounded man in quickly, sergeant! We don't want to hang around on the ground too long."

The sergeant waved to his men to bring the boy over and began to turn away. Spinning around quickly, as an afterthought, he roared. "Remember your chopper drill!" McEvoy grinned to himself as the three of them followed the sergeant's track through the grass. They quickly loaded Johnny onto the stretcher rack at the rear, handing up the plastic bag to the medic already busy with his patient.

Calling their good-byes, they crouched forward and ran out from under the rotor blades. Not pausing for even a cursory look at the helicopter as it lifted off the sergeant called out. "Defensive positions! Three-sixty degrees! Move!"

The small group ran to positions around the clearing ready to fire on anyone taking a pot-shot at the chopper. He was pleased to note that the new man, albeit very young and so far unnamed, was quick off the mark, rifle ready. The chopper rose quickly, turned a half-circle and headed toward base camp over the Nyanga Mountains.

The sergeant watched it disappear into the distance and cursed softly. "The poor bastard! Only a kid! They seem to get younger every year." He forgot in his anger that he had been only seventeen when he first joined the army. Was it only fifteen years ago or was it fifty or five hundred years? He could hardly remember his childhood on a farm near the Wangwe Game Park where he had learned his bush craft, tracking game and hunting as he ran wild around the place. He only remembered endless patrols, dead friends, crippled friends, friends who had left this war-torn country to find more secure environments in other places. His mind raced ahead of the helicopter to the base hospital in Katari where, already alerted, every facility would be geared up to receive yet another casualty of this interminable war. The helipad alongside the hospital would have attendants ready to rush the boy to one of the operating theatres. Yes he would get every assistance if he arrived alive and not D.O.A. Dead on Arrival, as was often the case. He straightened his shoulders.

"Right! Close up … Patrol formation!" He growled. The patrol fell into a loose formation and headed off. The new replacement took Johnny's vacant position on the left.

About a mile further on the sergeant found what he was looking for, a flat-topped Acacia tree, commonly called a 'shade' or 'umbrella' tree. Such trees all over the country had provided shade for generations of tribal chiefs when an Indaba or talk-in with the elders of the tribe was called for.

"Okay, lads! Take a break whilst I check out these new orders." He said. "Frank! Leave that radio and go with John and scout about a bit." Frank gratefully shrugged out of the radio harness and flexed his shoulders luxuriously. He set the radio against the tree and set off with John. They would move out about a hundred metres and then circle three-sixty degrees and take up positions on opposite sides, covering.

The sergeant eased his pack and sank gratefully into the shade, reaching into his pocket for the package. The other two stretched out under a tree a few feet away, one hand ready on the F.N.'s by their side. The sergeant read the typed message once, then again, slowly. Reaching into his pocket he withdrew a map and his stubby forefinger moved rapidly along and up the co-ordinates, stopping at a point which he marked with a pencil. He measured off the distance.

"Hum! Twelve kilometres," he muttered. Putting the map away he looked up to where the replacement lay and called him over. "Roy! Come here a minute!"

The boy got up quickly with his rifle and moved over. The sergeant stuck out his hand, which the boy took.

"Welcome to the gang, Roy. Pleased to have you with us. The report here says you were the best of your intake. I like what I've seen so far. With a name like Van Houston you must be a Jarpie, is that right?"

"No, sergeant! My family moved up from South Africa to farm at Marimba. I was born here in Nyanga.

"So you're not new to the bush!"

"Not really!"said the boy modestly, "but I have a lot to learn."

"Any problem, let me know!" The sergeant nodded, dismissing him. He put his fingers to his lips and sent out the high pitched chattering call of a weaver bird. It was answered on both sides. A few minutes later the two scouts moved back into camp.

The sergeant looked at them. "Anyone know the Chesterfields? They farm about twelve kilometres north east of here."

"Yes! I know them!" said John. "Henry, Louise, and two girls, Lisa and Caroline. They had a farm up near Kanyemba on the Zambian border. When the trouble started he sold out and bought this place. He reckoned it was safer but of course that was before Mozambique went. Why?"

"We've been told to check the place out. The neighbours say their Agric-Alert has been out of action since yesterday afternoon. Probably nothing but we'll push on fast. Be extra wide awake. Let's go!" He set his compass and shouldered his pack. The others prepared and moved off, taking up their positions.

Kelso looked up at the sun. He did not have to glance at his watch to know it was past one o'clock in the afternoon. So much had happened that it seemed incredible that the day was only halfway through. It would be dark by seven o'clock. If they wished to reach the farm today they could not afford to loiter. They were bound to be offered supper, most farming families liked to have a patrol stop off for a while. It was a pleasant thought.

CHAPTER TWO

There had been three changes of lead scout, which once again put Barry McEvoy in the hot spot and it was he who slowly came to a halt, left hand raised. The rest of the patrol stopped immediately, sinking onto their heels, where they were hidden by the long grass. Barry signalled the sergeant who moved cautiously across. Pointing to one side, Barry wrinkled his nose. It was not necessary. The sergeant also could recognise the smell of death that hung heavily on the still air. He would have known anyway, without the sawing drone of the thousands of flies that enveloped the dead man and swarmed in heaving black masses on the eyeless sockets and pools of dark congealed blood surrounding the body.

The rest of the patrol came up to where Barry and the sergeant stood. Roy van Houston took one look at the bloated, tortured body and paled under his tan. Sergeant Wilson looked up.

"Roy! Get under cover of those trees," he said, pointing, "and keep us covered!" Roy moved off gratefully. Barry glanced up at the sergeant, a speculative look in his eye.

"What do you think, John?" Asked the sergeant looking at Kelso, his hand sweeping the whole area. Kelso moved around the body not looking at it but into the grass and dust which was heavily trampled. He took his time and the sergeant waited patiently, appreciating Kelso's talent as a tracker, which on occasion surpassed his own considerable knowledge. Kelso finally turned to the body and appeared to be counting. At last he looked up.

"I'd say there were about twenty-five plus, mostly wearing boots, which would suggest they were well equipped and trained. A few were wearing 'tackies', or as our English brethren would say, 'plimsoles'; probably eight or ten; possibly recruits. They came from over there!" He pointed towards Mozambique. "And they are heading in the same direction as we are. This character!" He pointed at the corpse, "probably worked for Henry, a farmhand. He must have stumbled upon the terrorists by accident. They gouged his eyes out and systematically bayoneted him. I counted fifty-eight punctures. I think they kept him alive for possibly two hours judging by the amount of blood he's lost. If he'd died quicker there would have been much less blood." He glanced up with a look that asked how his interpretation tallied with the sergeant's.

"How long ago?"

Kelso studied a clearly defined boot imprint; sifted some fine dust through his fingers, glanced once again at the body.

"About twenty-four hours!" He said finally.

"That tallies with my impression too," said the sergeant. "I think the quicker we get to the farm the better."

They moved into the open farm land, quicker now in the coolness of the late afternoon and topping a low rise they looked down onto the homestead that nestled cosily amongst the trees, with sprawling outbuildings scattered around. At first glance everything seemed normal enough, except for the lack of movement. No farmhands were doing the million and one things that have to be done around a farm. There were no animals or livestock of any kind, just a brooding silence. Kelso pointed over to one side, to the village that had housed the labour force and they worked their way down the hillside, taking advantage of any cover that presented itself. Entering the village they were appalled.

The men, apart from the latest recruit, had seen the same senseless slaughter on numerous other occasions yet still could not fully understand the terrorists' total inhumanity towards their own kind when they chose to work for the white man. Bodies lay everywhere, twisted and grotesque in their agonised death throes. Most had eyes gouged out. One man, obviously the chief, had been virtually skinned alive, and his genitals had been hacked away. His wife, lying beside him had been raped many times and her stomach opened up from the breast to pubic. Her face was congested and dreadful to look upon. At which stage she had died it was difficult to judge. Hanging from the Indaba tree in the centre of the village was a horrifying fruit of mutilated children. They had been hung by their feet from the branches and cleaved in two by machetes. Three of the women had their stomachs opened and foetuses removed from the womb then skewered to the mother's breast with bamboo sticks. Most of the men and boys had their genitals torn away and long strips of bamboo were driven up the anus, to protrude sometimes through the neck or chest. Charred bodies lay in the burnt 'kias'. It was impossible to tell whether they had been burnt alive or thrown in after being tortured to death.

Barry muttered to nobody in particular. "And these are the bastards who want to run the country, what a fucking joke!" But no one was laughing.

They moved up to the farmhouse. The homestead was typical of all the farmhouses in the country at this time. Whether large or small, beautiful or ugly, they all had one thing in common, a three metre tall, heavy wire mesh fence that surrounded the house and outbuildings. It was topped by barbed wire set out at an angle with floodlights mounted at each corner, these were operated by a switch in the house. Across the road that led to the house were heavy gates, chained and padlocked. The house itself was sand-bagged up to window level and had grenade mesh above that. It was difficult to appreciate that the farming community had lived under these conditions for many years, knowing that at any moment of the day or night a bursting mortar shell, or a burst of automatic fire, could be the harbinger of a merciless attack, or that a husband could be ambushed as he left to visit his fields or to give directions to his labourers. Wives and children ran the gauntlet when visiting friends or going into town to do the shopping in the farm's mine-proofed Landrover. No wonder so many had left, heartbroken but happy to be alive. Those that stayed on were a special breed, and there were very few of them left.

Barry checked the gates, they were locked, but a hundred metres to the right a section of the fence had been cut away and hung inwards, leaving a gap about a metre across. With Kelso and the sergeant covering, the other three ran through the gap and took up defensive positions. The other two followed.

Rapidly they advanced on the house, sure that if any terrorists were around they would have been fired on by now. The outbuildings had been ransacked, and the food store was a jumbled mess of broken sugar bags, flour, tins, and tumbled shelves. On the counter facing the door was a severed head, lips peeled back in rictus from large white teeth. The body lay half hidden behind a pile of broken provisions. Ligaments, veins and windpipe stuck out of the blackened stump like limp spaghetti. Barry made a silent vow never to eat the stuff again.

Reaching the house, the sergeant signalled van Houston and Kelso to circle around the back whilst he, McEvoy, and Stevens moved cautiously onto the stoep and through the open door into the lounge.

The sight that met them brought a choking sob from McEvoy and a now familiar, gut-aching anger, terrible in its intensity, to the sergeant. Stevens stepped back onto the stoep sucking in great globs of air.

The girl, it must have been Lisa, was spread-eagled on the wooden floor, six inch nails had been driven through the palms of both hands. She had been raped many times, viciously. The skin between her legs and across her stomach was raw and caked with blood, blackened, and now crawling with flies.

As was normal with these savages, once they had finished with a woman, the stomach had been ripped open with a panga. But to the sergeant, the most horrifying thing of all was the face, set in death, showing the most awful pain and horror. From the child's eye sockets protruded kitchen knives that had been hammered deep into the head.

They searched the other rooms and found nothing but disorder and chaos. Drawers and cupboards had been ransacked and the contents strewn around in piles. Opening the door onto the back stoep they discovered Kelso, white faced and visibly shaken. Van Houston was doubled over retching uncontrollably. McEvoy, following close on the heels of the sergeant, took one look and began muttering over and over, like a continuous chant. "Oh my God! Oh Mother of God!" Stevens covered his eyes and began to cry softly.

Sergeant Wilson felt a cold sweat break out all over his body and he shook with the depth of his anger.

"Roy! Frank!" He snapped. "Check the rest of the outbuildings. Barry! Look in the bedrooms; see if you can find any blankets to cover these people up. Come on, move!" They gladly turned away to do his bidding. He looked towards Kelso who seemed to have aged in those last few minutes.

"What sort of bastards are they who could do that to anyone," he asked, "for whatever reason? In war people get killed, that's accepted. But to do this, they must have actually enjoyed it. How can supposedly civilised human beings sink to this fucking depth?"

The sergeant again took in the scene that would be forever etched on his brain. The woman, she must have been the mother, had been progressively hacked to pieces. Eyes, ears, nose, lips, eyelids and breasts lay scattered around. Feet, hands, arms and legs. Her agony did not bear contemplating. In the garden, nearby, a mortar shell had landed close to a metal rotary clothes line, severing the central steel pole about five feet above ground level. Impaled on this was the elder daughter. The jagged shaft entered between her legs and protruded from her neck, pushing her head over at a grotesque angle, her pretty blonde hair mercifully covering her face. Both hands, hacked off, were missing.

McEvoy arrived with a handful of blankets and they set to work covering the bodies. By the time they had finished darkness was descending rapidly, as it does in Africa. There is no lingering twilight as in European countries, rather a sharp, quick division. 'Just as you would expect,' thought Kelso, thinking politically. 'No gradual change, no shades of grey, just a quick switch from white to black. Light to darkness? Perhaps light to grey? Who knows! It seems inevitable that the whites will be forced out eventually. Hadn't they forced themselves in initially? Carved an Eden in the wilderness against the wishes of the incumbents. He had heard all the justifications and had believed them, because he was born here, as was his father and his grandparents. Does birth establish a right? Could the enforced juxtapositioning of nations be reversed? He thought not. Canada returned to the Eskimos? America to the Indians? Australia to the Aboriginals?

Europe and South America were a tangled mess of upheavals that could never be reconciled. Even the last world war had redefined boundaries. The Israelis had created a state at the expense of others. European and Asian boundaries had writhed in and out like the tortuous lines of a conga. In the past the world map changed constantly, might was right and few questioned it. Now, he realised, the world had entered an era of righting past wrongs, salving national consciences, overreacting because of guilt complexes. Political considerations overrode people; what are a few thousand white deaths when you are cleaning the national slate? Those pioneers and settlers of yesterday who created empires and won the gratitude of their nations are the embarrassment of today. No native alive today could have done more for his country than had his family. Assuming that they had to be brought into the twentieth century, it had certainly been done with a fraction of the pain experienced by other developed countries. No babies working in coal mines, no industrial revolution —'.

John's thoughts were interrupted at that point.

"John!" Called the sergeant. "Check the switches over by the Agric-Alert. See if the security lights are working."

John tried several switches before he saw one marked 'generator'. He made the switch and the lights throughout the house and around the security fence glowed and then brightened.

"Put those house lights off!" Roared the sergeant. John tried various switches and the house plunged back into darkness, leaving the area outside the security fence bathed in light. From the rear of the house came the steady throb of a diesel generator.

"I wonder why they didn't burn everything like they usually do?" Barry asked.

"Probably two reasons," muttered the sergeant. "One, They wanted the whites to see what they had done to frighten them off, and two, they were still here this morning, heard the helicopter coming for Johnny and probably thought it was looking for them and took off quickly."

"And Mister Chesterfield?"

"Dead I hope! The poor bastard."

Once again the sergeant pulled out his note book and code sheets and working rapidly coded a message which he sent back to base.

"The opposition have got so many listening posts around our borders now it's hardly worth the effort to code everything. They break our frigging codes just as soon as we use them," he said, adjusting the tuning on the radio.

"Stand by Sierra Papa One Five!" The static crackled eerily around the darkened stoep. There was a pause.

"Sierra papa One Five! Your orders are to stay at that loc., you will have cyclone support at first light. Do you copy? Over!"

"Echo Charlie One! Copied! Out!"

But before the sergeant could break the contact the radio burst into life again with another message.

"Sergeant! I thought you might like to know that your detail of this morning arrived D.O.A. I'm sorry. Out!"

"I'm sorry too," snapped the sergeant stabbing the 'off' switch viciously. The radio sank into silence.

Barry, hearing the last message, rose and walked slowly out into the garden and stood with his head bowed, hands in pockets, a figure of dejection. He felt the sergeant's hand on his shoulder.

"Barry," he said, "you did your best. None of the rest of us could have done as well. Believe me, every one of us appreciates your efforts." Coming from the sergeant, Bob Wilson that meant a lot, and Barry recognised the fact and was grateful.

"The operation was successful but the patient died," he murmured. The sergeant punched him lightly on the arm and walked away. Always the right thing at the right time thought Barry. Tough, sympathetic and understanding. His admiration for Bob Wilson was of long standing, well placed and durable.

Without any actual orders being given they moved out into the garden and stacked their packs around the trunk of a large jacaranda tree. Nobody fancied the echoing stillness of the house with all its horrors.

"Frank! You're a dab hand at cooking. Do you feel up to rummaging around the kitchen and knocking us up some scoff? Some hot food and tea would do us all a world of good. But don't hesitate to say no if you don't feel up to it."

"Ok, sergeant! I'm alright now!"

"I'll give him a hand," said van Houston quickly.

"Good lads, but cover up the windows before you put the lights on and switch them off as soon as you've finished."

"John?"

"Yes, sarge!"

"Take the first watch! They're not likely to come back, but we don't want to take any chances. Barry! You take over from John. I'll take over from you. Ok?"

"Fine!"

They all realised why the older men were on first. If there were to be an attack it would probably be in the early evening. That was the usual terrorist pattern. It gave them time to get away before daylight when the security forces could start tracking them. John Kelso moved off, his rifle seemed to be an integral part of him.

Roy and Frank moved quickly through the lounge, eyes averted from the blanket swathed shape vaguely discernible in the moonlit room. They passed down the passage and into the kitchen where they discovered that blackout curtains had already been fitted, these they drew across the window. Switching on the light they cleared a space amongst the chaos and set to work. Tins of meat and fresh vegetables were scattered all over the floor and the men took their pick.

"Wonder why they left all this lot?" said Roy.

"Probably couldn't carry any more once they'd loaded up at the store."

"Probably!"

They made a large pot of stew and a good strong brew of tea. Apart from Roy none of them had eaten a hot meal for five days. They ate ravenously, the sergeant taking over the guard duty from Kelso whilst he ate.

A while later Barry stood up and tucking his F.N. under his arm walked around the corner of the house to where John stood in the shadows. They talked quietly for a while then John, handing over the guard, walked back to the camp, removed his boots and stretched out on his sleeping bag.

"Ah, what more can man want? A full belly and a warm bed, the stars above and good companions around and the world's my oyster!"

"Hmm! Waxing poetic, John? Wouldn't you rather be at home with your family, knowing that tomorrow you would wake up to a hot breakfast and then be off to the university?" Asked the sergeant.

"I guess so, Bob, but a full belly does that to me. One good experience always takes precedence over a dozen bad ones. You look back on your life and what do you see. Not the sad or tragic things that happen but the times when as a kid you visited the seaside at Beira or Durban, or the time your father took you sailing. All the pleasant highlights. We have a tremendous in-built facility for convenient forgetfulness. You will remember the time your auntie gave you a piece of sugared ginger and yet forget the dozen times she cuffed you around the ear for being noisy."

"I'll go along with that," said Roy, "you do only think of the good things that happen."

Frank broke in. "You're a university man, John. What do you think will happen when the stuffin' blacks take over?"

"You're sure they are going to are you"

"Aren't you?"

"Steady on, Frank, I'm studying law, not politics."

The sergeant grinned. "I thought that was all university students did study these days."

"If you are thinking of the black students you could be nearly right!" Said John. "Very few seem to go in for medicine or any of the sciences. They seem to prefer politics, sociology or similar subjects. I suppose the minister of labour should liase closer with the education department, so that with forward planning, they could anticipate the needs of commerce and industry and hope to enrol students to fill the vacancies that will be occurring at the time they graduate. After all, how many political science graduates does a country like this need?"

"As far as I'm concerned, none! We've got enough causing trouble right now."

"I agree with that, sarge!" Said Frank. "But, John, shit! Being in a university you must have a better idea than we have."

"Frank! That's another misconception. University students have no special access to 'inside' information, neither are they clairvoyant. However there is a greater tendency towards debate and discussion where a whole variety of points of view are presented and argued over. So I suppose we do tend to get a fair idea of the general consensus of opinion. For years people have tried to categorise the differences between blacks and whites but neither can be pigeon-holed because within each group there are an infinite number of variables. We tend to talk about blacks being easily swayed to violence by agitators, but think back, did you ever see films of the crowds of whites being harangued by Hitler or Mussolini? It has been argued that if the races integrated and interbred all racial hatreds would disappear. Yet look at Mozambique! Black men married white girls and white

Portuguese men married black girls. There was no segregation there. Yet when the country was overrun there was still killing on racial lines and whites were burnt alive in their cars, some thrown off the tops of buildings.

"But, John!" Frank protested. "We've lived together for years, generations, without all this trouble. What went wrong? We always treated our servants well. If they wanted to change things why didn't they use peaceful means, demonstrations, petitions? That's how we would have done it. It's hard to know just what they do want, they seem to be killing indiscriminately, whites as well as their own."

John thought for a while. "African aspirations generally defy our logic because we ascribe our thought processes to them, when really their culture and environment must influence their thinking, as indeed our history and experiences have influenced ours. Throughout history strong nations have subjugated weaker ones, usually by force, making no effort to understand their culture or to build on what was there. We force an abstract God down their throats, eradicate their culture, violate their women, enslave them in various ways and then postulate how good we are to them. We assume they will welcome our democratic systems. We impose a British style of government, because we want it, but it doesn't work in Africa. Their tribal system usually operates within a dictatorship. What they want is a benign dictator, unfortunately you very seldom find a benign dictator among whites and the same goes for blacks. We in our arrogance assume that they welcome our organisational skills, our democracy, our legal system, our ambition and our haste. But in every society people find their own level. Rules are put in place and a pecking order established that suits them. They have their own gods and rituals, and for them they work. We tend to remove their historical stability and replace it with something that means nothing to them. They don't feel it or understand it. They have generally felt unsettled and abused, they watch with envy our wealth and decry our waste. We failed to take cognisance of their aspirations and as the controls established over generations by their own culture diminish so inequality takes root, and inequality is the blood brother of envy and a by-product of envy is violence. It doesn't always have to be structured violence. It is often violence for violence sake, to hurt, redress and acquire, to even out the disparities. After all Frank, the less you have the less you have to lose. Even life itself is poor coinage if your burden is too heavy.

"But we've given them so much, John, education, hospitals, work and a whole lot more".

"You are quite right, Roy, but the only right way to give is when the recipient is unaware that he is being given anything, also he should have a choice as to whether he wants the gift or not."

"That may be but they are a fuckin' sight more intelligent now than they were a hundred years ago".

John laughed. "You are getting confused between intelligence and education. They can exist with nature far better than most whites. They have lived off their intelligence for thousands of years. I sometimes think that most of the things we teach them they could well do without".

"But we have been very good to them, do you think they would be better off under a black government?"

"Roy! Even under the most tyrannous of regimes people find their own level of accommodation and life goes on. You must remember that the struggles and intrigues are always initiated by those at the top of the heap, those in power or aspiring to be in power. In any conflict the peasants are pawns with no power to change events, no say! The wars rage around them and they die, mostly without knowing why they die. If the ordinary people in the world could choose they would choose peace, but they have no choice, they are manipulated in the same way that a stockbroker manipulates share markets, with possibly less emotion. What a wonderful world it would be if politicians and power brokers had to fight the battles instead of coercing the populace by nationalistic jingoism and corruption. The displaced and disenchanted women, children and old men sit on their bundles, cold, hungry and despairing in their grief. Do you think they care who the hell runs the country? They should know that in spite of the promises, the assurances and the entreaties their lot will not improve one iota.

You see, Roy, whites opened a base in the Cape to replenish ships heading east for trade. There was nothing altruistic about it. They settled the area and moved northwards—it was a land grab, mainly for the minerals that lay under that land. They pushed the natives off their land. Would you like it?"

"No I guess I wouldn't but it was a long time ago. Several generations of whites have been born here. We have lived here as long as any living black, and after all, John, there were no countries as such with clear-cut demarcation lines only tribal homelands. They took what they wanted from other tribes, much the same as we did! We happened to be the better fighters!"

"That's not quite true either, Roy. The Zulus knocked the stuffing out of the might of the British army at Isandhlwana. The only reason they lost against the Boers at Blood River and the Brits at Rourkes Drift was because of the superiority of the gun over the spear. We could argue all night about what we have given them, but the whole point is did they want it? They want us out, and the Russians and Cubans are helping them to do just that!"

"It's all very interesting, John", said the sergeant. He stretched and flexed his muscles. "But that isn't our problem right now"! He said with a grin, "all we have to do is carry out our orders until we are told otherwise. I suggest we all try to get some sleep. We'll be away early. We've got a long day ahead of us tomorrow." The sergeant moved to his sleeping bag.

By the time the upper limb of the morning sun had lifted over the trees, the patrol had eaten a substantial breakfast and cleared a landing site for the expected helicopters. They stood around now spaced in a rough circle about fifty yards across, waiting to cover the choppers when they should arrive. They did not have long to wait. 'Must have left in virtual darkness,' thought the sergeant as he indicated the landing pad.

The two helicopters came in fast, landing almost together. The clatter of their rotors shattered the early morning peace, then all was quiet.

The preliminaries were soon over and Sergeant Wilson took Colonel Jameson and Captain White into the house and onto the back stoep. Hardened as they were, both men were deeply moved. Behind them came two police inspectors, a photographer, and two medical orderlies with large plastic bags. When the others had finished, the medics began the unenviable task of packaging the bodies ready for transportation. They did not attempt to remove the impaled girl but sawed the pole off using a hacksaw from the workshop.

For over an hour the army officers and police inspectors questioned the sergeant. At last the sergeant stood up, dusting off his trousers.

"Sir!" He said, addressing the Colonel. "Their spoor is still pretty warm. We'd like to get after the bastards. We reckon they hung around here until yesterday mid morning. They're cocky, and I don't think they will be moving too fast, but the border is only twenty five miles away."

"Any ideas as to what happened to Mr. Chesterfield?"

"Well, sir, we've studied the tracks and we think he is being dragged along with them. There are scuff marks and bloody footprints."

The colonel and the captain stood up, one after the other they shook the sergeant's hand. "Sergeant, we know your reputation, it's second to none as a soldier and a tracker. If you can catch up with these murderers herd them down to a position about here!" He unfolded a map and pointed to a place where the river between Nyanga and Mozambique shallowed to a fording point. "I'll organise a stop line with Number Three Commando. Good luck and don't get into any trouble." He smiled, and they all moved away to the helicopters.

"I'll send a detail back to bury the villagers," he said. They took off quickly and were soon out of sight.

"Right, men! Let's go!" Said the sergeant. The patrol moved out quickly through the gap in the fence and were soon swallowed up by the thick bush.

CHAPTER THREE

The patrol pushed on. The trail was easy to follow, signposted as it was with empty food cans, beer bottles, and packets of all descriptions. Sergeant Wilson was delighted to see it. It showed a lack of discipline and a gross overconfidence. The terrorists obviously considered themselves well away from any possible pursuit.

It was mid-afternoon when John, scouting well ahead, fell back on the rest of the group to inform the sergeant that he could smell something burning ahead. The patrol moved into a skirmish line and ranged ahead slowly and cautiously. Moving from cover to cover, listening for any untoward noise, sniffing. It was sometimes possible to smell a crowd of terrorists up to two hundred metres downwind, the smell was quite distinctive and generally objectionable. About a quarter of a mile further on they stood at the edge of a small kraal. The two pole and dagga huts were still burning just above ground level. The mealie field to one side had burnt for a short time and extinguished itself on the damp stalks. On the edge of the fire-blackened area lay a woman and her two children, all had multiple bayonet wounds. The patrol scattered around the clearing and it was Kelso who first saw a movement in the grass about fifty yards from the burning Kias. He was about to open fire when a bloody hand was raised momentarily and flopped back. Running forward, rifle at the ready for instant action, he found an African, badly wounded and obviously dying. The sergeant ran up at John's call.

"Who did this to you, Madala?" he asked. The old man struggled to speak. "Mad dogs baas, mad dogs from over there." He gestured towards the border.

"How long ago did they leave? We need to know. They have killed many of your people and ours!"

The man choked and fell back, his life ebbing. The sergeant shook him gently.

"Madala, we must know. How long?" He struggled to speak, finally raising a hand, three fingers extended.

"Three hours, Madala?" The old man nodded, then, "*bulala*

inyoga baas!" He fell back, dead. "Yes old man, we'll kill the snakes for you, and for the others."

John looked at the sergeant. "We've made up a lot of time, sarge, but if they are still three hours ahead of us, we don't have much hope of catching them this side of the border, unless they run into the stop line."

"They won't do that now, they're too far north. They must know of another crossing point. It's eight miles to the border and they must be nearly there by now. Let's press on, if necessary we'll chase them all the way to Beira!"

They moved off again, John ranging ahead, and for once luck was on their side. They had been on the move for just over an hour when John virtually fell right into a clearing, fortunately deserted. The grass around was flattened and blobs of mealie meal had been dropped around the remains of a fire. "Well I'll be damned!" Said Barry. "How sloppy can you get?" They even stopped to make mealie pap."

The bottom of the fire was still warm to the sergeant's hand when he scraped the charred wood away with his boot.

"Well, mealie meal is their staple diet. They hate going without it, but I would have thought they'd have waited until they got back into Mozambique." He said. "They can only be about an hour ahead of us now and just about at the border."

They pressed on faster to make the river before darkness made tracking impossible.

Darkness was falling fast as they caught the first glimpse of water through the trees. As they drew nearer they could see the water racing madly over a rocky shelf, making a difficult but possible crossing point. The trail led down to it. With his binoculars, the sergeant could see clearly where a large group had climbed the bank on the far side.

"Stuff it!" He said. "We'll have to camp here and pick up the trail again at first light. What a pity, so near and yet so far. Pull back a bit and find somewhere to sleep. I don't have to tell you, but I will, no fires, no lights, no smoking. Roy, you're first watch, then Frank, Barry, John, and me last, Okay?"

They withdrew fifty yards into a deep patch of bush and set out their sleeping bags. John passed around thick slices of biltong, sun-dried beef, known to the Americans as jerky, which they cut into thin strips and chewed. No one talked above a whisper, knowing how voices carried in the stillness of the night. Barry was on guard and had walked quietly down to the river, watching the far bank from the deep shadows amongst the trees. As he stood there speculating on their chances of catching up with the terrorist gang something attracted his attention at the outer periphery of his eye. He turned his head slowly from side to side, trying not to look directly at the spot. Yes there it was again. He moved quietly back into camp and shook the sergeant who rose quickly and followed Barry back to the river. The rest of the patrol, with an instinct born of many such incidents, lay fully awake, rifles in hand, waiting.

They were back in a few minutes. "Ok, lads, we can see their fire. We know where they are. We are going after them. Leave your heavy packs here. Just bring rifle, ammo, knives, and water bottles. Make sure nothing squeaks, rattles or bangs. You've got five minutes."

They waited in the brush opposite the causeway.

"John! Roy! When that big cloud covers the moon, you two cross over. Roy, hold on to John's belt and for Chrissake don't slip off those rocks. We'll keep you covered, you cover us when we cross. Right, off you go!"

The two stepped out carefully onto the slippery rock, inching their way forward, feeling for each foothold before transferring their weight. Towards the centre the water reached up to their thighs, swirling around them, forcing them to lean into the current that threatened to push them over the edge into the dark swirling waters below. A heavy branch suddenly appeared, moving fast, bearing down on them. At the last moment it caught on a rock and swung away. Roy let go his breath and struggled on. They floundered up the far bank and slid into the darkness beneath the trees. Nothing stirred. A few minutes later they were joined by the rest of the patrol. The sergeant led the way cautiously, the rest followed in single file. From time to time he stopped to peer closely at the luminous hand of his compass which he had set before crossing the river, lining up his course with the occasional flash from the terrorists' fire. He cocked his head from side to side, listening carefully, then raised his head and sniffed slowly and carefully, weighing up the various smells drifting on the cool night air. They had gone about three-quarters of a kilometre when he held up his hand and signalled them to wait. Leaving his FN with John he moved ahead, his boots making no noise on the leaf-covered ground. He smelt it again. Cigarette smoke. Lying flat on the ground he peered between the trunks of the trees trying to catch a movement or silhouette against the vague lightness of the sky. Then he found what he was looking for, the soft glow of light off to his right. He moved closer. He was within three metres and could smell the rank odour of the man who was sitting on a fallen tree, his back to the sergeant. Wilson moved forward, then froze as the man's head tipped back sharply. He thought he had been discovered. Then he saw the bottle glint in the moonlight and breathed a sigh of relief. Slipping his knife out of its sheath he raised himself into a crouching position and waited until the guard put the bottle to his lips once more. Then, under the cover of liquid noises, he moved forward, rammed the bottle with savage force down the man's throat whilst his knife sliced deeply between his ribs and into his heart. He lowered the body to the ground. He could see the terrorists' camp fire about one hundred metres ahead.

The patrol inched itself towards the light, arriving within thirty metres of the clearing without seeing any signs of other guards. They had a clear view of the camp and counted thirty men, either around the fire or sitting in the shadows. There was no need for silence, the terrorists were so confident of their security and so cock-a-hoop with their victories that they laughed and joked, slapping their legs as they danced around, drinking from bottles or stuffing food into their mouths. On one side was piled loot stolen from the farm. From where he lay Barry could see a case of Johnny Walker as well as cases of beer. On top of all the provisions he could see clothes, a yellow dress that must have belonged to one of the girls, coats, and trousers. In front, heartbreaking in its incongruity, was a cloth doll, looking at the Bacchanalian scene with smiling innocence.

On the far side of the fire, reflected in the dancing light of the flames, hung Henry Chesterfield, if indeed it was he. He was suspended from the branch of a tree by his arms which were tied above his head. His toes traced a bloody pattern in the dust as he swung gently from side to side. He was naked and his body was streaked with blood and dirt, as was his head where it rested on his chest. He could have been dead, but he was not.

As they watched one of the younger blacks pushed himself up from his position near the fire and picked something up off the ground. Moving towards the old man, he made a comment to the others which they found hilarious and set them rolling around the ground shrieking with laughter. He stood in front of the swinging figure and shouted into his face. There was no response. He hit him in the mouth and Henry opened his eyes with great effort. The black brought both hands forward, lunging at the man's chest and stomach, drawing his hands downwards towards the genitals. Whatever the objects were they gouged several grooves down the body and blood welled up, filling the grooves and running down the pale skin. His efforts evoked little reaction from the tortured man. The black shouted again, then said something to the old man who struggled to focus his pain-racked eyes onto the objects that were now lightly brushing his manhood. He was so exhausted and in so much pain that it took a while before he recognised the objects for what they were. His reaction was totally unnerving. His eyes opened wide and a horrifying scream broke from the depths of his throat. His body jerked with demoniacal energy in a frantic effort to pull his body away. His face was congested and foam collected around his mouth. His tormentor held the trophies high, and his peals of laughter joined in with the rest.

The sergeant's bullet caught him a few centimetres below his armpit, smashing its way through the rib cage, shattering the heart and lungs, and tearing a great bone-strewn hole on the far side. All around guns unleashed their fearful retribution. Fast, accurate gunfire poured into the mass of black bodies. Most never got up from where they lay.

Barry and the sergeant concentrated their fire on those in the shadows, determined that none should escape. Finally the firing died down as targets became scarce. As it stilled an overpowering silence descended in which the stentorian breathing of the wounded and dying sounded hideously loud. They waited a while then moved forward into the camp.

The sergeant found one man who had been shot through the hips, he was in extreme agony. He walked over to him intending to finish him off, then changed his mind. All around came the occasional crack of rifle fire, as the wounded were finished off and the dying helped on their way.

Wilson looked down at the black man. "How many of you were there, and which one was your leader?" he asked. He spoke the lingua franca of the mines, *fanigalo*, which is understood by most tribes up as far as Kenya, after which *Swahili* takes over. The black man remained silent, hatred shining from his eyes.

"I'll ask you once more," said the sergeant, repeating the questions. The terrorist spat. Taking a booted foot in both hands Wilson raised it and twisted outwards.

The black screamed.

"When you are ready to talk let me know," he said. He twisted the leg from side to side. He could hear the broken bones grinding. He felt the bile rising in his throat.

The black fainted. Dropping the boot the sergeant looked around and found a bottle of water, which he sloshed over the unconscious black.

"They can give it but they can't take it, can they?" He said to Barry.

"Barry! You and John make separate counts, see how many we've got." Barry moved off.

The black started moaning.

"Back in the land of the living are we? are you ready to talk yet?" The sergeant caught hold of the man's boot. The black screamed. "There were thirty-one of us."

"Where were you heading?"

"Villa de Manica."

"And your leader?"

"He was over there, by that tree," he said, pointing. The sergeant called to the others to drag all the bodies over to the fire so that the wounded man could see them. A while later he lifted the black's shoulders and asked him if he could see their leader. The black gave a triumphant leer.

"No, I think you missed him, white man."

"How many left here, John?"

"We have both counted, sarge," said John. "We make it twenty-nine, including the guard that you got earlier."

"So two escaped!" He turned to the wounded man.

"What is your leader's name, and the name of the other who got away?"

"I'll tell you, white man," he said, managing to convey an insult in the "white man" which he emphasised. "Our leader is Francis Chaka. Remember the name, white man. He is also called 'The Hammer'. You'll be seeing him in Government House in Katari soon, if you are still alive."

"And the other man?" Asked the sergeant.

"He is a section leader called Phillias Mutenda and he's a mean man, sergeant. He'll get you for this. You'll be a long time dying, white man."

"Unfortunately for you, black man," the sergeant also emphasised the words, "you won't be there to see it."

The terrorist raised himself on one elbow. "I claim prisoner of war … "

The sergeant's bullet cut him short.

They walked over to where Frank Stevens and Roy had laid out the old man. "He's dead!" Said Barry. "I think his heart just gave in."

"I'm not surprised," said John. "did you see what that bastard was scratching him with?" He pointed into the grass. Lying where they had been dropped were two slender hands. Sticks had been forced into the wrists and bound with grass. The fingers were long with beautifully shaped nails on which there were still traces of nail varnish. They had dried into claws.

"Oh my God!" said Barry. "His daughter's hands!"

They searched the bodies for papers, orders, anything to hand in to Special Branch when they returned to base. They smashed all the terrorists' guns and set alight to the supplies. When they were ready, they made a rough-and-ready stretcher, and carrying the remains of Henry Chesterfield, they returned to the river. Back on Nyangan soil, they took turns digging a grave in the soft earth by the side of the river, whilst the sergeant busied himself coding a message for base camp. He concluded the message with 'Operation continues!' Having passed the message he waited a while, listening to the voice crackling in the darkness.

" … you are to return to base!"

He picked up the handset. "Echo Charlie One! Echo Charlie One! I cannot read your last message. Say again!" He turned the set off.

Frank Stevens looked at his sergeant, a puzzled look on his face.

"I heard every word he said, sarge!"

Sergeant Wilson gave Stevens a long look and closed one eye slowly.

"You heard nothing, Frank. Ok?"

Frank grinned. "If you say so, sarge."

They buried the farmer by the bank of the river and marked the grave with stones. Each man felt the occasion deeply. With him they buried his daughter's hands. As the others retrieved their heavy packs, John and Barry stood and urinated all over the grave.

"No disrespect, old man," muttered John, "but this will stop any animals from digging you up, our apologies."

CHAPTER FOUR

They recrossed the river and set off in a direction south of the terrorist's camp, hoping to cut the tracks of the two who had escaped. They walked for a couple of hours along a game trail that lead in the general direction, then the sergeant called a halt.

"That's enough for tonight, we have cut down the distance a little. Get some sleep, we'll be away at first light." Once again they spread their sleeping bags and slipped gratefully into them.

Rising whilst the sun was still below the horizon, they made a hurried breakfast of corned beef and biscuits washed down with water after which the sergeant got every man to count his ammunition. They divided the rounds evenly. They had just over one hundred rounds each, five full magazines, plus a few spares. Consulting his map, the sergeant reset his compass for Villa de Manica whilst Barry buried the cans and trash. Once again urinating over the disturbed earth. They did not want rubbish lying around to show where they had been.

Keeping to the comparative safety of the trackless bush and avoiding open ground they pressed on until sunset. They had managed to collect a few bananas on the way and once chanced upon a native hut. It had long since been abandoned as a dwelling and was now used for drying groundnuts, to which they helped themselves. Once, hearing loud noises, they crept near to investigate and discovered a herd of elephants disporting themselves in a muddy water hole.

The huge bull stood to one side on guard whilst the babies played in the mud or wallowed joyfully. The grown-ups filled their trunks with muddy water and blew it over themselves, their offspring or any other elephants near them. It was a beautiful scene and the men stood watching, forgetting the war for a few stolen minutes, revelling in the uninhibited pleasure of it all.

They camped that night in a burnt-out farmhouse, in the garden of which they found paw paw, avocado, mangoes and a few overgrown carrots. They ate their biltong first, finished off with fruit and were well satisfied.

"Well, lads," said the sergeant, "we've made a direct line to Villa de Manica, so unless those two terrs managed to hit a road and get a lift we should be ahead of them. I propose to hole up on the west side of the town and cover the road. If we don't see them by nightfall we'll abandon the whole idea and make our way back to the other side of the river.

"How will we recognise them?" asked Roy.

"Well, they'll be dressed like those other terrs and will be about as tatty as we are. In any case nothing nor anybody is likely to use that road, not since the border was closed. If this 'Hammer' character is so important we must try to capture him alive."

"Hell, sarge," said Frank, "that goes against the grain a bit!"

"I feel the same way, Frank. We all do, but that's the way it's got to be. However, if we can't capture him we do the next best thing."

The next morning they worked their way around Villa de Manica until they hit the road, now in a sad state of disrepair. They scouted parallel to it until they found a rocky outcrop which was well shaded and they settled down to wait. From time to time a local villager passed carrying firewood or vegetables, and once, along the road from town came a young black couple, holding hands and giggling. Occasionally the girl would cover up her face with spread fingers and double up with laughter at some outrageous comment from the boy. As they came opposite to where the patrol lay hidden, the boy looked behind and seeing nobody quickly pulled the girl into the long grass behind some dense bushes.

Five pairs of eyes boggled at the quickest strip tease on record. The whole performance was over in four minutes. The couple dusted each other down and waited until the road was clear, then hand in hand sauntered back to town.

"Blimey," said Frank, "that must have been the fastest bang on record; I must drop a line to Guinness. Just don't ever say your sergeant never provides entertainment."

They settled down again.

Towards late afternoon a few donkey drawn carts trundled along, piled high with farm produce, heading towards the town. The sergeant looked at his watch and stretched.

"Well, lads, I think we must have missed them. They should have reached here by now; unless we can find out where they have gone we've had it." Wearily they slipped their arms through the straps of their packs, adjusted them for comfort, and moved off at right angles to the road. They intended to keep well away from habitation and head back to the border. However, they had not gone much more than a kilometre when they came to a barbed wire fence. Over to one side, through the trees, they could see a house. They climbed over the fence and keeping the trees between themselves and the windows they moved closer.

The house itself was a typical villa of the wealthier Portuguese businessman. A sweeping driveway encircled what once must have been a beautiful rockery, now badly overgrown, that curved away to a dirt access road. As they watched, an army lorry turned into the driveway and cut through several flowerbeds on its way to the porch where it skidded to a halt, throwing granite chips far and wide. Out of the cab stepped two soldiers. One made a comment as he walked around the front of the vehicle, which his companion found enormously amusing. They both carried AK rifles with the distinctive 'banana' magazine. They walked up the steps and on to the verandah and one raised his rifle to hammer on the door. Before he could do so the door opened and a short stocky man stepped out, closing the door behind him. The two soldiers moved close to the Portuguese who was obviously terrified. One put his face a few centimetres away from the man who promptly backed away until he came up against the door, his hands raised to cover his face.

The men hiding in the garden could hear the soldiers shouting and the protestations of the Portuguese but could not understand the contents of the argument.

"Well!" said Sergeant Wilson. "any friend of his is a friend of ours, and they just may have the information we need. Let's go!"

They moved away from the front of the house until a corner hid them, then one by one they ran over to the back door. Finding that the door was unlocked the sergeant pulled it open and moved into the kitchen which was unoccupied. A half-eaten meal was sitting on the kitchen table. A short passage led from the kitchen to the lounge door, where it turned right into a hallway. Stairs led upwards to the bedrooms. Shouting and the sound of blows were now coming from the lounge, so the sergeant assumed there must have been another door to the lounge from the hallway. He signed for Barry to check the upstairs and Roy the dining room and toilet, all were clear of occupants.

The noise in the other room had reached a crescendo when the sergeant, followed by John and Frank, casually strolled in. But there was nothing casual about the way they held their guns. The scene that met their eyes looked painful if slightly comical. The unfortunate Portuguese was lying flat on his back across a splintered coffee table, his legs in the air, trying to fend off a black soldier who seemed intent on pulling him to his feet with the obvious intention of knocking him flat again. The other soldier was standing near the fireplace; both rifles leaned against the wall. As the stick entered he made as if to move towards his gun, changed his mind, and stood with mouth gaping.

At the sergeant's "Allo! Allo! Allo! what's this 'ere then?" in his best imitation of a concert hall bobby, the other soldier spun around a look of incredulity on his face, he made no move at all.

The Portuguese, on the contrary, scrambled to his feet, dodged behind his assailant and dashed at John crying, "Ah! The Nyangans, the Nyangans. Thank God!" He seemed to think it was a general invasion.

John fended him off as best he could whilst Sergeant Wilson signalled the two blacks to lie on the floor, hands above their head. They obeyed with alacrity, probably also assuming them to be part of a large raiding force that periodically crossed the border to destroy terrorist bases.

Frank collected the two AKs.

Sergeant Wilson turned to the Portuguese. "What's your problem, Pedro?" He asked.

"Not Pedro, sergeant. Fernando Gomez! Welcome to my house!" He said with simple dignity, his composure obviously restored. "These vermin come here two or three times a week to rob me, they have taken everything of importance long ago. When I say I have nothing left they beat me, what can I do?" He shrugged his shoulders, raising his hands in a typical gesture of helplessness.

"Why didn't you get out before they closed the border? A lot of your people flocked into Nyanga. You would have had some time under this government so you must have known what life was going to be like."

"Sergeant!" He replied, "I applied for a clearance and a visa twice. After the second time they came to my house and accused me of being an agitator and sympathetic to your regime. They beat me, and then they took away my wife and daughter to a work camp. The last I heard of them they were working in the fields, stripped to the waist like native women. I have had no word of them for three months. What can I do?"

John walked to one of the captured soldiers and kicked him hard in the ribs.

"Do you know where the work camp is?" He asked. There was no reply. John looked at the sergeant.

"Not another one!" He said. Turning, he kicked the man full in the face knocking out several teeth. The black man looked at him, a baffled look on his face, but again he said nothing. John raised his boot again as the sergeant said mildly.

"Perhaps he doesn't understand English, John."

John lowered his boot. "I never thought of that!" He said sheepishly. He turned to the Portuguese.

"Ask him where this work camp is!" He said.

The Portuguese spoke to the black man for a while, he seemed keen to talk.

"I know where the place is now!" He said. "It's only eight kilometres west of here, on a farm of a friend of mine. That is, it was his farm before they killed him and turned his farm into a cooperative."

"Now ask them," said the sergeant, "if they know of a man called Francis Chaka, otherwise known as the 'Hammer'". He watched them carefully as he spoke the names. There was no reaction so he was not surprised when the Portuguese said that they had never heard of him.

Gomez became more and more agitated until he could contain himself no longer.

"Please, sergeant, could I have a word with you in private?" he said, glancing meaningfully at the two blacks. They walked into the kitchen leaving the others on guard.

"What is it, Gomez?"

"Sergeant, I would have tried to escape to Nyanga a long time ago but I could not because of my wife and daughter. Now when you and your men go, we will all be killed. What am I to do?"

"Well, at a pinch I suppose we could take you with us. How

does that suit you?"

"And leave my wife and daughter to be killed, sergeant? Surely you do not think I could do that!" Gomez drew himself up proudly. "I would rather die with them."

"Well either way they are going to be killed," said the sergeant.

"Unless," said the Portuguese, grabbing the sergeant's hand. "Unless you release them and take them as well. Please sergeant, do this for me. Please I beg you!"

The sergeant looked away from the pleading man, feeling embarrassed for him.

"Gomez, we're here for one reason and one reason only. There are only five of us. We are hungry, tired and short of ammo. We cannot possibly go chasing all over Mozambique taking on the whole Mozambique army, not to mention the terrorists. So the answer is no! No! No! I'm sorry."

Gomez seemed to shrink. "I will get you and your men some food!" He said. "Thank you, sergeant. I do understand; it was foolish of me to hope." He busied himself in the kitchen.

The sergeant turned around to find Barry and Roy in the doorway. Barry gave him a long level look.

"Barry, it's no good looking like that!" he said gruffly. "You know as well as I do that it's impossible."

"Ok, sarge! So they all die! Too bad."

"Will you cut it out, Barry! This is a war we're fighting. People get killed. They could get killed just as easy getting through the border."

"That would be a clean death compared to the one they're going to get!" Said Barry, turning away.

Striding angrily down the passage Sergeant Wilson flung open the lounge door and called John out. He explained the gist of Gomez's fears. When he had finished he waited for John's comment.

"We could always take him with us."

"He won't go without his wife and daughter."

"Then let's get his wife and daughter."

"Not you as well! I've just had that out with Barry. It's totally out of the question."

"Ok! Then we just go!"

"Yes!"

The meal when it arrived had all the makings of a total failure. Not that Gomez had not tried. He'd used up every scrap of food in the house in concocting a large pot of stew, with hunks of bread to go with it. Gomez, sitting on a stool by the sink, a picture of total dejection, did not help. Nobody spoke and they toyed with their spoons as if they were really not hungry. The sergeant sat morosely listening to the silence, punctuated at intervals by Gomez's sighs. Finally he slapped his spoon down loudly on the table.

They all jumped, startled.

"Alright!" He said. "We'll do it and don't blame me if we all end up dead!"

Grins appeared all around the table and the food disappeared as if by magic.

"I was going to anyway. I just wanted to make sure you all felt the same way," he laughed. "What a crowd of tough bastards you all turned out to be."

Gomez looked around him, baffled by the complete change of atmosphere. He looked at the sergeant who was grinning from ear to ear. Then, dubiously at first, then with certainty. He cried, "You are going to do it, sergeant! You are going to do it!"

He ran around the table shaking hands vigorously and slapping backs, until the sergeant sent him off to pack the things he would want to bring.

"Whatever you bring, Gomez," he said, "you will have to carry, and you'll have a lot of walking to do, so make it light."

Within fifteen minutes he was back down the stairs wearing a pair of good serviceable boots and carrying an army pack, similar to theirs. "It was my son's," he said in answer to their inquiring looks, "he was also in the army. He was killed on the northern border fighting these people." He pointed to the two men lying bound in the lounge. The sergeant handed him one of the AKs "Do you know how to handle this?"

"Yes!" said Gomez simply.

"Right, Frank, go out to the lorry and check the fuel, oil and water. And see if the lights work."

"Right, sarge," said Frank. He moved outside and Roy followed him to give him a hand and to act as another pair of eyes.

"John, untie that character whose teeth you have just kicked in and get him out to the lorry. Barry, make sure the other one is well trussed up. We can't have him getting loose until tomorrow. Gomez, I shall want you to act as interpreter and guide."

They walked outside and Gomez turned off the lights and locked the doors. He gazed at the house for a while and shook his head regretfully.

The sergeant walked over to where John held the black soldier.

"Gomez, tell him I want him to drive this lorry to the place where your family are. Tell him to take any route he thinks best so that we will not be stopped. When we get to the camp he can tell the guard anything he likes as long as it gets us in with no bother. If everything goes well he will be allowed to go free. If we run into any trouble he'll be the first to die. You got that?"

"Yes, sergeant!" Gomez turned to the terrified man and passed on the message. He nodded vigorously and climbed into the cab.

Sergeant Wilson sat beside him with a knife pressed into the man's ribs. Gomez squeezed into the front seat beside the sergeant. The rest climbed into the back and closed the canvas flap.

They drove back onto the main road turning westward away from the town and headed towards the Nyanga border post at Machiponda, now a fortified encampment. About two kilometres along the road they turned right onto a dirt road that twisted and turned to provide access to the various farms scattered over the whole province. About fifteen minutes later the driver turned the lorry into a small lane to the left.

"This leads to the camp," said Gomez. "It's about half a kilometre away."

"Make sure he has his story fixed," muttered the sergeant.

They approached the camp slowly, the gates were open. A small gatehouse stood to one side but no sentry was in evidence. They drove straight on and pulled into a car park where several other vehicles were standing. Without being told the driver switched off the engine and lights.

In the silence they could hear the radiator gurgling and the muffled movement from the men in the rear as they collected their gear. They sat a while, waiting to see if anyone was interested enough to come and investigate. No one was.

"So much for our worries about getting in, Gomez." Sergeant Wilson signalled the driver to get out and followed him to the ground.

He tapped the side of the truck and one by one the others emerged and gathered around. It was very dark but they could just make out the outline of several low timber huts to the right. Facing them about fifty metres away was another low building. The lights were on and they could see men moving around and hear snatches of conversation. To the left stood what was obviously the farmhouse, also lit. The raucous sound of music drifted over to where they stood.

"Ask him where the women are kept and where the guards are," he ordered.

Gomez addressed the driver. "He says that the first hut to the right is for African women, there are no guards there. The hut behind houses the European women and other women who need a guard. The guard is normally on the far side. The building in front is the guardhouse and accommodation. In the house to the far left are the officers. Behind the guard house is a cell block." Gomez translated.

Sergeant Wilson ordered the driver into the back of the lorry where he was securely bound and gagged. They were about to move off when the door in front of them opened throwing a path of light half way across the car park. Out stepped one of the guards his AK cradled under his arm as he tucked his shirt into his trousers, a cigarette hung loosely from his lips. Without looking either right or left he ambled over to the gatehouse, went inside and closed the door. They had obviously arrived as the guard had left his post to relieve himself. 'Good timing' thought the sergeant. Telling the rest to stay where they were he walked casually over to the first hut to the right, anyone looking would assume he was one of the guards. Reaching the deeper shadow of the hut he waited until John and Gomez joined him. They crept to the far end of the building and peered around the corner. In the doorway of the next hut they could just make out the features of the guard as he drew on his cigarette. John and the sergeant whispered for a while, then John padded silently back and crossed the gap between the two huts and up the far side of the European women's quarters.

The sergeant waited five minutes then stepped out into the open and walked casually over to the guard who tossed his cigarette away and stood up. The guard said something which the sergeant did not understand. By now he was only a few paces away and the guard repeated his first remark, louder now, and started reaching for his gun which was propped in the doorway. John came up quickly from behind and his arm went around the man's neck, choking off a cry, as his knife plunged deep into his back. The guard struggled for a while and then slipped to the ground.

"What kept you, John? I thought you'd gone to sleep!" John grinned in the dark.

Gomez came up and they pulled the dead man into some bushes where he was well hidden from sight.

John tried the door, it was not locked and he opened it slowly. The three men eased themselves inside and stood in the darkness listening.

Sergeant Wilson took out his torch and shielding it with his hand ranged it around the hut. The light picked out two rows of double bunks one above the other, spaced closely together. The meagre clothing of the women hung from wire hangers hooked over nails driven into the planking. A table with a scattering of chairs completed the furnishings. One or two of the women moved fitfully as the light touched their faces, but most slept the sleep of the dead. Wilson motioned Gomez to follow him and together they moved slowly down the room shining the light briefly into each face as they passed. Most seemed too exhausted to bother with the disturbance, but one girl who appeared to be about twenty five years old, sat up quickly as the light reached her and muttered in broken Portuguese, "Oh no, please, not again. Leave me alone!" Gomez patted her arm and reassured her, cautioning her to silence. They moved on, the girl watching them with a puzzled look on her face.

They had just started the second row when a low cry from Gomez indicated that he had found what he was looking for. He reached eagerly for his wife as the sergeant moved forward quickly pushing Gomez aside, his hand reaching out covering the woman's mouth. She raised herself up off the bed, struggling as the sergeant held her tightly.

"Say something, you idiot!" He whispered harshly. Gomez leaned over his wife.

"Maria! Maria! It's me, Fernando. Please don't make a noise, do you hear me? It's me Fernando, you must be quiet, do you understand?" She nodded violently and the sergeant released her. Then they were in each other's arms, both crying, the cries getting louder. Then the daughter in the bunk above awoke and added her tears and questions to the mounting uproar.

"Quiet!" Snarled the sergeant. "Do you hear me? keep the noise down!" It subsided into an excited rumble, but by now all the women around had begun to wake up and started to call out. "Who's there? What is going on? Are you all right, Maria?" The sergeant cursed Gomez in fierce whispers, making things infinitely worse.

Realising that the cat was out of the bag, he grabbed Gomez and hauled him to his feet. "If you want me to get you out of here, listen to me!" He shone the torch on himself.

"Tell them to be quiet!" He said, shaking Gomez by the collar. "Tell them what is happening and what we intend to do!" Gomez started talking quietly. From around came cries of "Ah! The Nyangans, thank God!" Women came running over to hug him and the sergeant. At the other end of the dormitory, John was getting his share of the general mobbing. Gomez at last managed to get them all quiet, but one, an obvious spokeswoman, stepped forward and rambled on in Portuguese for a few moments until Wilson intervened.

"What seems to be her problem, Gomez?"

Gomez shrugged his shoulders. "Sergeant, they all want to come!" He said apologetically. John turned away spluttering and the sergeant rounded on him. "Get yourself outside and see if anyone has noticed this bloody din," he snapped. John left with tears of restrained laughter in his eyes.

Most of the women had been in the camp for a year or longer. Their working day started at five thirty in the morning, summer and winter. They had a break of three-quarters of an hour for a midday meal and that was their only respite until five thirty in the evening. Their food consisted mainly of mealy meal, augmented by scraps of meat that somehow got past the cooks and guards, and occasionally paw paw and mangoes scrounged from the guards or field hands, and they had a price. No medical facilities were provided and washing and toilet arrangements were primitive. They were subjected to abuse and degrading advances by their guards who often whiled away their guard duty with some unfortunate dragged from her bed into the bushes. Pay night for the camp staff was a time of special apprehension for the women, when drunken guards forced themselves onto the defenceless prisoners. It was no wonder that the sight of Nyangan troops conjured up visions of release and that the dangers involved failed to daunt even the most timid. The women stood around quietly now and the sergeant shrugged helplessly realising how unfair it would be to take just two of the prisoners.

"Ok!" He said. "If any of you want to go with us you must realise you will have to walk. You may come under fire and some of you may be killed. We will guard you as best we can but we can promise nothing. Anything you take with you, you must carry yourself. Get yourselves dressed and get your things together. You have five minutes and if I hear any noise outside that door I shall leave without you. Do you understand?" They nodded.

Gomez's wife touched the sergeant's arm. She had tears in her eyes as she thanked him. Then to Wilson's utter amazement she said, "You have rescued the Nyangan prisoners, yes?"

"What Nyangan prisoners?" he asked.

"Did you not know? They were brought in here yesterday. I thought that was your main reason for coming."

"I didn't know anything about them! Where are they?" he asked.

"They are locked in the cells behind the guard house." She answered.

"Where are the keys to the cell block kept?"

"As far as I know all the keys are kept in a box on the wall of the office this end of the guards' quarters." Then her face brightened. "But, sergeant, it's now nearly eight thirty, at nine o'clock they feed the prisoners any slops that the officers or guards have left. Perhaps that may help you."

The sergeant gave her a hug. "That's a great help" he said. Then turning to Gomez he explained that they would be back for the women just after nine o'clock.

"Make sure they are ready to go and find out which is the best way out of the back of the farm."

Gomez talked quietly to the women for a while, then turned back to the sergeant.

"They say that with the guard gone they can easily make their way to the north boundary about half a kilometre from here, there's an old barn near a hill. I know the place and could easily lead you to there. It will save time and trouble, if that's all right with you?" The sergeant agreed happily.

Hurrying outside he signalled to John to follow him and they rejoined the others by the lorry. Strangely enough, apart from a low murmuring from the direction of the hut, they had not heard a thing.

"Blimey!" Said the sergeant, "I thought the whole camp would have heard them!"

Huddled down behind the lorry, out of earshot of the prisoner, he told them about the captured Nyangans and explained his plan for rescuing them. He told Gomez to un-gag the prisoner and find out what he knew about the layout of the cell block. He returned a few minutes later with the information that the sergeant required.

The cellblock had been part of the original complex of outbuildings. It was long and low with a central passage, modified to accommodate a series of cells with heavy doors with drop bars. Each door had a one hundred millimetre square, heavily grilled, viewing hole at eye level and a slot at floor level through which food was passed. There were six cells on either side of the passage and each cell was about three metres square. The sole furnishing was a galvanised bucket which served as a toilet en suite. Some cells contained just four occupants, others as many as eight. The stink from the buckets, which were only emptied when the guards thought about it, had permeated the brickwork and the area around, attracting flies in their thousands. During the heat of the day the conditions were appalling. Normally the cells would have held a few local malefactors, mainly because the camp was only twelve kilometres from the border well within the range of Nyangan commandos. However, a series of unconnected events had decreed that tonight the establishment would be fairly bursting at the seams.

Two weeks before, a mission hospital and school to the east of Nyanga's M'como area had been overrun by terrorists from Mozambique. The nuns and priests had been badly beaten, most of the nuns raped and several killed. The mission had been burnt to the ground and the surviving missionaries, together with over one hundred school children, had been abducted into Mozambique. For nearly two weeks they had been shuttled from place to place, constantly ill treated and abused and seldom fed. Their entreaties to the escorting terrorists for food and medicines for the children had resulted in two more priests being killed. This however did not deter the rest, caught up as they were in a kind of religious masochism. Eventually in exasperation the terrorists had herded the missionaries into a lorry, separating them from the children, and brought them to the camp where they had arrived two days earlier. They shared two cells all sixteen of them. The children were still walking.

Occupying six of the cells were some thirty-six Portuguese men and women. The two women should have been sent to the work force with Gomez's wife but they had been caught with guns in their possession and now shared the same fate as the men. There had been fifty-five men and women involved in a valiant but fruitless bid to cross from Mozambique into South Africa via the Kruger National Park in the eastern part of the northern Transvaal. They had made it as far as the high game fence that enclosed the park and had turned to walk along it hoping to find a gap, and had walked right into an army patrol. They had no real chance to fight it out as the soldiers had seen them coming and they were surrounded before they realised their predicament. All of these were scheduled to be shot in two day's time. Most of the women had been forced into the labour camp.

Two of the remaining four cells housed drunken Mozambique soldiers, sleeping off their hangovers, and in the last two cells were the Nyangans. There were eight men. Four from Number One and Number Two Commando who had been separated from the main strike force during raids into Mozambique. They had fought running battles with terrorists' gangs until wounded and captured. Often they wished they'd died. Two were black Scouts caught infiltrating terrorists' camps. They should have died a dozen times being, probably, the most hated and feared of all the Nyangan forces. One was a police reservist and the last was a farmer. Both the latter had been captured on Nyangan soil and brought back over the border. The police reservist had been detailed to help guard a farm, but he and the farmer had been caught unawares when the cook had opened the security gates and led a group of terrorists into the house whilst they were having supper. The servant had worked for the farmer for twenty-seven years.

All of them were battered, had black eyes, broken noses, split lips and missing teeth. Broken ribs and fingers were shared fairly evenly amongst them, although the two blacks had come off worse. For the past few weeks they had been paraded in towns and villages up and down the country. They had been dragged, bound, onto a platform, whilst the guards harangued the crowd for half an hour deriding the invincibility of the Nyangans. Then a crowd of soldiers would walk on and beat the prisoners up for five minutes. The louder the crowd roared, the harder the beating. The black Scouts took the brunt and were always carried back unconscious. Even in their own extremes of pain, the whites would tend their black comrades, setting aside a little of their meagre food for them, using precious water to wipe the blood from their battered faces. But time was running out for all of them. The following day they were to be paraded in Villa de Manica and the beat-up artists had been told to make it final.

Outside the cell block, well concealed, lay the patrol, waiting. At ten minutes past nine, from the direction of the house came two guards, their rifles hanging from their shoulders by the straps. They carried between them a dustbin in which slopped a revolting mixture of plate scrapings. They both held a pile of tin plates and the sergeant was pleased to note that both their hands were occupied. As they drew near they turned towards the door and that was when the patrol rose silently around them. Rifle butts descended and the two men were caught as they fell. Finding the keys took but a few moments, then the door swung inwards. Roy, John and Frank took up positions outside in the shadows. Inside, two bare light bulbs lit up the passage, but they were not strong enough to light up the cells. They removed the steel drop bars from the first two cells and opened the doors. The smell of beer mingled with puke quickly drove them out again. The sergeant tried the third door, he peered inside and could easily recognise the torn and tattered remnants of Nyangan camouflage. He moved inside and gently shook the arm of one of the badly battered men, his hand over the open mouth. The eyes opened slowly, focused, then recognising the uniform on the white man leaning over him he struggled to sit up his mouth working, trying to speak. The sergeant put his finger to his lips. The man nodded, tears springing from his eyes, something the terrorists had not yet managed to do.

"How did you know we were here?" he whispered.

The sergeant silenced him. "I'll tell you all about it later. How many of you are there?" The man struggled to his feet.

"Eight altogether in here and in the next cell. But, sarge!" He added," There are missionaries over there, and all those cells are full of Portuguese. They'll all be shot unless you take them as well."

"Ok! Get everyone awake. Quietly, do you hear? Quietly!"

They opened the other cells, waking the occupants and enforcing silence as they gathered in the passage. A lot were quietly weeping, all were ragged and haggard. Some limped, some had to be carried.

'Jesus!' Thought the sergeant. 'How the hell are we going to get this lot home?'

One man, a Portuguese, caught the sergeant's arm. "Our women, sir! what about our women?"

"Don't worry about the girls, we got them out first!" The man moved to embrace the sergeant who hurriedly stepped aside. He walked to the door and whispered to Frank who handed him the guns captured from the camp guards and the soldiers back at Gomez's house.

He signalled the Nyangans over. "Any of you guys fit to fight?" he asked.

"All of us at a pinch, sarge. But several have broken fingers and ribs which will make it difficult, but we'd all like to try." The sergeant handed over two of the rifles, the other two he handed to the Portuguese.

"I know all you people have been hammered about." He said. "you all have an axe to grind, but you come under my orders now or you don't come at all. If any one of you takes off on his own vengeance trail I personally will shoot him; is that fully understood?" He waited a while. They all understood perfectly.

"Right! We will move out of here. No talking! In a few minutes some of you will be meeting your wives and daughters." He turned to the Portuguese. "I don't want a lot of shrieking. You will be responsible for keeping them quiet."

'That passed the buck nicely', he thought.

They trussed and gagged the unconscious guards, tumbled them into a cell, and locked all the doors. The drunks in the first two cells had not moved, their snores and grunts punctuated the night. They all moved outside to where Gomez waited with the rest of the patrol. "Lead on, McDuff!" said the sergeant. He tossed the keys far out into the bush.

CHAPTER FIVE

With some of the Portuguese men helping the wounded, they all followed Gomez as he led the way towards the rendezvous. The sergeant counted them as they passed.

"Ye gods!" He muttered. "Sixty-three of them so far, and about another twenty-five women waiting; twelve kilometres to go and another seven hours of darkness!"

With John and Roy covering the rear and Frank and Barry on the flanks, the sergeant moved up alongside of Gomez as they made their way to the meeting place, where the women waited. As the two groups met a brief melee ensued as men and women searched frantically for their partners. 'All things considered,' thought the sergeant, 'they were fairly quiet and settled down quickly.'

John and the sergeant now scouted ahead. It was obvious they would not make the river that night. The pace was too slow, the bush was dense, and the wounded needed frequent rests. After about five kilometres, John found an ideal place to stop, a dip in the ground surrounded by rocks with a small stream winding its way through the middle. The party settled down. There was no lack of help for the wounded and they were washed and their wounds dressed with strips torn from the ladies' petticoats. The nuns were well trained and competent. The men of the patrol shared their biltong and the remainder of their provisions with their Nyangan compatriots whose needs were greatest. The men of the patrol and the Portuguese stood watch together as Sergeant Wilson called Roy to him.

"Roy!" He said. "You are the youngest here. Do you think you could make the river tonight? It's about seven kilometres."

"I'm sure I could, sarge! Why?"

The sergeant spoke quietly so that none of the people around could hear.

"We don't have an earthly chance of getting back with this lot," he said. "It will be light in a few hours and they will be on our track. The trail is obvious enough. We can't move very fast with these wounded guys. We will have to have some cover."

"I want you to leave your pack. Take your rifle and just two mags; angle slightly south and you will be sure of hitting the river below the ford. When you see the river, follow it up until you reach the ford. There is a permanent OP, observation post there and a couple of dozen guys. Take my torch and signal the other side." He paused to hand over his torch. "You know the old 'sevens' code, don't you?" Roy confirmed that he knew it. "Contact our chaps and explain our position. Get them to contact base."

"Why can't we radio from here, sarge?"

"Our radio is useless. The batteries went flat early yesterday," replied the sergeant wearily. "Get them to contact base for clearance to come over and give us a hand. Have you got it?"

"I've got it, sarge!" said Roy. "I'll get ready now!"

"Don't let the others know you're going!" Roy moved away and collected his pack and spare mags, which he left with the sergeant.

"And, Roy! Remember you could run into anything. Be careful and good luck." He patted the boy on the shoulder.

Roy moved casually towards the edge of the camp, paused to talk to Barry briefly, and was gone, swallowed up by the dark night.

At four-thirty the sergeant awoke and sluiced his face with water from the stream and filled his bottle. The rest of the patrol followed, and then they moved around shaking the others. As darkness started to lift they trailed out of camp, John ranging ahead and Frank and Barry bringing up the rear. Sergeant Wilson moved up and down the column urging them to increase the pace, giving assistance where it was needed. They had gone about two kilometres when John came running back.

"Get them off the track!" He called hoarsely. "There must be over a hundred school kids up ahead. They are headed in this direction on the same game trail, and I counted up to ten terrs with them." One of the priests overheard and came up to the sergeant.

"Sergeant!" He said quickly. "They are our children from the mission school. They were abducted at the same time as we were. They are being taken to Villa de Manica, then on to Beira. You must get them away!"

"We'll see what we can do, but right now get everybody off the track!"

They moved everyone back about two hundred metres to where a depression hid them. They left the Portuguese to guard them and the two fittest of the Nyangans were placed behind rocks about fifty metres from the track and told to cover the men if they got pushed back.

The patrol moved ahead to where they could see the school children strung out over a hundred metres or so. In front, talking amongst themselves, were six terrorists, following up at the rear were another four. The game trail was narrow, making it difficult for any of the guards to walk alongside the children, for which the sergeant was duly thankful. 'Thank goodness for small mercies,' he thought. His main worry was how to get rid of the guards without harming the children. He sent John and Barry about a hundred metres back down the trail with orders not to fire until he did. Frank and the sergeant moved into cover behind a pile of rocks, aiming their rifles towards the trail, a mere forty metres away. They waited. The early morning sun was still weak on their backs and casting long shadows across the land; the cicadas awakening to the sun started up their endless chatter and high above a buzzard turned in lazy circles. The column was level now, the men in front holding their AKs casually, laughing occasionally. Then came the children, some holding hands, some talking, most plodding along on tired legs, heads down and silent. Their khaki school uniforms were torn and dirty, and some children carried their shoes, laces tied together, over their shoulders.

The long line passed slowly and Sergeant Wilson looked back down the trail to where John and Barry were hidden. The front of the column was almost level with their position. It would have to be now.

He lined up his sights on the nearest terr. Frank took the next man. Both squeezed the trigger simultaneously and the two men fell. Down the trail he could hear the crack of FNs as Barry and John opened up. Shifting sights quickly, they both picked another target.

The children, petrified into living statues at the sound of the first shots, now ran screaming in all directions. Frank hit one man who fell, holding his shoulder, but the sergeant's shot was baulked as two children ran straight into his line of fire. Frank, ten metres away from the sergeant's position had a clear view and his shot drove the terrorist back onto some rocks.

John and Barry were having problems. John's first shot had gone true and he watched his man spin around and fall. Barry's shot caught a terr high on the shoulder, knocking him down but failing to put him out of the action. John's second shot went wild as he pulled his gun to one side at the last second to avoid a running child. His third shot brought down another, but by this time they had come under heavy fire from the remaining four. They were hampered by the screaming children who seemed intent on running everywhere except into cover.

John signalled to Barry and under cover of the rocks they ran back towards the position where the two Nyangan 'long stops' were stationed, pausing from time to time to drop into cover and scatter their pursuers with a few well-placed rounds. John dashed between two rocks showing himself briefly to the enemy, drawing them on. The ruse worked. The terrorists came running, firing at the fleeting shapes that dodged elusively from cover to cover. As they slowed John showed himself yet again as he dived between the two 'long stops' position. He felt the bullet hit his hand, or was it his arm? it threw him off balance and he crashed to the ground rolling over and over, ending up half concealed behind a towering ant hill. Still gripping his rifle, he pulled himself into cover.

The terrorists had seen him fall and ran forward shouting and baying like hunting dogs. The shouts died rapidly as the two 'long stops' opened up; John and Barry joining in a split-second later. Within seconds it was all over.

Even as the sound of firing died down the nuns and priests were running forward calling to their charges, herding the children together. Barry ran to where he had seen John fall and was relieved to see him sitting up nursing his wounds. A bullet had cut a groove across the back of his hand, over the wrist, and through the back of the upper arm. Barry slipped out his first aid kit and set to work.

In front of them the two Nyangan ex-prisoners finished off the wounded with cold satisfaction. Hardly pausing for breath the sergeant got them under way again, pushing hard for the river. John, insisting that his wounds were no real handicap, headed the column and Sergeant Wilson scouted ahead. They had shared out the terrorist's rifles between the Nyangans and the Portuguese but the ex-prisoners were in such bad shape that they had enough to do just to keep walking.

The sergeant came loping back. "Only one and a half kilometres to go!" He called. "Speed it up!" Everyone tried their best, willing hands half carrying the wounded who by now were on the fringes of total exhaustion. The sergeant gave them no rest. He knew that by now the enemy was close on their trail. He sent four of the Portuguese ahead to watch for any attempt to cut them off then, with John, dropped to the rear where Barry reported seeing large numbers of soldiers moving up fast behind them. He ran back to the column.

"Women and children run for the river!" He shouted. "You men without rifles take relays helping the wounded. You Portuguese with rifles, cover them! Move!" He roared. The children ran, the nuns and priests running with them, pulling them along. Some of the Portuguese women swung the smaller and slower children onto their backs and soon the whole column was strung out over half a kilometre, running, falling, crying, running. The sergeant ran back to his men, there were six of them now, two already near the limits of their endurance. The enemy closed.

With three men firing, the other three ran back thirty metres and dropped to the ground, covering whilst the others ran past them. Down, fire! Up and run. Down, fire! Only half a kilometre to go to the river.

"We'll make a stand amongst those rocks!" Yelled the sergeant. The men dived into the cover of a rocky hillock pulling the two trailing men with them. They picked their targets carefully, saving their precious ammunition. The enemy sensing victory drove forward, yelling at full pitch and 'ki-yipping' like mad animals. They flung themselves at the hill, were forced back, came again.

One by one, the guns of the patrol stilled into silence as they ran out of rounds and hand-to-hand fighting broke out all over the hillock as the Mozambique soldiers, realising the situation, attempted to take the Nyangans alive. Knives flashed and rifle butts arced as the two groups clashed.

Barry, swinging his rifle like a baseball bat, sailed into four blacks who had leaped at the sergeant. Screaming like a banshee, he clubbed left and right. Sergeant Wilson swung one man over his shoulder his knife flashing, raking up through the soft skin of the stomach. Twisting fast he drove the knife into another's throat and he was clear. With Barry beside him he ran to help John and Frank who were standing astride the two now-unconscious Nyangans, fighting off about ten assailants. John went down clubbed behind the ear and Barry cleaved his attacker with his rifle butt. Frank was struggling to wrestle an AK from one towering black whilst another hung around his neck trying to throttle him. The sergeant was everywhere, lunging, stabbing, slicing. He went down with three blacks on top of him his head ringing from blows. He was bleeding from a dozen wounds and a blood haze settled behind his eyes as he struggled mightily to rise.

Barry, with his back to Frank, sank slowly to his knees as the enemy pounded his head and body, he felt his senses going.

The women running towards the river never noticed the tanned, lean men who passed them running flat out. They never saw huge Sergeant McGrath, his face congested with rage and effort as he pounded along to help his lifelong friend, Sergeant Wilson.

They may have seen Roy van Houston pass, sobbing in his exhaustion. He had already run fifteen kilometres that night, having gone too far upstream he had turned back, throwing caution to the winds in his haste. Now his last reserves were being expended in a desperate effort to reach his comrades, even just to die with them.

They would not notice the men of Number One Commando as they raced past carrying a heavy M.A.G. machine gun between them, bands of ammunition draped across their shoulders. They could not help but hear the roar they gave as they closed with the enemy. A roar filled with hate for the enemy and encouragement for their comrades fighting for their lives on the hill. It was a roar of iron hard men fighting for what they believed.

The machine gunners threw themselves flat, rammed in the

lead of the first belt and sent hail raining among the enemy ranks. The rest were charging straight for their comrades on the blood-soaked hill, firing as they ran.

The enemy heard that terrible roar and felt the anger. They broke and ran and as they ran they were cut down. Sergeant Wilson tasted his own blood as the sun was blotted out by black bodies. He felt his senses ebbing and a numbing glow settling over him. Then as unconsciousness began to overtake him he saw with curious detachment those same black bodies spin away. He heard the roar drawing nearer, he smiled to himself. 'Ah! Here comes the cavalry. Right on time!' He fainted.

As the women and children reached the ford, a line of soldiers standing in the water, passed them one to the other, then on to more men standing on the bank who pulled them to safety.

On the hill the men of the relief force gazed with amazement at the scene of carnage around them. Sergeant Wilson and his men were lying where they had fallen, dead bodies piled around them and over them. Over eighteen enemy soldiers had died in that last terrible melee, more were strewn on the slopes, and yet more on the veldt below.

Sergeant McGrath walked over to where his friend lay, cursing as he threw the dead bodies aside and dropping down he cradled Bob Wilson's head in his lap. Sergeant Wilson was covered in blood, great clots of it, mostly from his dead assailants. As McGrath sat there rocking in his grief he saw Wilson's eyelids flutter, the eyes opened struggling to focus. "Ah! McGrath!" He murmured weakly. "I didn't know you cared!"

McGrath's face split into a happy grin as he raised his water bottle to Wilson's cracked lips.

All around, McGrath's men were working quickly, dragging the dead off their comrades, bandaging, taping. John Kelso was sitting up, nursing a lump the size of an egg behind his ear. Frank Stevens was dead, a bayonet lodged in his back. Barry McEvoy was still unconscious and bleeding from several injuries but seemed likely to live. The other two had escaped serious injury, but total exhaustion had beaten them.

One of Sergeant McGrath's men hurried over to where his sergeant sat.

"Thought you'd like to know, sarge, there's a whole mob of

locals headed this way. They are only about a kilometre off!" The sergeant jumped to his feet.

"Ok, men, pick up our dead and wounded, and let's get the hell out of here!" He shouted.

John could walk with a man each side assisting him the rest had to be carried, four to a body. They made the river just as the first of the enemy force topped the rise, but a blanket of withering fire from the rest of the troop plus the Portuguese on the Nyangan bank drove them back whilst McGrath's men withdrew with their burdens.

They moved back several hundred metres to a camp carefully hidden in a depression surrounded by dense bush where all the refugees had collected. As the bodies were set down gently under the shade of an acacia tree an anguished silence descended on the camp. All were convinced that the bloodstained and battered men were dead. Then Sergeant Wilson moaned and tried to sit up and with shouts of joy the women took over.

As soon as he was able the sergeant wrote out a short report and handed it to McGrath. It read simply, 'Sierra Papa One Five will be returning to base tomorrow. E.T.A. approx. 1000 hours. Escorting missionaries and schoolchildren from St. Francis mission M'Como and a number of Portuguese nationals. Regret death of trooper Stevens. Request cyclone lift for eight Nyangan nationals and Stevens.' Sergeant McGrath walked away as he read the message. The message relayed was slightly more explicit.

Base camp was about eight kilometres away as the crow flies. There was no road or trail from McGrath's camp so Sergeant Wilson allowed four hours to make the journey. The helicopter would be making two trips and would arrive at about eight o'clock, so he made arrangements to leave at six o'clock, it would be fairly light by then.

The column moved out of camp in the early light of dawn anticipation putting a spring in their step. The sergeant and John scouted ahead, Barry and Roy followed up at the rear, for even here they were not completely safe. Three hours later they struck the road about half a kilometre from the base camp. They had seen the helicopter shuttling overhead some time previously.

The sergeant called to his men.

"Ok, lads! Let's look a little bit like soldiers. You lot!" He called, his glance taking in the refugees and the missionaries, "close up so we can at least look as if we were protecting you!" Laughing, they formed three rough and ready ranks, Sergeant Wilson and John on the near side, Barry and Roy on the other.

As they neared the camp they saw a large crowd of people standing in the road near the gates. They were cheering and waving. It took the sergeant a few moments to realise they were cheering them. He raised his chin another notch and held himself erect against his pain and fatigue. The crowd jammed the gates and lined the wire fence that bordered the road, running along to keep up with the column. As they drew level, someone in the crowd started to sing 'Knick knack Paddywack,' and the whole crowd took it up, clapping in tune.

The significance was lost on the sergeant, who had not seen the film where the heroine shepherds a column of children to safety as they all sang that song. But John and Barry had and they grinned.

There were members of the Portuguese Association from Umdali there to welcome their countrymen, church officials and black men and women. The girls in the 'opps' and radio rooms had left their jobs to lean out of the windows and cheer.

"My God!" Said Captain Peterson, out from England one year. "Will you look at that!" His throat contracted involuntarily at the sight. Sergeant Wilson strode out, his head swathed in bloody bandages. His shirt and trousers were ripped into blood-soaked tatters that flapped around him as he walked. He had an air of magnificence about him that was awesome. John Kelso, one arm supported by a bandage, his hand and upper arm covered with bloody rags and his bandaged ribs showed through his torn shirt. Barry was no better. All of them caked with dirt and blood.

"They've been out for three weeks, fought virtually every inch of the way. They must be bone weary and starving, but just look at them! How can you beat men like these?" he asked. An expression that was applied to the Spartans crossed his mind. 'They were never beaten, only killed!'

The sergeant, looking a little self-conscious now, headed the column through the gates, the cheering crowd parting to let them through. Then all was chaos, everybody milling around shouting and laughing. The sergeant extracted himself with difficulty and made for the office block where Colonel Jameson and Captain White stood with the rest of the officers on the shaded stoep. Before he could mount the steps they were striding towards him, hands outstretched. When the preliminaries were over Colonel Jameson told the sergeant to muster his men at the sick bay where the medical staff were waiting for them.

"Get yourselves cleaned up and fed then catch up on some sleep. When you're ready, sergeant, we would like to see you for debriefing. You are all booked in for R.and R. from midday tomorrow."

"Thank you, sir!" Said the sergeant. "They could use a break, but I would like to get the debriefing over as soon as possible, so if you don't mind I'll tidy up and be back in an hour and a half."

"That's fine by us, sergeant, if you're sure you are up to it!"

To the minute, the sergeant was back, showered and freshly shaved, his khaki drills knife edged and his boots gleaming. The only signs of his recent ordeal were a fresh bandage around his head and a stiffness in his movements.

Present at the briefing were two Special Branch men, to whom he was not introduced, Colonel Jameson, Captain White, a Police Inspector from Katari, and an immigration official whom the sergeant supposed had the problem of dealing with the Portuguese refugees. There was also a rather attractive stenographer. The immigration officer asked a few pertinent questions, then excusing himself from the meeting he left to sort to out his own problems.

Colonel Jameson chaired the meeting but it was the two Special Branch men who asked most of the questions. The Colonel passed around several pages of a report, closely typed, which they all studied for a while in silence. Then Colonel Jameson turned to Sergeant Wilson.

"Sergeant! We have here copies of your report up to the Chesterfield Farm incident, if you have read it and are satisfied with it would you please carry on with your report from there! You have been in this position a thousand times so I need not emphasise that what you may think trivial could be of vital importance to these gentlemen." He pointed with his pipe to the two men from Special Branch. "Take your time sergeant."

The sergeant gave a clear outline of events leading to crossing the river into Mozambique and attacking the terrorists' camp. As soon as he mentioned Francis Chaka the two Special Branch men sat up.

"Are you sure that was his name?" one asked. The sergeant confirmed that it was.

"And he escaped?'

"Unfortunately!"

"That's a great pity, sergeant. No fault of yours of course. You did a magnificent job, but Francis Chaka is 'the' top man on the other side." He emphasised 'the'. "He is well above such people as Samora Kachel."

"More like a Castro!" said the other.

"Yes, he has been very specially groomed by his Cuban masters for a particular role in this part of the world. He disappeared from Africa a few years back. I'm surprised they risked him in the field!"

"Probably wants it known that he personally participated in the 'struggle'," said the other. "Associate himself with the unwashed masses!"

"If we could carry on please! Sergeant."

The sergeant picked up where he had left off. When he got to the point where they had crossed into Mozambique Captain White produced a copy of the sergeant's radio message and passed it around. The S.B. man looked up. "You did not receive the message telling you to return to base?"

"No sir! The signal was very weak. I think our batteries were low."

Captain White, in an aside, muttered. "The sergeant's radio always packs up when he gets an order he doesn't want to obey!"

The stenographer looked up, trying not to laugh at Sergeant Wilson's red face.

"Do I put that in the report, sir?" She asked amidst general laughter.

"Good God! No!"

The sergeant hurriedly continued his narrative. When he reached the end there was silence for a while.

Clearing his throat, the Colonel said. "Sergeant! you and your men did a first class job. Besides the military aspect, which was brilliantly executed, the rescuing of the missionaries and the school children together with the release of the Portuguese people will be a morale booster second to none. I need hardly add that a full report will be forwarded to Command Headquarters."

"Thank you, sir!" Said the sergeant.

Then the men from Special Branch started in with questions, probing his mind for any details he may have forgotten.

"Do you have any idea where Chaka could be now?"

"I was only told that he was heading for Villa de Manica."

"Do you suppose he was going to witness the execution of the Nyangan and Portuguese prisoners?"

"It was possible, but I don't know, sir."

"How many troops did they manage to muster at short notice to pursue you on your way back to the border?"

"I thought about a hundred, sir, Sergeant McGrath thought nearer one hundred and fifty, but more came as we were being carted away. McGrath knows more about that than I do."

"Yes, we have his report. Did you see any of the terrorist groups mixing with the regulars?"

"No, sir! I don't think they get on too well."

"What was your impression of their army discipline?"

"Generally very sloppy."

"How about the terrorists' discipline?"

"Worse!"

"How well do they fight?"

"Better than they did a few years ago."

The questions went on and on until eventually, after two hours, the colonel interceded. "Gentlemen! I am sure Sergeant Wilson must be near exhaustion. If he isn't I am. Have you nearly finished?"

"Just about, sir." said one. "Just how well do you know John Kelso?"

The sergeant was taken aback. "Kelso, sir?"

"Yes!"

"He's a first class soldier, a true Nyangan, and on top of that he's my friend," said the sergeant with some anger.

"Well, he couldn't have a better recommendation than that." He laughed briefly. "I'm not suggesting he isn't all of those things, sergeant, so lower your hackles. It's just that he was known as a bit of a radical when he was at the university, very sympathetic to the blacks."

"So were a lot of us a few years ago!" Sergeant Wilson retorted. "But since that time a lot of friends and relatives have died and that tends to polarise your sympathies to your own kind. Unfortunately this kind of conflict hardens attitudes and destroys respect."

"Thank you, sergeant! That's fine, and don't worry about your friend!"

"I wasn't going to!"

The colonel rose. "Thank you, gentlemen." He said, "and, ah! lady!" He smiled. "I need not remind you that everything talked about in this room is classified. Sergeant! If you will come to my office I'll give you those passes for you and your men."

He walked out of the room, followed by the rest of the officers.

Sergeant Wilson sat there for a while as waves of exhaustion swept over him. He hardly noticed the stenographer shuffling her notes.

"You must be tired, sergeant," she said. He started up, opening his eyes. He had almost fallen asleep. "Oh! Sorry, miss. What did you say?"

"I said you must be tired." She smiled.

"I think that's a bit of an understatement", he said.

"So you will be going on leave tomorrow?"

"Yes! Katari!"

"How will you get there?"

"Oh! I suppose they will lay on a wagon as far as Umdali. Then we'll catch a train."

"I only asked because I'm going to Katari tomorrow, and I have my car here. I've just got to type this report and then I'm clear. If you would like a lift you are welcome. I would be pleased to have the company, especially on these roads."

"I suppose they lay on a convoy from Umdali don't they?" he asked. "If you wouldn't mind dropping off Barry, one of my chaps, there. Roy goes to Marimba, right on the way, and John and myself to Katari."

She smiled ruefully. "It will be no trouble at all, sergeant."

"Well! We can't keep calling each other sergeant and miss can we? I'm Bob Wilson."

"I know! I'm Sally Ferguson!" They smiled and shook hands. He stood talking to her for a while on the stoep then having arranged to meet the following day at noon by the gates he walked over to Colonel Jameson's office to pick up the passes.

Sally watched him walk away, whilst ostensibly tidying her notes.

CHAPTER SIX

John, Barry and Roy were already at the camp gate when Sally arrived. They stowed their kit into the spacious boot of the Citroen and the three of them squeezed into the back seat. At two minutes to twelve, Bob Wilson strode out of the Sergeants' mess carrying only a small bag, apart from his FN.

He tossed the bag into the boot, made sure the boot was secured and got in alongside Sally. As the car moved out into the road he cocked his rifle, making sure that the safety catch was on. The rest followed his lead and the windows were wound down. It was merely a precaution to facilitate returning fire should they come under attack.

In the back, John and Barry were laughing and finding everything amusing, their comments, often outrageous, were always funny and brought a smile to Sally's lips. Occasionally they would burst into song and the others would join in. The sergeant, whilst listening to Sally, noticed that Roy was not joining in the general hilarity and in a flash of intuition, realised the cause. A while later during a lull in the conversation he turned in his seat as if the thought had just occurred to him and grabbed Roy's hand.

"Roy! I haven't had a chance to thank you for what you did, bringing up the cavalry. It was a terrific job. It couldn't have been easy getting through in the dark. It is very much appreciated. We wouldn't be here now if it wasn't for you. I won't forget it!"

In the mirror Sally could see the boy's Adam's apple working as he strove manfully to hold back his tears and only then did she realise that there had been a problem, that the sergeant had recognised it and without fuss had solved it. She reached for Bob's hand and squeezed it. Barry and John, realising that the boy was blaming himself for Frank's death soon dispelled his fears and within minutes he was singing and joking with the rest, obviously much relieved.

When they reached Umdali they drove to the 'Wise Fox' hotel, where they all piled out and headed for the bar to have a beer with Barry before driving him to his flat. Then it was on to the police station to join the convoy assembling for the run to Katari. There were twenty-two vehicles in the convoy, which finally pulled out at two o'clock, with a mine-proofed Land Rover at the front and another following up behind. The police reservists stood in the back behind a browning machine gun, wind goggles screening their eyes, swinging the gun from side to side whenever they passed a likely ambush site.

At Marimba they left the convoy and turned into the shopping centre where Roy's father was waiting with the farm pick-up truck to take him home. There were introductions all around and before they left the sergeant arranged to meet them, together with Roy's mother, at the Rhodes Hotel in Katari in two days time.

An hour later they drove into Katari, past the drive-in cinema and on to Independence Avenue. Sally turned her head. "Where do you want to be dropped off, John?" she asked.

"Up by the university if it's not too far out of your way!"

Bob looked up. "I'm in North Street, Sally. If you drop me off first, then John, you can go straight up the Glendale road. You live in Greendale Park don't you?"

"Yes! That's right," said Sally, biting her lip. John smiled to himself. It was obvious that she wanted to get Bob on his own. He leaned forward.

"Sally! I don't know if you realise it but the Glendale Road is under repair, it has been for a long time. You would probably be better off coming back up the Enterprise Road." He mentioned an alternate route to Greendale Park. "So it may be better if you dropped me off first, then dropped Bob off on your way back."

She looked back quickly, saw his grin and smiled her thanks.

"Thanks, John, that's a good idea."

They left John standing in his doorway. "See you at the Rhodes!" Bob called as they drove off. John waved.

Turning into North Street, she drove into the car park at the rear of a block of flats, opposite some playing fields.

"You didn't have to drive all the way in," he said, "but thanks anyway." He got his bag out of the boot.

"These flats look very nice," said Sally.

"They aren't bad at all," said Bob, hefting his bag.

"Which one is yours?" she asked, staring around the tiered banks of windows.

"It's that one," he answered, pointing, "on the third floor, with the yellow curtains." He started to move forward.

"You must have a gorgeous view!"

"Not bad at all, it looks over the playing fields."

Sally was getting desperate. "Oh Bob, I wonder if your wife would mind if I came up to wash my hands. They are all sticky from driving." She saw a shadow flit across his face.

'Oh God!' She thought. 'He's going to put me off!' She could feel the colour rising to her face and turned away in embarrassment.

Bob turned towards her, an apologetic look on his face. "Good grief! Sally. By all means, I should have invited you up. Will you stop for coffee. Excuse my bad manners!"

They were both embarrassed for different reasons and stood looking at each other for a while, then they both burst out laughing. They were still laughing as they reached the lift.

'He didn't fall for that one!' she thought. 'I wonder if he is married, please don't let him be married!'

Bob led the way to his flat, opened the door, and standing back invited her to enter.

"It's probably a bit musty," he said. "It's been closed up for weeks." He moved past her and opened the windows.

'Well there can't be a wife then,' she thought, 'at least not here!' She looked around the flat.

"Do you mind?" she asked.

"No go ahead! I'll get some coffee on."

She walked into the lounge. It was beautiful. A thick tufted rug covered the floor, the autumn shades matching the long curtains that hung full length the whole width of the room. White lacquered shelves along the walls were full of books. One wall was almost covered with framed ancient maps. The whole room sparkled with life and character.

'Oh! Oh!' she thought. 'There seems to be a woman's touch here and a clever one at that.' She sat on the settee and was immediately engulfed in soft leather comfort.

Bob came in from the kitchen with two steaming mugs of coffee and a plate of biscuits. "The bathroom is over there!" He said, pointing. "You said you wanted to wash your hands."

"Oh yes!" She said, jumping up. She felt herself blushing again as she remembered the excuse she had used. "I won't be a minute!" She dashed off.

When she returned he was standing on the balcony in the gathering darkness, drinking his coffee. She picked up her mug and joined him.

"Peaceful isn't it," she said. "You would hardly know there was a war on would you."

"There's always a war on," he replied, "if it's not against a conventional enemy or injustice then it's an internal thing. A battle for what you want out of life; a battle to lay personal ghosts."

"Do you have personal ghosts?"

"Don't we all? Don't you have an Aunt Mabel who died two days after you had that senseless row about nothing? Don't you feel guilty that you didn't take the trouble to walk round and make up?"

"I suppose so!"

"Isn't there something you would like to forget, that time doesn't heal?"

'Keep it light,' she thought, 'it's too early to get into this sort of conversation.'

"Put like that, I guess we do have our own battles." She turned away and put her cup on the table. "Give me your cup, I'll wash them up quickly."

"Oh! Don't bother, Sally! I'll do it later, after I've eaten."

"Are you going out for a meal or eating at home?"

"I'll pop over to the take-away. I'll have to stock the fridge tomorrow."

"Why don't you come with me, out to my folk's place? They are expecting me and they always cook far too much. Do you have a phone?"

"Yes! The phone is over there, but I couldn't possibly impose like that," he replied, smiling.

Sally ignored him and picked up the phone, dialled a number and waited. Soon her mother answered and all was settled.

As she turned to him she caught again that fleeting look on his face and again failed to place it.

'Damn it!' She said to herself, 'I've done it again, I'm pushing him too hard.'

She put her hand on his arm. "I'm sorry, Bob! I didn't think! Perhaps you have something else to do, or perhaps you wanted to be on your own tonight."

He looked at her troubled face and cursed his own churlishness.

"Please! I'd love to come. It's not very often I get the chance of home cooking. Pour some drinks while I get changed. That cabinet over there!" He pointed.

"Just casual!" She called. "What do you drink?"

"Good! And a whisky and soda."

"What was that?"

"Good! I'm glad it's casual and I drink a whisky and soda!" he called from the bedroom.

"Ok!" She poured the drinks, making herself a gin and tonic. She was reading the titles of the books when he returned.

He was wearing a brown-green, lightweight thorn proof tweed suit, brown brogues and a knitted tie. Her heart lurched at the sheer maleness of him. He had removed the bandage and a raw gash with stitches puckering up the skin into an angry furrow, ran from his eyebrow to his hairline.

He handed her a piece of lint and a length of wide adhesive tape.

"Would you mind taping that on for me?" he asked.

"Good grief!" She said. "That's terrible. It looks awfully sore. You should have left the bandage on!"

"It got soaked when I showered, anyhow this looks less piratical." He smiled at her.

He leaned forward slightly and she placed the strip of lint over the wound, getting him to hold it in place whilst she taped it. His face was very close to hers and she could smell his after-shave lotion. As she reached up she brushed against him, his hands moved to her waist to steady her. She drew the moment out pressing the tape down gently. She could feel his breath on her cheek. She swayed towards him, willing him to kiss her.

"That's fine!" He said, stepping back, "I think we can be off now, unless you would like another drink?"

She shook her head mutely as she walked past him to the door. 'You dumb bitch!' She thought, 'why don't you just throw him on the floor and rape him. You couldn't be any more obvious. What is the matter with you? You've never been like this before.'

Bob locked the door and they walked to the lift.

"I think I'll take my own car, Sally, and follow you. It will save you running me back."

"Alright! I'll wait for you on the road outside."

She drove towards home and because she was angry with herself she drove fast. Bob, following behind in his Toyota, kept a wary eye open for police cars as he was forced to exceed the speed limit in order to keep the tail-light of the Citroen in sight.

As they were expected the gates to the driveway had been left open and they drove straight in, Sally to her own carport beside the garage, leaving Bob to park parallel to the driveway.

Her parents had been sitting on the stoep having a traditional 'sundowner' drink and enjoying the coolness of the evening breeze. Hearing the cars arrive they stepped down to the garden and walked over to greet their daughter and her guest.

Sally ran to meet them, hugged her father, gave her mother a kiss and introduced Bob. Then, with hardly a pause said, "I must go and change out of this uniform. You can come and talk to me mother whilst I change. Would you be a dear and look after Bob for a few minutes, dad?" She dashed off.

"Well! That was short and sweet," said her father. "You wouldn't think we hadn't seen her for weeks," he added with a smile.

Her mother noticed Sally's flushed cheeks and the covert looks she gave Bob, knew instinctively that at last their daughter had caught the love bug good and hard and she sighed. No wonder she had dashed off, no girl in that condition wanted to sit around in a creased, none too flattering uniform. 'I have a feeling,' she thought, 'that this is going to be painful for all of us.' She excused herself and followed her daughter into her bedroom.

As she entered the room Sally threw her arms around her.

"Isn't he gorgeous?" she cried, spinning around and dancing back to the bed, where dresses had been discarded as they were dragged from the wardrobe.

"He does seem very pleasant, dear," her mother replied, "but I've hardly had time to get to know him!"

"You'll love him," she said with certainty as she stripped off her uniform and tossed it onto the floor, opening drawers, throwing fresh undies onto the already crowded bed.

Her mother watched her as she ran from place to place. 'She is a beautiful girl,' she thought. Her dark hair, free from pins, tumbled across her tanned shoulders. She had always been beautiful, even as a child, her large brown eyes, thoughtful and questioning, had captivated hearts as long as she could remember.

Sally had suitors by the dozen, but even though she had gone out with boys from time to time, no one had made a permanent impression. Now, at twenty-six, she had met a man against whom she had no defence and her mother prayed, 'please let it be right, please don't let her get hurt.'

"Oh, mother! I haven't got a thing to wear!" She cried, as she pulled out the umpteenth dress.

"What about the new one you bought just before you left? It cost a fortune. It's in my wardrobe. I'll fetch it!" Her mother turned away as Sally slipped under the shower.

She returned with the dress over her arm, still in its plastic dust-coat. A few minutes later, Sally, showered and hair washed, dripped across the bedroom carpet, a towel wrapped around her head.

Her mother held up the dress.

"Just the thing, mother, just what I wanted!"

Her mother smiled. A few weeks ago when she had bought the dress on impulse, loving it's rich red colours, Sally had discarded it because she said the low neck line and flared skirt made her look like a gipsy wanton. Now it was just perfect.

'Ah, well!' She thought, 'love makes all women wantons.' She laid the dress carefully on the bed.

"I see he has a plaster on his head," she said. Has he been fighting?"

"Mother!" She said, all indignant. Her mother laughed.

"I didn't mean brawling, darling. I meant soldiering. You said over the phone that he was a sergeant!"

"Oh!" Then, "Mother! I'm not supposed to tell you this but … It will probably be in all the newspapers tomorrow," she concluded.

"Just he and four men did all that?" Sally's mother said. "He must be quite a man!"

"He is!" said Sally, brushing vigorously.

"I'm surprised a good looking man like that hasn't been married off long before now." She saw the brush stop, and a stricken look touched her daughter's face.

"He isn't married is he dear?"

"I don't know, mother, he doesn't talk about himself. I don't care if he is," she added defiantly. "if he is I'll fight her!" Tears flooded her eyes.

Her mother walked over to her daughter and put a hand on her shoulder. "Don't cry, darling, you'll make your eyes all red. It's no use getting upset over pure speculation. He's probably not married anyway." But a coldness touched her heart.

"I'd better get back and see that father isn't neglecting our guest," she said. "Don't be long dear, he won't enjoy being dragged out here and then left to the tender mercies of us two old fogies."

She need not have bothered. Bob and Sally's father found they had many things in common. John had fought in the 1939-45 war as an officer in the Argyles and was now with the Ministry of Agriculture. They were deep in conversation and totally absorbed.

Bob rose to his feet as she entered the room, his eyes looking behind her for Sally.

"Sally will be right out, Bob, she won't be long. Has John been looking after you?"

"Of course I have!" said John. "Anyhow! The lad's big enough and ugly enough to look after himself!" he chuckled.

She could tell immediately that they had hit it off, so she excused herself again to check the dinner arrangements.

A while later there was a call from Sally. "Mother, can you come here a moment please?" Her mother walked through to the bedroom to find Sally facing the door.

"How do I look?" She whispered, brushing the front of her dress, tucking a wisp of hair into place, showing every sign of acute nervousness.

Her mother paused, tilted her head to one side and said dubiously, "Well ...!"

Sally's hands fluttered.

"Darling, you have never looked so beautiful as you do now!" She said smiling. "He doesn't stand a chance!"

"Promise?"

"Promise!"

The two men were deep in conversation when Sally entered the room, neither of them looked up.

Sally's mother said quietly, "John! Would you get Sally and me a drink please?" At this point both men looked up.

Sally's father instinctively stood up. He would not normally have done so for his daughter. He started to speak.

"Wow, who's … " His wife silenced him with a look.

Bob started to rise, saw Sally, jerked upright so quickly that he knocked his chair over, spun around to pick it up, blushed, took another look, stepped forward, stammered "H-h-hello, Sally!" Then he stood there staring. His open admiration was all she could have wished for. She walked forward confidently, all woman. From behind her, her mother breathed a sigh of relief.

Bob's surprise was total. Sally had left him in a crumpled uniform that gave no hint of the woman inside, her hair pinned up to fit under her hat and flat shoes completed the picture of mediocrity. The woman who now confronted him had gleaming black hair that bobbed on her shoulders; a red tiered dress complementing her dark skin and crimson lips, snuggled into her tiny waist. Her breasts were small but beautifully shaped and curved above the bodice. Raised sandals and stocking drew his attention to her long slender legs. His overall impression was one of movement and sparkle.

"How is your drink, Bob?" said John. "would you like another whisky and soda Bob? ah! hum! Bob?"

Bob tore his eyes away.

"I beg your pardon, John. Yes please!" He said.

Dinner was a sparkling affair. Margaret Ferguson watched her husband drink more than she had seen him drink in years. He joked and laughed, mainly directing his conversation towards Bob in whom he had obviously found the son he'd always wanted. Bob could not take his eyes off Sally, and Margaret rejoiced.

After dinner they moved into the lounge, where John showed no signs of letting up. He would normally have retired to bed before ten o'clock.

Margaret had tried several times, unsuccessfully, to turn the conversation into a more personal channel, not because she was more inquisitive than the average woman but in the hope of quelling Sally's fears as to his marital state. Sally also tried but Bob was completely switched off on that channel.

It therefore came with a considerable shock to both women when a while later, John, with his bluff innocence, sailed straight into the question with both feet. He had just roared at a comment of Bob's and turning he slapped him on the shoulder and remarked, with no quile at all. "Surprised a strapping fellow like you has not married. Had more sense I suppose?"

Both women held their breath whilst trying to make light conversation.

There was silence for a moment, then Bob said quietly, "I was married once."

"Oh!" Said John. "Divorced?"

Sally saw the same shadow cross Bob's face and suddenly she did not want to hear his reply.

She looked up quickly. "Dad, that's Bob's business. Please don't embarrass him!"

Her father looked surprised. "Oh! sorry, lad. Didn't mean to pry. Just talk."

"I know you didn't, John, but I'll tell you all the same."

Sally looked up. "Not if you don't feel like it, Bob."

"I was married once!" He said. "Had a son! He'd have been three years old now. We lived on my parent's farm just outside the Wangwe Game Park. My wife, son, mother and father were all killed when their car ran over a landmine planted just outside the security fence."

"Oh God!" said Sally. "No!" Tears started from her eyes and rolled unheeded down her cheeks.

In the silence that followed John brought more drinks.

"So sorry I was instrumental in bringing those memories back to you, boy," said John gruffly. Margaret thought 'How can Sally fight a ghost? It would have been better had his wife been alive.'

"I'm sorry to have put a damper on what has been a wonderful evening," said Bob. "I felt so comfortable and at home here with you that I felt like telling somebody, just once. But now I think it's time I was going and let you good people get to bed." He rose.

Margaret walked over to him, pulling his head down she gave him a kiss on the cheek.

"I'm so glad you feel at home here, Bob. We would like you to treat it as such. You are always welcome."

John started to walk Bob to his car, caught his wife's eye, and said his goodbyes on the stoep. "It's been a real pleasure, Bob. I hope you can come again."

Bob looked at all three of them.

"I've arranged dinner at The Rhodes tomorrow evening. I hope you will be my guests. Can you make it?"

They thanked him and arranged to meet in the 'Can Can' bar at seven-thirty.

Bob reached for Sally's hand. "Will you see me off the premises, Miss?" he asked with a smile. They walked down the path to his car.

They stood by the door, neither knowing quite what to say, suddenly shy in each other's company.

"That was very kind of you to invite us all out tomorrow night. There will be quite a crowd. It's a pity Barry won't be there."

"Don't bank on it. He knows all about the arrangements. I wouldn't be surprised to see him turn up. Never known Barry to miss a night out yet!"

Sally laughed. "I hope he comes. You are all very good friends, aren't you?"

"It's a friendship born under tough circumstances, Sally. We all owe each other our lives. That must count for something."

"Men are so lucky! Women can never have friends quite like that. I wish sometimes I were a man."

He laughed. "In that dress, you'd certainly be a hit!"

He turned her so that the light caught her face. "Wear that dress tomorrow, will you? I'd like my friends to see you."

"You like it, do you?"

Bob smiled. "There's only one thing nicer."

"Oh! and what's that?"

"The filling!" He said, drawing her into his arms.

He slept late, had a leisurely shower, then drove around to the shopping centre to stock up with most of the things he would need for the next nine days, including four dozen cans of beer.

Then leaving his car at the flats he walked into the town.

He had a light lunch sitting under a large multi-coloured sunshade at a sidewalk cafe in the centre of town and watched the slim, sun tanned girls doing their lunchtime shopping. He noticed that the stores and office blocks still had security guards checking hand luggage and once during the morning he had been caught in a search cordon. Apart from that everything looked peaceful and calm.

He bought a newspaper and read about a security force raid into Mozambique, and it was only when he read, 'during the raid, eight Nyangan prisoners were rescued from certain death at the eleventh hour by a daring attack on a prison ... ', that he realised that the article referred to his recent efforts. For no accountable reason, he felt a rush of embarrassment and looked around guiltily. He turned to the 'deaths' column and noted that the 'In Memoriam' lists were getting longer but he was relieved when he failed to recognise any names.

He walked back slowly to his flat and let himself in. He felt once again the familiar swamping rush of loneliness that engulfed him. It was his own fault of course. Since all his known kith and kin had disappeared in the blinding flash of a landmine he had deliberately shunned company, avoiding friendships or any emotional entanglements.

He had taken the flat in town, furnishing it with bits and pieces from the farm and cut himself off. He had sold the farm stock and machinery, locked everything up and left it. One day, perhaps he might be able to sell it, but not now. He would never be able to go back again. It held too many memories.

He had loved his wife dearly and when a son arrived he had wanted nothing further. Eventually the farm would have been his and Jane's, to enlarge and make successful as an inheritance for his son, now it was all gone.

His hatred for the kind of people who could kill innocent men, women and children indiscriminately was all consuming. It was this hatred that made him take chances, risking his life time after time in the field, building up a reputation second to none. It was this reputation that was being discussed at that very moment at Command Headquarters, where recommendations and citations for bravery awards for him and his men were being passed from hand to hand.

He took a can of beer from the fridge and walked into the bedroom, kicked off his shoes, and dropped onto the bed.

And now there was Sally!

He knew without any doubt at all that he was falling in love again, something that he never thought could happen. He knew that Jane, wherever she was, would approve, she was like that. He'd had plenty of opportunities to date other girls, his big problem was putting them off without hurting their feelings. It was not that he did not want them, sometimes he ached to hold a woman in his arms. Once or twice he had nearly given in to his feelings but the same thing stopped him.

In a vague way he believed that when he died the family would all be reunited. That his wife and child were looking down at him. The thought of them watching whilst he made love to another woman was off-putting to say the least. He also thought that his chances of surviving this war were remote and he wanted to join them knowing that nothing had come between them.

He had tried to explain this to John once. It was at a party that John had talked him into. During the evening a particularly attractive woman had virtually thrown herself at him and John had watched, amazed, as Bob had discouraged her time after time until she finally gave up and joined a group of air-force types.

"What was that about?" he'd asked. "If you didn't want her you should have passed her over to me! I don't mind being second choice!" He looked at Bob, screwed up his face in a 'Long John Silver' take-off and said, "You're not goin' funny are ye, me hearty?" They'd both laughed.

John had pressed the point and as Bob had a need to unburden a little they had ended up sitting on an isolated part of the garden wall. When Bob had explained the way he felt John sat for a while thinking.

"Bob!" He said finally. "I understand the way you feel, but if there were any logic in what you say life would be unbearable. What about all the people we've killed. Could you bear the thought that they would all be 'up there' waiting? Even if in this brave new world all antagonism was forgotten, it would still be embarrassing. Why, you'd even hesitate to go to the loo, or think bad things because if they can see through walls they can surely read your mind. Think of all the good people who have remarried once or twice. That would take some sorting out. No Bob! It would be just as embarrassing for the watcher as it would be for the watched. It's not on!"

"So what are your thoughts on the subject?" Bob had asked.

"Bob, everyone thinks about life hereafter. Some people need a religious peg to hang their hopes on, that's possibly why a lot of older people make a last minute sprint with good works and church-going just in case there's something in it. Others evolve their own theory, one that suits them, one that they can use as a buffer or a salve to ease them over the edge of the unknown into death, or rebirth, if you like. You may recall some experiments carried out by the Americans a while ago, Bob. They tried to find out what happens if you withhold dreams from somebody for a long period. They connected up some electrical gadgets to the brains of several people and when increased activity signified that person was dreaming an electric shock woke them up. This went on for several days until the subjects were on the brink of insanity. They deduced from this that dreams were an essential part of our life, a recharging process. Now, I recall that as a child I was very active in my sleep. I would be sword-fencing like one of the Three Musketeers and leap right out of bed whilst dodging a sword thrust. I walked in my sleep. I remember hearing my sister cry out in the night, she had been dreaming she was sniffing flowers and had hit her nose on the wall, making it bleed. What it all adds up to is that I think dreams are all powerful to us."

"I don't see the connection," Bob said.

"Bear with me a moment Bob and I think you will. Isn't it possible that life as we know it is all a dream? When we have completed our 'three score years and ten.' we rub our eyes, shrug our shoulders, and say 'funny dream I had last night, I was on a place called earth'!"

"But," said Bob, "everybody doesn't die at three score years and ten!"

"Does everybody sleep the same length of time?" replied John. He continued. "They then go through a whole day in whatever media they live in and then go back to sleep again. That would explain reincarnation, why people sometimes feel 'I've been here before.'"

"Are you suggesting that earth, as we know it, is merely a play ground for our dream time?" Bob asked.

"Partly that and partly a reversing process, like matter and anti-matter, like flowers breathing in carbon dioxide by day and replacing oxygen by night, whatever it is we use up during our day, the process is reversed at night."

"But wouldn't that mean that in this other life of ours one day would be roughly three times three score years and ten, or two hundred and ten years?"

"So what?" John had replied. "Time is all relative. If you are having a good time, time flies, if you were being burnt at the stake each second would seem an hour. If you could only walk one metre an hour then a kilometre would take you one thousand hours, if you could fly at sixty kilometres per hour, then one kilometre would take only one minute. Everything is relative. You say, 'My! That girl has a lovely skin', but if you shrunk down to the size of an ant you would see pit holes all over her face and feel sick!"

"So what are you trying to say?"

John looked at Bob for a while. "What I am trying to do is give you an alternative theory to replace yours, so that you can start to live again. If you accept mine that life here is all a dream, you have the excuse that we are not responsible for our dreams, so do your own thing without regrets. Nobody is watching you, you have nothing to repay, just live and enjoy your dream."

It had sounded plausible to Bob at the time, but it had made no real difference. Confronted with similar situations he had felt the same restraints and nothing had ever matured.

Looking at his watch Bob discovered that it was six o'clock already and the sun was low in the sky. He must have dozed off. He got up and straightened the bed, then stripping off he stepped under the shower.

He arrived at the hotel a few minutes after seven o'clock and made his way up to the 'Can Can' bar to find John already two drinks ahead.

John had barely time to order a whisky and soda for Bob when a large hairy hand descended on his back and with a joyous "Hi!" Barry arrived.

"I told Sally you couldn't resist a party!" Bob laughed as he shook his hand.

"Oh! Is she coming along tonight?"

"Yes, and her mother and father," Bob said.

"I see! Chaperones. They must have heard of your reputation," said Barry. "She seemed a pleasant, quiet girl."

Knowing Barry, Bob took it to mean 'plain and uninteresting' and reminded himself to watch his face when she arrived.

"You've met her parents then?" asked John.

"Yes, she invited me back to dinner last night."

John thought, 'Well, he's had a lot prettier women chasing him. I don't think she stands a chance.'

"That's nice," he said.

Bob and Barry were on their second drink. Bob's back was to the door when Sally and her parents arrived. His first intimation was a low whistle from Barry.

"Gees! Just look at what's arrived," he muttered, obviously not recognising her.

John looked up appreciatively. "That's really something!"

Bob walked over to welcome them and took Sally's hand, drawing her to the bar. "You've met Sally," he said. "This is Mrs. and Mr. Ferguson. Er, close your mouth Barry, you look like a goldfish," he added laughing.

They all shook hands as Barry muttered something about uniforms for girls should be banned. Sally revelled in their obvious appreciation and turning to Bob she held his arm with both hands. She tipped her face up for a kiss, thought he would not approve in a public place, and changed her mind. Bob put his arm lightly across her shoulders and kissed her forehead.

'Well! That's a turn up for the book', thought John 'Don't tell me our Sally has worked a miracle and brought Bob back into the land of the living.' He sincerely hoped so.

Bob had just ordered drinks for the newcomers when Roy and his parents arrived, and everyone became tied up with introductions again. It appeared that John Ferguson and Henry van Houston had met before at the Ministry of Agriculture and various other farming community meetings. They immediately became engrossed in tobacco quotas, much to their wives' smiling objections.

Barry eased himself into a position beside Sally and proceeded to flirt outrageously, much to everyone's amusement.

At eight-thirty they moved into the dining room, where a large table had been reserved for them. Bob ushered Sally to the far side where she would have a view of the band and the room in general. Barry winked at John and they quickly moved either side of her, cutting out Bob. Sally looked around for Bob, panic on her face, half rose, sank down again looking quite dejected. John, laughing, stood up and offered the seat to Bob who smilingly refused, saying he would sit opposite where he could keep his eye on all three of them and talk to the other two ladies as well. He pulled a face at Sally who tossed her head and looked away pretending she was not talking to him, which pleased Barry enormously.

As soon as Bob sat, however, Sally's foot, minus a shoe, slid onto his knee. He tried not to laugh.

Sally's father leaned across to Henry. They spoke for a while, Henry nodding briskly. They called the wine steward over. A few minutes later iced buckets of champagne appeared. Henry turned to Bob and informed him that as he was paying for the dinner Sally's father and himself insisted on buying the wines. They had different wines with every course and between courses they danced. They laughed a lot, talked a lot, and thoroughly enjoyed themselves. At one stage of the evening, whilst Roy was dancing with Sally his father spoke quietly to Bob. "You're his idol, Bob. He thinks the world of you. I'd be grateful if you would keep an eye on him. I'm not asking you to mollycoddle the lad. He's tough, he's fit, and he's got guts, but he's all I've got. Without him there's nothing, do you understand, Bob?"

Bob was to remember those words at a later date.

It was one o'clock in the morning when they finally left the hotel, expressing their thanks to Bob and calling out their goodbyes. As a gesture Bob asked the Ferguson's if they would care to call in at his flat for a coffee or nightcap. They refused in spite of Sally's urgings until her mother laughingly said, "Sally, it's all right for you young people to stay up all night, but we older ones are dead on our feet. If you want to go to Bob's for coffee you go with him, but it means he'll have to run you home afterwards."

"Well that's settled then!" she said.

When they arrived at Bob's flat Sally busied herself in the

kitchen whilst Bob removed his jacket and tie. Coming up quietly behind her he slipped his arms around her waist letting his hands rest lightly on the softly rounded curve below her navel. She leaned back against him, turning her head, and he kissed her. She twisted slowly to face him, her hands reaching up crossing over behind his neck. Her body arched into his, their tongues met and explored each other. Bob's breathing became tinged with urgency. Then he stepped back holding her at arm's length. "Come on, young lady. Let's drink our coffee and I'll run you home. It's past your bedtime."

Sally moved forward and rested her beautiful head against Bob's chest. "You know I'll stay the night if you want me to. You only have to ask. I've absolutely no shame where you're concerned." she whispered.

He reached past her and turned off the kettle. "Young lady, pick up your bag. I'm taking you home right now before I change my mind. Tomorrow when I see your parents I want to be able to look them straight in the eye so they can say, 'well, that's a nice chap, he may even be good enough for our daughter.' He smiled and handed Sally her bag.

She sulked a little going down to his car, but before he moved off he put his arms around her and said gently. "As a child, whatever meal I had, I always kept the 'bestest' bit till last. I carefully ate all around it, then right at the end I would eat the 'bestest' piece, and that piece was better than the whole of the rest of the meal put together." He kissed her and drove off.

Her parents were still pottering around when Sally let herself into the house. She hung up her dress and was sitting on the edge of the bed when her mother knocked gently on the door.

"Come in mother," called Sally, "I'm not in bed yet."

Her mother walked in and sat on the stool facing her.

"What a charming man Bob is," she started. Sally burst into tears and dropping to her knees she put her head in her mother's lap and sobbed as if she would never stop.

Her mother just sat there brushing the shiny dark hair up from her neck and saying over and over again. "There, there, darling, it can't be as bad as all that."

Between sobs she said, "I offered to stay the night, I wanted to. I wanted him to make love to me, do you hear? I don't care!"

"And he turned you down?"

"Yes, he wouldn't even let me have coffee. He said he wanted to be able to look you and dad in the eye the next time he saw you … " She stopped crying and suddenly burst into bubbling laughter as she told her mother about his 'bestest bit', then she started crying again.

"My darling! You are in a state aren't you? I'm afraid we all go through it some time."

Her mother talked to her as she got ready for bed, then as Sally slipped between the cool sheets, she tucked her in as she used to when she was a child. Within seconds she was asleep.

She was still sleeping the next morning when the phone rang. It was Bob. She ran down the stairs in her nightdress to take the call.

"Hello, Bob. Are you there?" She said breathlessly. Her mother, who had handed Sally the phone, murmured. "If he could see you like that he wouldn't be sending you home without coffee." She walked away smiling.

"If you'd give me a chance to answer, I could confirm that I am indeed here," he said, laughing, "you were still in bed and it's eight-thirty. Don't tell me I've got myself a degenerate for a girlfriend!"

"I didn't get into bed until two o'clock, and I need my beauty sleep!"

"Yes that's true," he said blandly.

"Pig!"

At that stage her father walked past on his way to breakfast, and gazed for a while at his daughter who was standing on one leg, the other hooked behind it. Her frilly pants peeped out beneath her shorty nightdress. "Catch pneumonia standing around like that," he muttered. He slapped her bottom with his newspaper. "Give him my regards," he mimed. She nodded.

"Sally, are you listening?" asked Bob.

"Yes! Dad sends his regards."

"Thanks! Give him and your mother mine! Listen … "

"Are you coming out today?"

"Sally!" said Bob, exasperated, "if you will listen for just a few seconds, I will tell you. I rang up to let you know that I will be out of town for two, maybe three days. Do you hear me?" Pause.

"Yes I heard, but has it anything to do with last night?"

"Yes in a way, but not the way you're thinking."

"Where are you going?"

"I'll tell you all about it when I get back."

"Will you ring me."

"The very second I arrive back!"

"I'm sorry about last night," she said, with a catch in her voice.

"Don't be, I kicked myself all the way back to town."

"Don't lie to me," she said.

"Sally, I must go. I'll call you the minute I get back. Good-bye darling."

"Bye!" The phone clicked and he was gone.

Sally's mother heard the phone being replaced and called out. "If you have finished out there, slip on your dressing gown and come and have breakfast!"

Sally, running back to her room cried out tearfully, "I don't want any!" Her door closed behind her.

"What was all that about?" asked her father, looking up from his newspaper, a bewildered look on his face.

Her mother started getting a tray together.

"I don't know, John, I'll take her up a tray and she will probably tell me."

"She's been acting strangely lately," he persisted. "Wonder if she needs a tonic. Always seems to be either crying or dancing around singing."

She looked at him shaking her head. "Don't you think Bob may have something to do with it?"

"But he seems such a fine young lad."

"That's just it, John," she said, "your daughter is desperately in love for the first time and she doesn't know how to handle it. Luckily Bob seems to have enough sense for both of them. She's trying hard to throw away every moral value she has ever had and then regrets it and thinks Bob will despise her for it. She's all mixed up. She has a very strong emotional feeling for Bob, wanting to give him everything without restriction, when Bob doesn't take advantage of her emotions she feels cheapened, but she can't help herself. She is very unhappy."

John got up, laying his paper aside. "Oh! In that case," he said, "she needs her father. Give me that tray!"

She handed it over gratefully, knowing that in spite of his seeming unawareness, his love for his daughter was boundless. There had always been a rapport between them that could not exist between a mother and her daughter.

He climbed heavily up the stairs and knocked on Sally's bedroom door.

"Yes?" She said in a tearful voice.

"It's me, can I come in?"

"If you want to!"

He ambled in, closing the door behind him, placed the tray on the edge of the bed and sat down beside it.

"Right!" He said gruffly. "Who's been upsetting my baby? Tell me who it is and I'll go around and knock him down!"

Sally had to laugh in spite of her tears. Ever since she could remember whenever she had hurt herself her father had picked her up and said the same thing. Sometimes he would look all ferocious and bring his fists up like a boxer and dance around her punching at an imaginary enemy. Once or twice she had fallen deliberately, making out to cry just to hear him say it. Then he would cuddle her for a while and whisper into her ear. 'You were only just pretending weren't you?'

He looked at her for a while. "Painful is it, baby?"

She nodded tearfully.

"Well he's a grand lad! I've no doubt he's worth a few tears." He looked at her for a few moments, collecting his thoughts, then he said musingly. "Do you remember those children's parties your Aunt Mary used to have? They were always very popular. There was always plenty to eat and lots of fun and games. She always invited about a dozen kids. The thing you all liked most was the special cake she gave you as you left. Every cake had the child's name on it. Oh, they weren't so big, you could hold it in the flat of your hand. Most of the wretches had eaten theirs before they reached the gate, but you always brought yours home whole, so you could show it around. Then every so often you would take a knife from your doll's house, cut a very thin slice off and make out to feed your dolls. You always ended up eating it, or passing pieces to your mother or me. In that way you would make that cake last two or three days and get a tremendous amount of enjoyment out of it and give other people enjoyment just watching you." He stopped and seemed to be lost in his own thoughts.

"Meaning, dad?" She knew that this was not just idle reminiscence.

"Well, baby!" he said, "in Bob you have a man a notch or two above the average. Don't use up all the new experiences at once. Draw them out so that you can feel the beauty of it for a long time, like thinking back on your first pair of high heels, your first dance, the first time you saw snow, the first time you smelled chestnuts roasting. The second time loses something. It's never quite the same. A marriage has to last a long time, don't wear off the newness all at once," he smiled, "and if you keep crying like this and stop eating Bob will wonder what he's taken on, so take this tissue and dry your eyes and eat up this breakfast before it gets cold." He started to walk away. "And as an expert on women, er.. from my younger, wilder days of course … I would say you have nothing at all to worry about. Bob doesn't stand a chance."

"Promise?"

"Promise!"

As he closed the door he saw her pick up her fork.

During the next two days, Sally never left the house. She tried to be cheerful and threw herself energetically into all manner of jobs, but the moment the telephone rang, she dropped whatever she was doing and ran hopefully to answer it, only to be disappointed time and time again. Her mother tried unsuccessfully to draw her out of the house with shopping sprees, cinema shows and visits to friends, but to all suggestions she remained adamant. She would stay in case Bob should ring. When he finally did ring, late on the third day the whole house seemed to breathe a collective sigh of relief.

In answer to his 'hello!' Sally asked him if he had eaten yet.

"Good grief, Sally! I have not closed the door yet!" he said, laughing. "I've been driving since six this morning and only stopped once all day."

"Well, we've had our dinner already but there are plenty of cold meats and salads so why don't you come right over and eat here?"

"Well! If you're sure that's not an inconvenience, I'll just have a shower and change and will be there within the hour."

"Right! See you then." Sally ran into the lounge. "Bob's on his way over. I said we would fix him up with some cold meat and salad."

Her mother rose. "I'm sure he would prefer a thick steak and vegetables. I'll get it ready."

"Thanks, mum, I'll just tidy myself up." She called on her way up the stairs.

"Do I have to put a tie on?" asked her father with assumed seriousness, but she never heard.

"Don't tease the girl, John. She hardly knows what she is doing now!" Margaret Ferguson said.

Bob arrived wearing slacks and open necked shirt. He barely had time to close the car door when Sally came running across the lawn to meet him. He held his arms out and she leaped into them, her arms encircling his neck. The kiss was long and lingering. Sally stepped back and looked at him quizzically her head on one side. "And what is the verdict?" she asked.

Bob looked puzzled. "Verdict?"

"Yes! I've had the feeling I've just been put through some sort of test."

"You little chump!" He said, smiling. "If there was any test, that welcome should have told you the result."

She walked beside him to the stoep, both her hands on his arm, her head against his shoulder. "I've been so worried." She said.

Mrs Ferguson had set a tray for Bob in the lounge and he ate ravenously. Before he had finished Sally's parents had excused themselves and retired to bed.

After clearing the dishes away, Sally brought Bob a beer and sat on the carpet in front of his chair looking up at him.

"Well, darling!" She said finally, "are you going to tell me all about it? You don't have to if you don't want to." She added quickly.

"I want to tell you, Sally. But give me a few minutes to collect my thoughts. One thing I do want to make clear right at the beginning. There was no test as you put it. My feelings for you were never in doubt and nothing would have turned me from you

...?" He paused. "I drove all the way up to Wanwge to the little churchyard there, where my parents, my wife and my son are buried. I did not go there to ask permission or to justify my actions, no, I went there to restate my love for them all. As I stood by Jane's grave I tried to explain that I love you very much, but that my love for you did not in any way detract from the love I had for her. I would never compare one with the other. It's like trying to compare the taste of an orange to the taste of a peach. Each one is delicious but different. I cleared my mind of Jane and I felt her approval. She is dead, as is my son. Nothing will recall them. I shall always treasure their memory, but I will not mourn their passing. From now on Sally, in all the years to come, you will have all of me, all my love, with no regrets. There will be no ghosts in our bed and our love will be new and fresh to both of us, finding our way together. " He smiled at her tear brimmed eyes.

"In case you don't recognise it my love, that's a proposal of marriage, or do you want me to go down on one knee?"

CHAPTER SEVEN

The following day Sally and Bob spent the morning going from one jeweller to another whilst Sally tried to select an engagement ring. They finally ended up at a wholesale distributor, the owner of which was a personal friend of Bob's. He was delighted to hear their news, he promptly turned over his office for their use and had tray after tray of rings of every conceivable variation brought in.

Bob, who hated shopping at any time, watched Sally trying on one after the other, choosing first one, then another, only to abandon the latest choice when another tray was bought in. Two hours later his smile was cracking slightly. His normal shopping routine was clear cut and simple. If he wanted socks he would go to a reputable men's outfitter, buy the socks and leave, no shopping around for the cheapest, no changing his mind over colours or shades. His purchases in the supermarket were the same. He knew clearly what he wanted, bought it, and left. Sally sensed his growing impatience and kissed him lightly. "Nearly finished darling. It's a choice between these two," she pointed. They looked the same to Bob, but he smiled and told her to take her time. It was another half-hour before the choice was made and the ring paid for.

Sally's parents were delighted and insisted on an engagement party. The two women immediately plunged into an orgy of organisation. Bob got the general impression that he was in the way so he took himself off, picked up John and some rods, and drove out to Henry van Houston's farm for an afternoon's fishing. Henry had an irrigation dam almost a kilometre long and half a kilometre wide at the dam wall.

Most of the indigenous trees had been left and in various selected sites he had planted jacaranda and flamboyants, creating beautiful shady arbours. The dam itself had been stocked with 'tilapia' of various kinds. Bob had been pleased to accept Henry's open invitation to fish there at any time.

As they drove through the security fence and up to the sprawling farmhouse, Roy came charging out to meet them, pleased to have their company. Mrs. van Houston joined them on the stoep, followed a few minutes later by Henry, his arms full of ice cold tins of lager.

"Saw you coming down the road and thought a cold beer might go down well." He shook their hands warmly.

Once John had informed them of Bob's engagement, the whole gathering took on a party atmosphere, they laughed and talked and forgot all about the fishing as the sun dipped over the horizon.

At seven o'clock, Bob stood up to leave, inviting them all to the party.

Henry shook hands and said. "Why don't you two come out for some fishing some time!" They all laughed. "And don't you forget to bring Sally with you next time you come," called out his wife. They waved their farewells as they drove out past the security fence, Henry walking up behind them to lock the gates.

The party was arranged for Saturday evening, two days ahead. Sally's leave finished one day before Bob's, which meant she would have to be back at camp on the Sunday. Bob insisted that he should drive her back and spend the night with Barry in Umdali, reporting back with Barry the next day.

Because of the short notice they spent most of the evening phoning friends to tell them about the party. Mrs Ferguson had already arranged the catering and the drink, together with barmen and bar tent, which would be set up in the garden.

Bob spoke to Sally's mother, explaining that he would like to take Sally up to Lake Karina, stay one night and return on the afternoon of party, but he realised that there was a lot of work to do … "Nonsense, Bob! It's a lovely idea; most of the organising is done now. Go off and enjoy yourselves. You will have finished your leave soon and you won't get the chance again for a while."

They joined the early morning convoy that left at six o'clock and were at the Makuti turn off to Lake Karina by eleven o'clock. The convoy stopped at the hotel for refreshment and then moved on again to the beautiful scenic drive into Karina. The whole convoy was held up at one point whilst a herd of elephants drifted slowly across the road. The big bull blocked the way whilst the cows and calves disappeared with surprising suddenness into the shadow of the trees. The police reservists were cursing under their breath, swinging the Browning machine guns to cover the convoy as they waited.

Bob had always considered Karina to be the most creditable and beautifully developed area in the whole of Nyanga. The roads that swept around the hills, climbing and twisting, were always in a good state of repair and the verges immaculate. The view from almost anywhere was outstanding, from the towering immensity of the dam wall itself to the unbelievably blue island-studded lake that disappeared into the misty haze of distance. Elephants sometimes walked right into the township and baboons and monkeys abounded. When the sluice gates on the dam wall were opened the wind-tossed spray soared high above the gorge, often creating a rainbow that hung in the air for hours each day.

They drove down to the Carribbea Bay Hotel that sits, like a Spanish villa, right on the edge of the lake itself. Bob had reserved two adjoining single rooms and they checked in. They unpacked their cases, showered, changed into shorts and sandals, and walked down to the small beach.

Sally, lying on her stomach alongside Bob, was piling up small cones of sand in ragged lines. "Where are we going to live when we are married, darling?" she asked.

"Well, first of all, I suppose we had better decide on a date for the wedding," he replied. "I was thinking about it last night. We have the black takeover soon and the army will no doubt have to be on stand-by for that. I would prefer you to be out of the country at that time so that I could concentrate on my job without having to worry about you. You know what the first few weeks could be like as far as whites are concerned.

"As soon as things have settled I should be able to sell the farm and perhaps buy another nearer Katari. I would then leave the army and concentrate on farming."

"So when does a marriage fit in?"

"Well! I thought in about seven months. Everything should have settled down, and we could go overseas for our honeymoon, perhaps England ... "

"That's an awful long time!" Said Sally, pulling a face.

Bob smiled. "It's open for negotiation, within reason."

"How about tomorrow?"

"Chump!"

She lay there for a while, then … "Why did you have to book single rooms?"

"Because you are special and I am giving you the special treatment."

"Is that negotiable?"

"No!"

She pulled another face but felt a warm glow at the knowledge that he did not consider an engagement ring as a key to her body, that he was going to try to save her as his 'bestest bit.'

Bob stood up brushing the sand from his shorts, took her hands and pulled her to her feet.

"Come on lazy-bones, let's take a drive out to the crocodile farm. I haven't been out there in years. Have you seen it?"

Sally shook her head. "No! I haven't. Odd really, considering the number of times I've been up here. Never got around to it. Let's go!"

When they reached the farm they only had three quarters of an hour before it was due to close for visitors, but the black attendant showed them around the various ponds and even let Sally hold a small crocodile, less than six months old. Even at that age, it took up quite an aggressive attitude and Sally hurriedly handed it back, much to the attendant's amusement. Right at the end of the tour he showed them a separate pond which housed just two enormous beasts. They looked as if they were carved from stone, until he threw a lump of meat near them, then their speed was quite impressive.

When they arrived back at the office, they strolled around the shelves, packed with hundreds of items of interest to tourists. Sally went into peals of laughter over a small stuffed croc that had been badly treated so that its eyes drooped sadly, giving it a most droll expression. Bob insisted on buying it for her and she sat it on the front shelf in the car where it stayed until they arrived back in Katari.

They arrived back at the hotel to shower and change for dinner. Bob had left the door open between the rooms so that they could talk to each other. Sally said something that he did not quite understand. He walked to the door to ask her to repeat it and looking into her room he could see Sally standing by the bed. She was struggling to clip the back of her bra strap. She was wearing snowy white, lace edged panties, and her long slender limbs were beautifully curved and golden. Her dark hair was hanging over her face. As she bent forward he could see the white skin where the tan ended as she adjusted the cups around her firm, pointed breasts.

She raised her head slowly, tossing her hair to one side as she saw him standing in the doorway, a towel wrapped around his waist. His scarred body was strongly muscled, and his tan much darker that hers. They looked at each other for a long moment, Bob's urgency becoming more obvious every second. Sally felt a delicious ache starting from her lower belly and spreading upwards to her hardening nipples. They moved towards each other, arms reaching out, mouths joining, tongues probing. She could feel the hardness of him pressing with more and more urgency against her. She felt herself lifted into his arms and being carried back to the bed. She realised then, not without some secret joy, that Bob had lost all control, for the first time since she had known him his iron resolve had failed. As a woman she rejoiced in the knowledge, but intuitively she realised that he would hate himself afterwards.

That he was saving her until after they were married was a special proof of his love for her; that would be gone forever.

Every part of her cried out for him, she wanted to scream, "Now!" Her senses were reeling.

He laid her roughly onto the bed. His hands were tugging at her panties, trying to pull them over her buttocks. His urgency proved too much and with one cry he tore them from her. She wrenched her mouth away from his, twisting sideways, trying to get his body from between her legs. "Stop it!" She cried. "Stop it! Stop it! Oh, please, Bob, stop!"

He watched the tears flowing down her face, saw her luxurious hair sticking sweatily, to her forehead, felt her body heaving under his. He shook his head slowly from side to side as his eyes seemed to focus from a long distance. He heard his own breathing, harsh and rasping. She watched the dawning horror on his face as he realised what was happening. He swung himself from her to kneel by the side of the bed, his head on her shoulder. "Oh my God! What have I done?" he moaned. "Oh, Sally, I'm so sorry, I didn't mean to hurt you!"

She put her arms around his head, her lips against his cheek. "Darling, you didn't hurt me, I hurt you. I wanted you to make love to me. Don't blame yourself; It's my fault as well as yours. Ever since I have known you I have wanted you, I should have stopped you sooner, Bob, but I couldn't."

He took her into his arms and gently kissed her eyes, her nose and lips and she kissed away his failure. Then sitting up she removed her bra and kicked off the shreds of her panties. Then she laid back. "Bob, darling, I'm all yours to do with as you please. I only stopped you because you did not know what you were doing and you may have regretted it. If you want to make love to me now I would welcome you, now and any time. I have no shame with you; I love you more than life itself!"

He looked over her naked body slowly, his eyes moving from curve to curve, seeming to carve the shape into his mind. He kissed the little tuft of hair at the bottom of her belly.

"Sally!" he said, "you are the most beautiful of all God's creations. To look at you is to see heaven itself."

His voice was a husky whisper. "I love you more than you can ever know and I will spend the rest of my life showing you new facets of love that you have never dreamed of."

He rose to his feet and walked back to his own room.

Dinner by candlelight was all that Sally could wish for, their conversation never flagged. It was as if an entirely new dimension had entered into their relationship. It seemed that the episode in the bedroom had altered them both in some subtle way. His loss of control in the face of her beauty had added confidence and a surety that had been missing and in some abstruse manner brought him within her reach. Their positions had undergone a readjustment. A certain amount of urgency had disappeared from her emotions. She still anticipated their final coupling with delightful impatience but now felt confident of her ability to wait until after the wedding, if that was what Bob wanted.

After dinner they drove up to a position overlooking the dam wall, which at night was floodlit, even though the border was only a few hundred metres away. They passed several groups of silent men standing behind their artillery pieces, ready to retaliate should the terrorists start hurling mortar shells into Karina, which they had done on several occasions, two actually landing in the grounds of Carribbea Bay. It was a magnificent sight even with only three of the sluice gates open. Millions of litres of water arched out into the gorge, tumbling into a fearful maelstrom at the base of the towering wall, to race away to the open sea north of Beira in Mozambique, many hundreds of kilometres away. The sheer immensity of the project befuddled the mind and made one wonder at man's audacity.

As they watched they could see the police boats of the Marine Division moving out under cover of darkness on their way down the lake to take up patrol stations. Just a few boats to cover the largest man made lake in the world; nearly three hundred kilometres long and over a fifty wide in some parts. The job of this branch of the security forces was to stop terrorists crossing the lake from the north on their way to rape and pillage. The unit mostly comprised of volunteers; their fighting took place in the dark of night. They hunted with radar, striking, hiding up in the shelter of an island during the day only to move out again as night fell.

'What a great pity,' thought Sally, 'that such a beautiful lake should be abused in such a manner.'

They drove slowly back to the hotel.

The next morning Sally woke Bob up by squeezing a wet flannel over his head. She dodged back into her room, and he heard the key being turned before he was halfway across the room.

He tapped the door. "Let me in!" He called softly.

"No! You are going to get your own back!"

"No I'm not. Promise! I just want to kiss you good morning!"

"Promise?"

"Promise!"

She unlocked the door and stood back. Bob walked in, looked at her lecherously from her toes, which started to wriggle with embarrassment, slowly up her legs, until he reached the baby doll pyjamas. His breathing quickened and his eyes narrowed.

"Take those things off and get on the bed!" He muttered. Her eyes opened wide and she started to speak. Then without a word she pulled the top over her head, hesitated for a second and then rolled down the panties. She looked at him, her eyes troubled.

"On the bed!" He said through his teeth. She sat on the bed and swung her legs over. Her hands moved to cover herself.

"Don't! Leave it!" he snapped.

He walked over slowly to the bed, knelt down and took her into his arms, kissing her, slowly with love and tenderness.

"Good morning, darling!" He said and standing up walked back to his own room.

"Don't be long, we're water skiing after breakfast." He closed the door. A double thump heralded the arrival of two slippers as they hit the door.

"Pig!"

After a light breakfast they changed into swim suits and walked down to a small jetty where the boat was waiting. They slipped their skis on and sat back in the water as the slack on the tow-rope was taken up. Then they were off. Neither knew how well the other could ski and were both pleasantly surprised. They crossed over time after time, zipping far out on the flanks and tearing back into the boat's wake. When Bob kicked off one ski, going slalom, Sally followed. For thirty minutes they darted and weaved, finally casting off the tow and sliding towards the beach where they dropped into a metre of water, laughing and splashing each other. They showered and changed, checked out of the hotel, and were on their way back to Katari with the ten o'clock convoy. Arriving back in town just after four-thirty. Bob dropped Sally off at her house and hurried back to the flat to get himself ready for the party.

Sally and her mother walked around the house and garden where she was shown all the arrangements. The caterers and bar staff had been and left their bits and pieces. The bar tent was up and the bar erected and glasses polished. A braaivleis had been set up near the pool where the caterers would serve the hot, fire cooked steaks so beloved by all. The lounge was cleared for dancing. Sally was delighted with everything, running from one place to the other, bubbling with excitement. She must have kissed her mother a dozen times and when her father arrived downstairs after his nap, he came in for his fair share.

"Did you have a nice time at Karina, darling?" she asked.

"Oh, mother, you can't believe how wonderful it was," she cried. "Everything was perfect! Do you like Phred, spelt with a 'ph'?" she showed them the stuffed crocodile and they all laughed at his sad expression. They watched her as she danced away to start getting herself ready.

"Oh, John!" said Margaret. "I'm so happy for her. I have never seen her like this before."

"Yes! Love certainly adds a polish, that's just how you used to be when I came a-courting!" he replied.

Margaret looked at him and smiled. "You still do that to me, even after all these years," she said. He gave her a kiss and they wandered back into the house arm in arm.

Bob was back at the house, as promised, by seven-thirty ready to welcome the guests as they arrived. He looked truly magnificent in his dress suit, which Sally insisted he wore for the occasion. Sally herself was not yet ready so he wandered around feeling somewhat lost until John took his arm and guided him up to his den.

He poured them both a stiff drink of Remy Martin.

"Brace you for the coming ordeal, Bob!" He said, raising his glass. "I wanted to see you on your own for a minute before the rush starts. I'm not a demonstrative man, lad, but I wanted to offer my congratulations. I always wanted a son, but it never seemed to happen, but if I'd had one I don't think he would have measured up to you. You are all I have ever dreamed of for my Sally." He paused. Bob started to speak, but John raised his hand to stop him and continued.

"I've got something here that I would like you to have. It would have gone to my son, if I'd had one, it's been in my family a long time and I know that you will treasure it." He handed Bob a small, highly polished wooden box, almost black with age. The lid had an inset silver panel, exquisitely engraved. He opened it carefully, and resting on a blue cushion was a gold 'Hunter' watch. He lifted it out and turned it over. The back was ornately engraved with a Scottish coat of arms and an inscription in Gaelic with the family name. Bob was enthralled, having never seen anything like it.

"I don't know what to say, John, except thank you! It's the most beautiful timepiece I have ever seen," he murmured. "It must break your heart to let it go, I am very honoured."

"It's a pleasure to give it to you, Bob, normally it is kept in the bank. I got it out this morning."

Bob closed the lid and took John's hand. "John I told you the first evening I was here that I felt at home, I feel more than that now, I feel part of the family."

He handed back the box. "John! I accept this gift and all the tradition that goes with it. But I have nowhere to keep such a treasure. I would be grateful if you would look after it for me until Sally and I have our own place where it can rest securely."

They walked out into the hall as Sally stepped lightly down the stairs. Once again Bob was transfixed. She was wearing an ivory toned dress that clung to her beautiful body. Her dark hair was piled on top of her head, around her throat was a glittering display of antique jewellery with earrings to match. The whole effect was simplicity, good taste, and timeless beauty.

"My God! Sally," he said softly, as he walked towards her, "I have no words to describe you."

She coloured slightly under his gaze and took his arm. John, standing beside Margaret, held her hand and squeezed it gently as she fumbled for her handkerchief.

The first guest to arrive was Andy McGrath, he had driven all the way from Fort Albert where he was spending a few days hard earned leave.

Bob and Sally moved to meet him, Sally wondering who this huge great bear of a man was. Bob shook his hand warmly, pleased beyond words that his friend had come all that way to be with him on this occasion. Bob introduced them. Andy took her small hand into his massive one as he looked at her with open admiration.

"You must be 'The' Andy McGrath," she said and reached up in a gesture that endeared her to him for life. Standing on tip-toe she pulled his head down and planted a kiss full on his lips. "That's for what you did for Bob," she said.

Bob smiled at his friend as Andy blushed and shuffled his feet with embarrassed pleasure.

"Sally!" He said. "If that's the reward for helping my friend, I'm going to follow that lucky bum around for the rest of his life!"

She slipped her arm quite naturally inside his and led him inside the house to introduce him to her parents.

John, Barry and Roy arrived soon after, seeming to sense that he would need his friends around when all of Sally's guests arrived. Barry had arrived at John's house in the early afternoon and Roy had driven in at midday. Both were staying with John for the night.

John remarked to Sally on how beautiful she looked. She smiled her thanks, Barry and Roy were struck dumb.

She led them all to the bar where her father and Andy were chatting away like old friends.

John Ferguson looked at these men and discovered that they all had one thing in common, a quiet self assurance that can only be acquired in the tempering ground of a battle field or some other extreme of danger. It contrasted strangely in Roy and Barry, with an unworldly shyness that slowly disappeared as alcohol wore away their inhibitions.

Bob managed to join his friends for a quick drink and was then pulled away by Sally to meet incoming guests.

"It's started, Bob!" Called Andy. "That's how it's going to be from now on. No more drinking with your pals, no more nights out. So get used to it!" Sally joined in the general laughter.

People came and went in a kaleidoscope of faces and names. Bob made no attempt to remember either, knowing that only time and familiarity would etch them into his mind. He accepted their congratulations and comments as they shook his hand and he laughed when his head was pulled down to receive a kiss from some of the more adventurous ladies. He generally received a nudge in the ribs from Sally's elbow on these occasions and retaliated by licking his lips in obvious enjoyment.

It was almost nine-thirty when Bob turned to Sally. "How many more friends do you have Sally? You seem to have half the population of Katari and a few from outside. I suggest we pack up and just circulate."

They made their way over to the bar where Bob got Sally a drink.

"Has she let you off the hook yet?" called Andy. They made their way to the end of the bar where the big man was the centre of a small crowd, mostly women.

"Not yet," replied Bob. "By the way, how are Betty and the kids?"

Andy looked puzzled for a brief moment, then as one or two of the women around him started to drift away with looks of disappointed exasperation on their faces, he said pleadingly, "Aw! Bob, that was naughty, you know I'm not married. Tell them it's a joke." He looked at the women who were outraged innocence personified. Bob took Sally's arm and guided her away, shaking his head sadly.

"Bob! Come back here!" Andy cried. Bob kept on walking.

"Is he really married?" asked Sally in surprise.

"No of course not, he's a confirmed bachelor. He's been fighting off female limpets for as long as I can remember."

"Oh! Bob, that was not a nice thing to do, you have probably spoilt his fun now, how could you?"

"Never fear, my love, Andy Mcgrath will undoubtedly get his own back before the evening is through."

They moved from group to group with Sally briefing him on names and backgrounds as they approached. Her circle of friends was vast and seemed to cover the whole industrial, educational and commercial spectrum. Quite a lot of the men looked at Bob with naked envy in their eyes. Bob suspected that the crowd held more than a few of Sally's old flames.

He took her hand and led her into the lounge where one of the many travelling discos played non-stop dance music. Taking her into his arms he glided onto the crowded floor, taking advantage of one of the slower pieces of music to hold her close. Sally rested her head on his shoulder and drifted around in a dream world of her own.

Later, walking across the lawn to where the braaivleis had been set up near the swimming pool, they saw Barry and Roy deeply engrossed in conversation with two young girls. They walked over. The two girls looked up and inspected Bob with undisguised admiration.

"So this is your sergeant, Barry?" one said. "Barry tells me you personally killed fifteen terrorists single handed," she continued. Bob threw a glance at Barry that should have withered him on the spot but did not.

"Not exactly," he murmured. "I had to use both hands!"

"Oh!"

"Have you all eaten?" he asked. We are just going to try one of those steaks."

"We have eaten, thanks," said Roy.

Sally and Bob continued towards the braai. and were joined a few minutes later by John, accompanied by a tall willowy girl wearing large tortoiseshell spectacles which made her eyes look enormous.

"Bob, Sally! This is Rita, she's a school teacher but in spite of that appears quite intelligent," said John.

"Damned cheek!" she replied.

"I'm trying to wean her away from her primary school outlook and into the realms of adult conversation. She hasn't discovered what life is all about yet." She took his arm, pulling him away.

"Come on genius," she laughed. "Let's sit on that swing over there. I'll propound one of my pet theories, and you can pull it to bits." They wandered off.

"I'd love to hear that. Only John could discover someone who could discuss evolution or something similar, at a party."

Bob changed his mind when they reached the fire and chose a kebab and salad. They found a seat beside the pool away from the main crowd and ate their first meal since breakfast.

John was not sure how it had come about that he and Rita had paired off. He had been talking to Roy and Barry when three girls had come up to them. Barry had immediately started them laughing with some outlandish stories. Two of the girls were in their late teens and the other in her early twenty's. He had studied the older girl covertly for a while, noting her shyness. She was not beautiful by most standards but had a wide generous mouth and a lovely smile that fluttered on and off, transforming her face and presenting a lively, intelligent aspect.

He had never been interested in the accepted standard of beauty, in his experience many of the most attractive girls relied too much on their looks and seldom offered anything else, whereas the less attractive ones made a greater effort to be interesting and pleasant. He realised that was a generalisation that must contain a whole host of exceptions.

He was deep in thought and it was several seconds before he noticed the girl watching him. She started to look away, a flush of embarrassment suffusing her cheeks. His sympathy was instrumental, initially, in his over-reaction. Taking her arm he walked her over to the dance floor where, during the following half an hour they discovered a mutual liking. They walked back to the garden seat.

"Alright!" He said, "let's hear this pet theory of yours!"

"In a minute, John, but first of all tell me about yourself. You have at least four wonderful friends here who obviously think the world of you, yet you try to stand aloof. No! Not aloof, it's more as if you are frightened to let yourself go. You are a lot older in your attitude than the others."

John raised his hands, about to speak. Rita quickly interjected. "I'm sorry, John, I'm not trying to be rude or prying. I just think you are a bit lonely and isolated from life and I'm trying to help."

John looked at her contrite face and choked back the sarcastic comment he would have made to any other person who tried to invade his privacy. He felt her interest and sympathy and for the first time in his life the urge to unburden himself was too great to withhold.

He told her of his childhood, of his parents, both professional people tied to a social life that found their young son an encumbrance. He told her of his holidays from school, spent with an uncle on a farm near the Zambian border, where an old Shangaan tracker had taken him on long treks into the bush; taking a delight in his white protégé, teaching him the skills and tricks of the tracker's art that was to prove so useful in the years ahead. He told her of the lonely evenings and weekends when his parents were overseas attending conventions with the legal fraternity, or at 'unavoidable' cocktail parties. He spoke for nearly an hour and Rita gave him her whole attention, introducing a question from time to time, making the odd comment that showed her interest. At the end of that time he ground to a halt, mentally drained, surprised at himself and apologetic.

"Hell! Rita, I'm sorry about this, drivelling on all that time, you must find me the world's most monumental bore." He took her hands in his. "Why didn't you stop me?"

Her smile was warm and understanding. "I didn't stop you, John because I was tremendously interested. You must have had a very lonely time. I know you would never talk about these things normally and I am truly flattered that you felt able to talk to me."

"Well you've heard my tale of woe, now let me hear your theory."

"All right as soon as you get me another drink!"

"Sister!" said John, "this had better be worth it!"

He returned a few minutes later with two glasses of beer.

"I somehow knew you would be a beer drinker," he said with a smile.

She raised her glass. "Cheers! I'm hoping it will help me put on some weight!"

"You're fine just as you are."

"Liar!"

"Now your theory?"

"I don't mind discussing it with you, you can pull it to bits, but don't you dare laugh!"

"That's a promise!"

She started to speak and then looked at her watch. She paused for a while then said. "It's nearly midnight, John. Do you want to stay on here for a while longer?"

"Not particularly. I think Bob has enough back-up crew with him. Why?"

Rita looked flustered for a moment, then she said with an obvious effort, "I rather wondered if you would like to come back to my flat and talk over coffee ... that's not a 'come-on', John," she hastened to add, her face beginning to colour up.

"You forward hussy, you!" Laughed John. Then added quickly as she started to protest, "I'll accept that offer gratefully, the way it was intended." She smiled her thanks.

"I'll just tell Roy that I may be late and give him the house keys, my folks are away so they can let themselves in." He returned a few minutes later and after saying their good-byes to Sally and Bob they wandered off deep in conversation.

"Well! Do I sense another romance?"

"I hope so, Bob, Rita is a really great girl, I know they'll suit each other perfectly!"

"Matchmaker!"

"Pig!"

Just after midnight people started to leave, but it was nearly three o'clock in the morning before Bob managed to shove Andy, Barry and Roy into their cars. They disappeared down the road to a cacophony of hooters and shouts.

"They are all staying at John's house tonight. He'll probably have complaints from the neighbours tomorrow. What a noisy lot!"

"What a lovely lot, Bob. They are just about the nicest guys I know."

"Did you enjoy yourself Sally?"

"Need you ask?"

CHAPTER EIGHT

Bob had already decided to cut his leave short by one day and return with Sally. The following morning they joined the Umdali convoy and reached the camp in the late afternoon.

Word of their engagement had preceded them and as Bob entered the Sergeants' mess he was greeted with comments from all sides.

"Why did you come back a day early, Bob, don't you trust us?"

"Hell, Bob! That was quick work!"

"I was just building up to a proposal myself!"

He called for drinks all round from the mess bar and accepted their chaffing with good grace.

By midday Monday, John, Barry and Roy had arrived and Bob was summoned to Colonel Jameson's office where, as he entered, Captain White shook his hand. "I believe congratulations are in order, sergeant. That was quick work!" he smiled.

"Oh! What's all this about?" asked the colonel.

"Sergeant Wilson has just engaged himself to Miss Ferguson, sir," the captain explained.

The colonel gave the captain a long look in which a question hovered. Captain White started to speak, then gave a slight, almost imperceptible shrug and closed his mouth again.

To Sergeant Wilson there seemed to be a slight awkwardness to the colonel's effusive congratulations.

The colonel signalled Sergeant Wilson to sit and stood puffing his pipe for a while before he spoke.

"Sergeant, I have some good news and some bad news," he said. He walked behind his desk and sat down. "As you have just returned from what was obviously a very pleasant leave, I'll give you the good news first. With regard to your highly successful sortie over the other side," he paused and pointed in the general direction of Mozambique, "you have been given a commission and this time we are not accepting your refusal," he added, slapping the table with his hand.

Sergeant Wilson opened his mouth to speak. The colonel waved him into silence and continued.

"Kelso also gets his third stripe and McEvoy becomes a corporal." He paused. "Young van Houston gets a very high recommendation that will ensure a quick promotion as soon as he turns eighteen. In addition, all of you, including Stevens, will receive awards for bravery. Any comment so far?"

"I take it, sir, that you will tell the others yourself?"

"Yes, sergeant, as soon as we have finished with you, the others will be sent for." Said the colonel.

"Right, now for the bad news," he continued, "and I cannot tell you how sorry I am to thrust this at you, especially having just heard of your engagement, er … I'll let Captain White explain the situation." He nodded and the captain, turning to the wall map, began to speak.

"First of all, sergeant, let me assure you that this is only a rough briefing to prepare you for a more comprehensive briefing tomorrow, to give you time to think up questions and answers, as it were.. During the past week we have been getting numerous reports of terrorist action in this area." He pointed to the map and circled the north east corner of the country, including M'Como.

"European farms, native villages, a sub post office, several stores and some residential houses have all been attacked. The signs are that your old pal Francis Chaka is leading them. Special Branch has more information which they have obtained from a captured, wounded terr. You will hear about that tomorrow. Chaka is quickly building up a reputation for invincibility; he has to be stopped at all cost. We have discussed this ad nauseam and as unfair as it may seem, you are the only man who stands a chance of doing the job. I am very sorry to have to ask and I do stress the word 'ask', you to do it. Should you, considering your changed circumstances, decline the job we will have to find some … "

"You don't have to go on, sir," said the sergeant. "You know I'd be pleased to have another go at that bastard!"

"I thought you would!" Said the captain, with a sigh of relief. "We believe the gang to number about thirty. You can pick your own men and armaments, but sergeant, this gang is tough. With Chaka leading them they are fanatical, you will not have an easy task."

There was a long silence.

"Anything else you need to know at this stage, sergeant?" asked the colonel.

"What time is the briefing?"

"Nine o'clock tomorrow morning."

"Can I start sounding out my men?"

"Yes, but caution them to silence!"

"There's just one other thing. If you don't mind we'll leave the promotions 'till we get back. It will only cause confusion. Ok?

"I understand. That's fine, sergeant."

"When would we leave?" asked the sergeant.

"Wednesday at the latest," said the colonel. The sergeant rose and took his leave.

Two hours later he sent a messenger to call John, Barry and Roy. When they arrived he ushered them into his room and handed them a can of beer. They had all been told of their promotions and awards, but for some reason known only to themselves, they were reluctant to discuss them.

There was silence for a while then John looked up. "You didn't call us over here just to give us a beer, Bob," he said.

Bob grinned. "Don't you think heroes deserve one?"

Barry toyed with his beer can to hide his embarrassment, Roy laughed self consciously.

"Ok! I'll come to the point," he said. "I have been given a job to do entailing 'Nailing the Hammer', if you will excuse the pun. It won't be an easy job or a safe one. Now I know you have all been told of your awards and will probably be feeling cock-a-hoop, so I am not going to ask any of you for a commitment today. I want you to sleep on what I am going to tell you, in strict confidence, and give me an answer tomorrow, first thing. I shall also want one extra man."

He took a sip of his beer and then went on to explain the task ahead. At the conclusion, as Bob stopped speaking, all three of them volunteered.

"I'm not listening!" said the sergeant. "if you still want to come tomorrow, let me know."

John ignored him and as if all had been decided, said, "you said you wanted one more? Well, you remember that chap we brought back with us from Mozambique? From Number One Commando? He was badly knocked about but all guts. Well his name is Greg, Greg Bartlet. He came back off R.and R. yesterday and was keen to join our outfit. He was talking to me about it earlier on."

"Yes," said Sergeant Wilson. "He's the tall, rangy lad, when you leave see if you can find him and send him to me." As they rose to leave he told them of the briefing and arranged to see them afterwards. He had already accepted the fact that they were all going.

He worked for some time on his arrangements, ate a hurried supper, and walked across to the other side of the camp to where the girl's quarters were. Sally was waiting for him outside their common room. He opened his arms as she flew towards him and she felt herself engulfed. Bob kissed her and she pressed herself to him fiercely, kissing his mouth, his chin, his cheeks. There was a wildness about her that Bob had not seen before, a tinge of desperation.

'She knows!' He thought. 'I wonder how she found out?' But knowing the camp telegraph he was not surprised.

They walked through the common room and on to the stoep at the back. The two girls already there discovered they had other things to do and smilingly left. Sally chatted away non-stop about nothing at all whilst Bob listened, waiting for the crisis he knew would come. He took her hands and drew her to him. She looked into his eyes and saw love, pain and compassion and knew that she was not fooling him for one moment. Burying her face against his chest she spoke bitterly.

"Why you, Bob? Why you? You have done more than your share, it's not fair!" she cried. He held her close, not speaking.

"You don't have to go, do you?" she said with a catch in her voice. "They say it's very dangerous."

Bob cursed the unknown 'they'.

He held her at arm's length and looked at her for a long moment, seeming to imprint the beauty of her onto his heart for all time.

"Darling!" He said, "it's a job. I have no reason to believe that it is any more dangerous than others before it. You are quite right in saying that I do not have to accept it, but the powers that be believe that I am the most experienced and stand the best chance of completing the job and getting myself and my men back in one piece. I am also confident of my ability to do it. If I wasn't, then for your sake alone, I would have refused it rather than expose you to the misery I know you would feel should anything happen to me. But, darling, if I turn it down then somebody else would have to do it, somebody perhaps with less experience than me. His chances would be less than mine and if he were to be killed because of that inexperience, then that would be on my conscience for all time, I know you wouldn't want that."

"Will John, Barry and Roy be going?"

"Yes!"

"Bob," she sobbed. "I know what you say is right and that I shouldn't interfere. One part of me understands what you say, but the other part doesn't want you to go, doesn't care if everyone else in the world gets killed as long as I have you. I don't care if that's selfish, I don't care what anyone thinks. I want you!"

He stayed with her for a while, comforting her, reassuring her and then reluctantly he made his way back to his own quarters.

At nine o'clock the next morning he was in the briefing room awaiting the arrival of Colonel Jameson. Captain White sat alongside Sergeant Wilson, opposite sat the two men from Special Branch. The sergeant noticed that Captain White had not called upon Sally to take notes and was pleased.

Everyone rose as the colonel entered the room and sat again at a wave of his hand. He took his seat and called the meeting to order.

"Sergeant," he started, "you have been given some information about this proposed sortie in order that you might have time to prepare yourself. These gentlemen, whom you have met before will give you more detailed information that may be of assistance to you, you know the drill. If at any time there is anything that is not clear say so. It's your last chance." He smiled and gave a sign for the men sitting opposite to start.

One of them stood up and pointed to a large-scale map of the north-eastern area of the country. Another map covering the area up to the southern part of Lake Malawi was folded and pinned partly over it. He picked up a pointer.

"This is the area in which you will be operating, sergeant," he said. "We have reason to believe that the group that we are interested in came from Tambara, south east of Tete on the

Zambesi. We were fortunate in capturing a wounded terr who has given us a lot of valuable information. Apparently there is a large training camp there with about ten Cuban instructors, advisers. It is a very important discovery for us because this is no ordinary training camp. The Cubans have selected about two hundred top terrorists and are giving them intensive training in terrorism, subversion and infiltration. They have neatly blended traditional African witchcraft and all the usual charms and *muti*, medicines, and a variety of talismans that are supposed to deflect our bullets and put the fear of God into our security forces. The witchdoctors have been bought and are being used, just as ours were in the early days. This camp is being used as a show-piece, the reason we haven't heard of it before is due to the terror that the witchdoctors have instilled into the locals. Anyone who opens his mouth will die and of course as you and I know, they will. I have no doubt that a few murders by the Cubans have created the right atmosphere. An almost religious fervour hangs over this camp. They are told constantly that they are the 'elite', God's chosen, that very special tribal gods watch over them, guide them and protect them.

They are being sent out on specially selected targets. Every possible precaution is taken that none get killed. This would shatter their belief in their invincibility. They are given 'soft' targets that have been carefully scouted by civilian spies, paid locals and even by bought servants. They have been shot at by their instructors dressed in Nyangan camouflage who, of course, carefully miss, then run away. Everything possible is being done to make them believe they are supermen. When they have finished their training each one will be sent to command a terrorist band for a concerted attack on us." He paused and sipped some water. "To create a godlike figurehead, somebody to whom they will attribute supernatural powers and follow blindly, they have been using one man. A man trained for years in Cuba. Previous to that he was given a university education, paid for by the World Council of Churches and English government grants and he attended the London School of Economics. He is a very intelligent, utterly ruthless man. We have reason to believe that he has been trained for a very special role, I wish we knew what it was. That man, sergeant, is your friend Francis Chaka, otherwise known as the 'Hammer'. Any questions so far?"

The sergeant remarked. "What a pity we didn't get him last time! But surely the fact that we wiped out most of his men must have been a disillusionment."

"Not necessarily. You said yourself that only two escaped your last attack, Chaka and one other. That other one could have been in the know and kept quiet, or else Chaka would have ensured that he never returned to camp. He could then have made up some plausible story, such as having had them transferred to Zambia or some other camp in Botswana and nobody would have been any the wiser." He paused. "But I'll tell you this, sergeant, don't ever get caught alive, you or your men. You personally have a very attractive price on your head and you are well known in this and other camps. I don't know where he gets his information, I wish I did, but he appears to be well informed. You are considered enemy number one. You would be a great prize.

Finally, before I hand you over to my colleague here, I would just like to say that if 'super' terrs are allowed to spread around other camps it could start some sort of jihad which, once started, becomes totally fanatical and difficult to stop. We could hit this camp with Commandos, Scouts, or S.A.S., and believe me we will, but we could not guarantee to get Chaka. He could be in the field, operating away in Beira, anywhere. We want him dead and above all discredited, his invincibility shattered. If you can get this man, sergeant you will have broken the back of terrorist morale for years to come." He sat down.

His colleague stood up, picked up the pointer and cleared his throat.

"Ahum! As you have already been told, the present super terrorists groups have come from their base near Tete at Tambara, here!" he pointed, "on the Zambesi. They are believed to have crossed the Conresi River here at Cotemani, north-east of M'como, and are operating in this area bounded by M'como, Shamra, Mount Darwinian, and the Mavuradonha Mountains." His pointer traced out an area of almost a hundred square kilometres. "Two European farms were attacked about a week ago. In one incident a farmer was killed whilst talking to his labourers in the field. Most of his workers and their families were murdered. In the second incident, a faithful servant of some twelve years stole the keys to the security gates and let the terrs in. They gave the farmer, his wife and two children the full treatment. I won't go into details, sergeant. You are well aware of them. Then two days later three native villages were burned down and the unfortunate villagers mutilated. They were accused of assisting our security forces. Then in quick succession, they hit a sub post office, two native stores and then surprisingly, two residential houses on the outskirts of Mount Darwinian. In both of the latter attacks the families were warned by, in one case the cook and in the other, by the gardener, both of whom heard about the impending attacks just before they were launched and risked their own necks to warn their employers. I'm glad there are still some loyal ones left. You have the dates and details on that sheet of paper in front of you," he added.

"Now the latest report to come in, just this morning, is that a family living near the 'Bradey Institute' were attacked yesterday afternoon. It's not on that sheet, sergeant," he said as Sergeant Wilson glanced at the paper in front of him. "We didn't have time to include it. The husband maintained the pumping station on the local dam. There were the husband, wife and four children. They were all killed except the wife. There really wasn't any point in killing her, sergeant," he said in answer to the sergeant's raised eyebrows, "they forced her to watch her children and her husband being tortured to death, there were twenty-five bayonet wounds, for God's sake, in the four year old son. What they did to the others is beyond description. The mother is now in the psychiatric ward in Katali General Hospital. The bastards tore her eyes out, she's totally insane."

Captain White glanced at the sergeant who had made no comment. The veins on Wilson's neck stood out like cords and his lips were pressed into a thin white line. Captain White thought grimly that he would hate to have this man on his trail. He knew the sergeant's tragic background and wondered, not for the first time, how Wilson kept his balance between a single-minded killer, coldly efficient and the warm-hearted man who had just become engaged and was widely liked and admired.

The Special Branch man continued. "The gang is believed to number twenty-nine or thirty now. When last observed they were moving northwards along the bank of the river that flows past the eastern side of the Mavuradonha Mountains, probably heading back towards Tete. We propose to drop you and your men off near Rusambo by helicopter. It's then up to you and I wish you and your men every success!" He started to collect his papers. Looking up he asked the sergeant if there were any questions.

"I have a completely free hand in this?" asked the sergeant.

"Absolutely! Captain White will sort out all the practical points, such as transport, maps, codes, supplies and recovery and so on."

"Then I have no other questions," Wilson said.

The two Special Branch men nodded and left.

"Have you decided how many men you are taking, sergeant?"

"Yes sir! There will be Kelso, McEvoy, van Houston and Bartlet."

"Just the five of you?"

"Yes sir!"

"And equipment?"

"We will travel light and fast, living off the land where possible. In addition to our FNs, I want four grenades per man and one of those new lightweight radios that you got in last week and won't let us have a look at." He smiled at the captain's grimace.

"I thought I had hidden those well, they are very expensive and very good. Of course you can have one, sergeant. At least it shouldn't start fading mysteriously at convenient moments." He laughed at the sergeant's discomfiture. "The batteries have four times the life of the old sets."

The sergeant continued hurriedly. "Knives, no boots, just veltskoens, one of the small compact medical kits, maps, codes, five kilos of biltong per man, six magazines and three hundred rounds each, two water bottles each and two torches, one large and one small. The rest of the things I need I have already."

"How about sleeping bags, ponchos, rations …?"

"We don't need them, sir."

Captain White opened his briefcase, drew out all necessary maps and handed them over together with code sheets to the sergeant. Then he brought out an official looking letter in a plastic sleeve.

"This is your authority, signed by the man at the top. Any branch of the security forces is commanded to render any assistance possible at any time!" He passed it over.

"The helicopter will arrive at the camp at thirteen hundred hours tomorrow," he said. "As long as you are all equipped and ready to go, you are free to do as you like. Passes are available if you need them. All that remains is for us to wish you and your men good luck and a safe return."

He shook hands. Colonel Jameson followed suit.

The whole briefing had taken less than one and a half hours, so Wilson called his men together, got them equipped and explained the situation to them, advising them to check their next of kin forms and wills, if they had any. This was normal procedure and raised no comment.

That evening John, Barry, Roy and Greg took Sally and Bob into Umdali and treated them to an early show at the local cinema, and then to dinner at the Wise Fox. Sergeant Wilson was glad of their company, which was lively and humorous. They made a special effort to keep Sally amused and not once did they mention tomorrow.

It was not until they returned to camp and Bob was walking Sally back to her quarters that she began to cry, very quietly.

CHAPTER NINE

The helicopter circled the camp once, gaining height for its run over the Nyanga mountains. The five men were wedged uncomfortably in the seats with their packs jammed into every conceivable space. Even the pilot had very little room to move and performed the necessary functions with stoical good humour. They climbed steadily and the men in their cramped positions shivered as the temperature dropped, but no one complained as they stared ahead, each one immersed in his own private thoughts.

An hour later the mountains began to fall behind and Mozambique appeared eastward as the chopper swung in a slow arc to the north and west, heading for the north side of the river, some fifteen kilometres from Rutambo where the dropping-off zone was.

The pilot flew low over the river looking for a suitable clearing in this wild and desolate area. He pointed out a mud bank in the middle of a wide sweep where dozens of crocodiles lay in sleeping rows, like sawn trees waiting to be floated down to a sawmill. As the chopper approached they slithered down the banks into the murky water with hardly a splash.

"Ugly bastards," muttered the pilot. "I'd hate to land amongst that lot!"

Sergeant Wilson turned to his men. "Remember your chopper drill lads. John, you follow me out and cover south. Leave your pack. The rest of you unload the gear and cover three-sixty degrees until the chopper leaves, and watch your head!"

Being unable to find a suitable clearing the pilot finally decided to hold the helicopter two metres above the river bank, balancing with great skill, whilst the men jumped out. They unloaded and scattered into the shadow of the trees whilst the pilot, with a wave and a grin spun away and headed back to Katari. 'Better you than me', he said to himself as he watched the rugged, frightening landscape flash past below him. There was almost impenetrable thorn bush sliced through by, mostly, dry river beds, which he remembered were known locally as 'dongas', and the Mavuradonha Mountains, black and menacing, a towering, evil backcloth to the drama that would be enacted there in the next few days. As a South African he took his hat off to Sergeant Wilson and men like him who fought year after year, ill equipped, greatly outnumbered, world opinion against them. But they were fighting with a tenacity and courage that confounded their critics, surprised their foes, and brought grudging admiration from all sections. 'I wish we could do more!' he thought.

Sergeant Wilson called John to him and the two of them pored over a map whilst the rest of the stick covered. He stuck his finger on a spot by the side of the river. "This is our position now and this is the last known position of Chaka's group," he said, pointing to a spot twenty kilometres away.

"You've hunted these mountains, John. Put yourself in Chaka's shoes. After the havoc he's caused he knows our security forces will be after him. He'll try to get back into Mozambique. Which is the most obvious way back?"

John thought for a moment.

"He's a long way from Tete," he said at last. "He must know we'll be covering his crossing at Cotemane so he is not likely to return that way. His best bet as I see it is to follow this river up to Chioco and then on to Tete, but that's a bit obvious," he concluded.

"Is there any other track that you know of not quite so obvious, one that might offer a little entertainment on the way?"

"Well!" Said John. "There is the old Mavuradonha game camp at the foot of the mountain. It's a beautiful spot and has lots of game. It started off well but is so difficult to get to that it never became popular. Now with the war nobody goes there. The last I heard a young couple were holding the place together by running a store for the locals." John pointed to a spot on the map. "It's about here, some fifteen kilometres west of us."

"Do they have an airstrip?"

"No! it's too wild. That's one of the reasons why it failed."

"How about Agric-alert, or radio?"

"I don't think so, the nearest place to them is Mount Darwinian, that's eighty kilometres away. They tried a radio telephone at the beginning, but the camp is low down and with the mountain in between it never worked."

The sergeant brushed the sweat from his eyes. "Well, John, I think that's where they'll head for!"

"A bit of a long shot isn't it, Bob? If we miss them there we'll have to chase them right back to their base camp!"

"It's not such a long shot, John, those last two attacks got him little in the way of supplies or loot and their ammo must be getting short. By hitting a soft target like this he gets his supplies, plenty of loot for the gang to take back and only a short distance to carry it, with a morale boosting murder or two just before popping back over the border. If he goes any other way all these advantages are lost, plus the chance that a run-in with our guys is more likely."

John saw the logic in the sergeant's argument. "In which case the sooner we get there the better," he said. "I suggest we follow the river for about eight kilometres before heading west. The country levels out a bit and there are less thorn trees. There are lots of dongas to use for cover and we can make twice the speed."

Sergeant Wilson called in the rest of the patrol and they moved off carefully, parallel to the river but avoiding the open spaces, keeping to the shadows, ever watchful.

They passed several small, cultivated clearings and helped themselves to ground nuts, paw paw and mangoes. They saw no villagers although occasionally a kraal could be seen nestling in the folds of the hills. They reached the point where they intended to turn off just as the sun made its frantic dash over the horizon to disappear in a magnificent outburst of colour peculiar to Africa alone.

They slept that night in an abandoned hut, the roof of which had mainly fallen in, allowing a glimpse of heavenly bodies as they moved with cold indifference along their allotted paths.

At first light they chewed strips of black biltong, washed them down with mouthfuls of lukewarm water from their bottles and watched the rising sun chase the stars from the sky. The African soil came alive as myriad creatures started their daily dashing from nowhere to nowhere.

The patrol headed westward, Sergeant Wilson or Kelso scouting ahead, checking the ground for signs of recent passage, finding likely trails. Several dry river beds allowed a faster pace until their meanderings northwards towards the Zambesi River rendered them useless.

Towards midday they were climbing slowly towards a plateau that overshadowed the dry rocky bush country and folded itself around the base of the mountain. It was greener than the lower plain and the stubby bush was broken up by large areas of mopani trees, acacia and fir. For the first time they could feel the soft stirrings of a breeze. The sergeant, scouting ahead, raised his hand and signalled them to cover. Kelso moved forward stealthily.

The sergeant swung his head in a listening attitude and Kelso, who had been sucking a round pebble to keep his mouth moist, spat the stone into his hand and allowed his lower jaw to drop. The sergeant noted the action, typical of the tracker. Both knew you can hear better with an empty mouth and a slack jaw. He listened a moment and then pointed ahead and to the right. They moved away from each other and were swallowed up by the tall grass and shrubs. The patrol waited, each man confidant that both men were totally competent in this environment and could well fend for themselves.

Ten minutes passed and then came the high pitched chatter of a weaver bird, answered immediately from a distance. Barry signalled the patrol forward. They found the sergeant and John standing quietly in the shadows watching a herd of water buffalo at a waterhole. There were about thirty of them, the bosses of their huge curved horns massive, black and powerful. These were amongst the most savagely aggressive animals in the whole of Africa, they allowed no liberties. The patrol watched, down wind and well hidden by the dense bush. They took their time. The cows and calves drank whilst the young bulls playfully butted each other. One large bull, obviously the leader, stood to one side, on guard, looking disdainfully at the young bulls then searching the surrounding bush for any signs of danger. He bridled slightly as a pair of leopards stepped daintily down to the water's edge, but the rule of the water hole prevailed, and the two drank their fill and moved back into cover. At last the herd moved off and Sergeant Wilson signalled the men, one at a time, to fill their bottles whilst the rest covered.

There was barely an hour of daylight left when they finally saw the store and game camp, difficult to distinguish set as it was amongst the trees at the foot of the mountain, blending well with its surrounds. The isolated cabins had a desolate look about them and grass grew up around the steps and paths. The house itself however seemed well maintained and as they watched a young man came out of the store, barring and locking it behind him. He walked slowly up to the house; he seemed to be checking a list as he went, his feet unerringly avoiding tree roots and rocks without his conscious knowledge.

"Doesn't seem to have a care in the world," said John quietly. "No fence, no security lights, no gun, house unprotected." Probably so far off the beaten track that the war hasn't reached here yet. We'll wait until dark and try not to let the locals know we're here," Sergeant Wilson added.

They sat in the growing dusk and watched the African villagers drifting slowly towards their kraal, some carrying bundles of sticks, some large jugs of water on their head, others with grass or farm produce. Then suddenly darkness was upon them.

They rose slowly, stretched their cramped muscles, and easing into their packs followed the sergeant in a silent file to the house.

"John! Roy! Round the back," he whispered. "Any servants you find, bring them into the house and make sure they stay. Barry, Greg, come with me." He signed for the two to stand in the shadows either side of the door. He knew it was extremely dangerous calling a man to his door these days and did not know what to expect. He tapped quietly on the door, standing to one side. Nothing! He knocked again, louder.

A man's voice called out. "Who is it?" Sergeant Wilson did not answer. Again. "Who is it?" with a touch of exasperation. Then the door opened and silhouetted against the light was a young man just under two metres tall, fair-haired, his shirt-sleeves rolled up. To Wilson's surprise he carried no weapon of any kind and seemed totally oblivious to any danger. Taking no chances the sergeant gently pushed him back into the room with his FN and with the other two following moved in behind him and closed the door.

"What the hell's going on?" he began. His wife, entering from the kitchen gave a short gasp of fear, stepped quickly to his side and clung tightly to his arm. They both spun around as the kitchen door opened silently and John and Roy slid into the room, closing the door behind them.

"What's the meaning … ," he began again.

Sergeant Wilson held up his hand, smiling. "I'm sorry to have frightened your wife," he began tactfully. "Please don't be alarmed. But first of all, are there any servants in the house?"

"No, we don't have them; my wife is more than capable, but…"

"One moment please," interrupted the sergeant, "are you two the only whites around here?"

"Yes, we manage the place and run the store. We have been here nearly two years."

"You have no security fence, floodlighting, or defences at all, aren't you worried about terrorist activity?"

Without waiting for an answer the sergeant stuck out his hand and introduced himself and his men. The young man hesitated at first then grasped the hand and said, "I'm Peter Gunning and this is my wife, Jane. I would be pleased to hear some explanations. Er … sit yourselves down, if you can find a seat."

The sergeant sent Roy and Greg outside. "Scout around and don't, under any circumstances be seen. I don't want anyone to know we're here. Well, Peter, I'm surprised at your lack of security. Aren't you worried at all about being attacked?"

"Why should we be attacked? We have a good rapport with the locals, we treat them fairly and honestly. We run a store for them and buy some of their produce. Jane helps the women with dressmaking. There is no reason for anyone to attack us."

The three soldiers looked at him, John's face reflecting a mixture of scorn and pity. Barry muttered something that sounded like, "You are out of your mind!"

"What do you think makes you different from all the missionaries who have been murdered, school teachers, traders, social workers, farmers …?"

The young man looked sheepishly at his wife. "I guess we never think about it," he said. "We have very little contact with the outside world. We only hear about such things when the owners re-supply the store, about every three months."

"Well it may come as a shock, but we are here because we think you are about to be attacked by a band of about thirty terrs who believe themselves to be something really special. They believe they are immune to our bullets, totally invincible, sadistic killers. A band who have already murdered men, women and children. A band who drove a woman totally insane after torturing her children to death in front of her, finally plucking her eyes out. What do you say to that?"

The sergeant was deliberately trying to shock some awareness into these insular minds, totally divorced from the realities of the times.

"There must have been reasons ... ," he began hesitantly, "provocation perhaps.. I can't see that they would attack us."

John exploded. "When you've seen a tenth of the things we have," he gritted, "you wouldn't talk like a stupid English, philanthropic, idealistic.."

"Easy, John," the sergeant interjected. "Simmer down!" John subsided, muttering.

The woman looked from one to the other with wide frightened eyes. "What do you want us to do?" she asked.

"Do you have any guns?" he asked, addressing himself to the husband.

"I believe there is an old shotgun and a box of cartridges here somewhere, the owner used them when he was hunting. I suppose they are still useable." He had a worried look on his face.

"You had better get it out and clean it up later." Turning to the woman he said. "I want my men billeted in the house. Nobody, and I mean nobody must know we are here. Don't trust any of your local natives, when they see a crowd of terrorists they will be so scared they'll tell them everything they want to know. We will scout out under cover of darkness and be back here before daylight. If they are coming they will be here tonight or tomorrow."

To the husband he said. "Go down to your store with one of my men and bring back anything you may need for a short siege. They will not stay long, either they will wipe us out and loot the store, or we'll beat them. Either way they will head for the border fast. Do you have plenty of water?"

"There's a forty gallon tank on the roof, it's pumped up from a well in the garden."

"Good! Make sure it's full. Whilst you are at the store bring back about two hundred metres of strong twine, you have some?"

"No! But we have nylon fishing line that the owners brought in when they hoped to organise fishing safaris, there's miles of that."

"That will do fine, the strongest you have. That's all. We will see to the rest."

The woman looked up quickly and said. "There's plenty of room sergeant. We have four bedrooms and more than enough supplies. You must all be very hungry. I'll have something ready for you all within the hour."

She seemed to have accepted the situation and her reactions were a lot quicker than her husband's. He still stood awkwardly bemused an uncomprehending look on his face.

Roy and Greg slipped quietly into the room. Sergeant Wilson looked at them, his eyebrows raised.

"The front is fairly open sarge," began Roy, "there's a clump of rocks about forty metres from the house. It could be approached by somebody without him being seen by anyone. There is also a stone trough about three metres long and a metre high to the right with trees behind it, not much other cover." Wilson nodded.

Greg continued. "There's a well about fifty metres out back and several outhouses, all of which could provide cover. There is also an old tractor over to the right and a cluster of rock with a 'gomo' behind them. They could get quite close without us seeing them." Wilson nodded again.

"Well lads," he said, "as soon as we have eaten John and I will scout back a few miles. Barry, organise a watch, one man is to be inside the house to watch front and rear. Get as much sleep as you can. Greg, go with Peter to the store now and bring back a few things." Peter and Greg moved to the door which now had a curtain over to keep out the light, organised by John and Jane. The sergeant called Barry aside and spoke to him quietly for a few moments. Barry nodded and slipped out the back door.

Well within the hour they joined their hosts in the seldom-used dining room where huge Kudu steaks and piles of fresh vegetables had been set out. They set to with a will and conversation dropped dramatically for the next twenty minutes. After the meal Sergeant Wilson caught John's eye and they thanked Mrs Gunning profusely for such an excellent meal.

"Now, if you will excuse us we'll take a bit of a walk to help digest it," said the sergeant. Mrs Gunning was not fooled. "Do be careful," she said, nervously.

They left everything except FNs and two magazines and moved outside, where they stood for a while until their night vision established itself. Then they moved off quietly into the night, their soft veltskoens making no sound in the thick dust of the track.

They passed the store and took a trail that led over a hill and skirted around the foot of the mountain. It was the only trail that the terrorists could take. They were grateful for the four-day old moon that afforded little light, but even so they kept close to the overhanging trees that bordered the track.

They had travelled about two kilometres and were quite expecting to carry on for another five or six before returning to camp. Sergeant Wilson guessed the terrs would be close by now. Should they not find them that night he intended to scout the track back ten kilometres or so the following day. He was certain in his own mind that the terrs would come that way and at that stage had not even considered his plan of action should his guess be wrong.

Suddenly both came to an abrupt halt as a loud laugh rang out, seemingly not more than a few metres away. Instantly a low sharp order was given and the laughter died to a splutter. The originator having obvious difficulty choking it off.

They slowly withdrew back down the track about fifty metres and angled into the trees. Placing their feet very carefully they circled around until they were downwind and crawled forward.

Both could now smell cooking fires and the musky smell of unwashed bodies. Then they caught an occasional view of a screened fire between the trees. Sergeant Wilson, not wanting their presence known, or to lose the element of surprise, signalled John to stop and they lay in the undergrowth watching. This was the terrorist band, there was no doubt about that. They could see the occasional flash of light off a gun and although it was impossible to count heads there were obviously a lot of men around. Several women could be seen cooking 'mealies', corn on the cob, and handing them around to the men. He tugged John's arm and they eased their way back away from the scene, all senses alert for any sign of sentries. Returning to the track they retraced their steps back to the camp.

Once inside the house he called the others together and told them what they had discovered.

"When do you think they will attack?" asked Peter, nervously.

"Well, in normal circumstances they would attack in the late afternoon or the early evening," replied the sergeant. "But in this case I don't think they will. Normally they count on our security forces getting after them quite quickly so they need the cover of darkness to get as far away as possible. But here there is no need. They know the store is here, they know that you two are here and they have probably been told that you are unarmed and have no means of communication with the outside world."

"How would they know that?" asked Jane.

"Quite easily. Your locals have never seen Peter with a gun and would assume that he didn't have one. They obviously know he has no means of calling outside this area. The terrs will know all about you by now, make no mistake about that. The locals know that the terrorists are close and they know you will be attacked …"

"One of our friends is bound to come and tell us," said Jane. "We are great friends with lots of them."

"I wouldn't bank on it," said John.

"No I'm afraid past history doesn't leave much hope of that," Bob remarked. "They, the terrs, will have no idea that we are here, so my guess is that they will hit at first light hoping to have a couple of hours fun with you two, loot the store and be over the border into Mozambique before darkness."

"I still find it difficult to believe they will attack us," argued Peter.

"There's only five of us," said the sergeant coldly, "get your shotgun out and make sure that its working. If they get past us, I would sincerely advise you to shoot Jane's head off and then your own. If they catch you alive, you'll be a long time dying. Then it will be a little too late to wish you'd listened. Ok, men, one of you on watch and the rest sleep. We'll stand to at oh-four-thirty hours!"

Jane Gunning put her hand on the sergeant's arm.

"Thank you, sergeant, and your men, for all you are doing for us. I know you are right. I'll have tea and something ready for you all to eat before it starts."

Bob looked at her. She was in her late twenties, he guessed. Not long out of England, living in an entirely new dimension but as full of pluck as the early pioneers. His glance travelled to her husband who, with Greg's help was stripping and cleaning the shotgun, his face was flushed but his jaw was firm and his hands were steady. He knew that when the time came they would come through with flying colours. He smiled his thanks and reassurance.

Well before 0430, Barry had collected a grenade from each of the patrol and busied himself outside in the still dark garden. Jane Gunning passed around mugs of steaming tea. She was followed by Peter bearing a very large tray of egg and bacon sandwiches. After he had finished eating Roy spent some time with Peter and Jane showing them how to load magazines and fire an FN rifle. The sergeant, Barry and Roy settled themselves at the front of the house. Greg and John were at the rear. Their spare mags were near to hand and extra rounds were piled next to them.

The sergeant looked towards Jane and her husband. "If one of us gets killed take up his gun and keep firing, and good luck! They nodded mutely.

Twenty minutes passed, half an hour. The only sounds were the occasional scuffle of a boot or rustle as cramped muscles were eased. Nobody spoke and all eyes strained into the darkness outside as slowly, almost imperceptibly, mysterious blobs materialised into discernible outlines and outlines filled in with recognisable detail as the first flushes of daylight chased the darkness ahead of it.

Roy's whisper cut into the silence.

"Something moving down by the store, sarge." Wilson's glance shifted.

"I've got it, Roy." He turned his head and quietly called Peter. "Do you have any booze in your store, hard stuff or beer?"

"Not a lot, only for our own consumption. We don't sell it. There's about six crates of beer and about a case each of whisky, gin and vodka."

"Good! They aren't likely to attack for another hour and then with luck they'll be half drunk. They must be really confident or Chaka would never let them hit the store first."

Faintly, but clearly a rasping noise was carried to them on the early morning breeze, and shadowy figures could be seen crowding into the store. They made little effort of concealment, probably hoping that the white man would be down to investigate, thus saving them the effort of winkling him out of his house.

Bob looked at his watch, just six o'clock. It was quite light now. Light enough to see the African kraal up on the hill and to notice the absence of people or cooking fires. They had obviously made themselves scarce.

He called Peter's attention to the fact.

"So much for your loving friends," he said. Peter shrugged resignedly.

Down at the store goods were being dragged outside and piled against the walls. Terrorists with an AK rifle in one hand and a bottle in the other were laughing and jabbering away as the spirits took effect. Then from amongst the trees below the village emerged a crowd of villagers, women, men, boys and girls. There were about twenty of them. They were being jostled along by four terrorists who obviously did not believe in 'sparing the rod'.

They were driven along to the store where one of the guards shouted something at them accompanied by blows and they fell to sorting and piling the goods into carry-sized bundles. They had been rounded up to act as porters.

One girl was bending down piling up goods, straight legged, bending from the waist as only African girls do. Her dress dragged up at the back showing her long brown legs and an occasional glimpse of unadorned buttocks. Inevitably one of the drunken terrorists saw this and with a joyful laugh stepped behind her and dragged her dress up over her waist and pulled her to him. She tried to straighten up and turned to fight him off but a heavy blow knocked her to the ground. Her assailant put his boot on her neck and ripped her dress from her. She wore nothing underneath. To a roar of approval from his friends he proceeded to rape her. She struggled for a while then lay there mute as a line of men started to form, awaiting their turn. By now all the women and girls were naked and spread-eagled on the dusty ground. Their sons and husbands turned their heads away in shame.

"My God! That's Sabina," cried Jane, peering over the sergeant's shoulder. "She's one of the girls I teach dressmaking. Can't you stop them, sergeant?"

"No! I can't, Jane. Her own stupidity got her where she is. I will never understand the African mentality as long as I live. They only had to walk over that hill to be safe, but no, they'll hang around a hundred metres from their kraal where they stand a good chance of being caught. Apart from which, without the element of surprise that lot could easily wipe us out. Then Jane, I'm afraid you would be in the same spot as she is. I'm sorry but it's every man for himself." Jane shuddered convulsively and turned away.

Beyond the store in the shade of the trees stood two or three terrs, partially screened by a rocky outcrop. Sergeant Wilson had noticed them some time back but could not see them clearly. They did not participate in the looting or the rape but just observed, talking amongst themselves. Chaka was probably one of the group and Wilson hoped for a clear view through his sights when the action started.

Eventually one of them moved forward and shouted an order, pointing towards the house. It took some time to get them out of the store and away from the women but eventually about twenty of them started moving towards the house, a small group moving away to circle around to the rear.

"Peter! Jane! Get behind that fireplace wall and keep down!" Sergeant Wilson spoke quietly.

"Roy, take the right hand man. I'll take the left. Barry, the middle. Fire when I do."

The terrorists came on laughing and shouting to each other. One or two fired an occasional round towards the house but their attitude was completely casual. They were obviously expecting no resistance and made no effort at concealment. A chicken, flushed from hiding from beneath a bush, weaved wildly across the advancing line, neck outstretched, squawking madly. Three or more terrs, hooting with laughter, opened fire, and puffs of dust kicked up all around the frenzied bird. Miraculously it was not hit and disappeared behind some rocks amidst general merriment.

Sergeant Wilson carefully aligned his sights on a target, they were now only fifty metres away. He squeezed the trigger and quickly shifted his aim as his man was flung backwards. Roy and Barry were now firing and shots could be heard from the rear as John and Greg opened up. Cartridge cases bounced off the walls and spun across the floor as the sharp incessant fire raked the ground outside seeking targets. The drunken terrorists, shocked into sober awareness, threw themselves behind any piece of available cover and tried belatedly to return the fire.

The ground leading up to the house was strewn with the dead and the dying. The wounded who were trying to pull themselves into cover were shown no mercy and were cut down.

The firing died away as targets disappeared behind rocks or trees, then suddenly from the side of the house where the dense bush grew close came a surging tide of blacks, screaming profanities as they dashed for the house. On their guns were tied talismen and charms given to them by witchdoctors to ward off bullets. The sergeant could not make out what they were from that distance but was amazed to see a terrorist still running for the stoep, knowing that his last shot had hit him just above the heart.

Such was the power of their belief that they kept coming on, even when hit two or three times. One black had almost made the distance to the house as Barry's shot hit him just above the bridge of the nose, his momentum catapulted his body onto the stoep. His feet hit the wall under the window where Roy crouched.

Two more went down under the hail of bullets before the rest broke and scattered. A group of the survivors were now entrenched behind the rocks and another three behind the trough and these were pouring automatic fire in lethal swathes at the house. Bullets were ricocheting off the stonework and buzzing around like hornets.

Sergeant Wilson nodded to Barry who reached out for the heavy fishing lines which lay coiled on the floor, the ends disappearing under the door. He separated the lines and taking one in both hands he took up the slack. Roy, watching from the window, saw a line of dust spurt up as the slack was pulled in. Then having got the line tight, Barry pulled sharply.

Behind the rocks the crouching terrorists had not noticed the small black grenade wedged and tied tightly between them, nor did they hear the twang as the loosened pin sprung out to fly thirty metres away, whipped by the spring in the line.

As the grenade exploded two terrs were killed instantly, another reared up clutching his head. He was knocked back behind cover as Roy's bullet smashed into him. Two others broke away and ran for the trees and were cut down. Barry reached for the other line and again took up the slack but this time the line jammed. Barry pulled hard to release it but it was well and truly stuck. Roy watching from the window could see where it was wedged into a crack in a small clump of rock. "It's no good Barry," he called, "you'll break the line."

Barry, cursing, looked out of the window and shook his head. It appeared that the terrorist who had rushed the stoep had accidentally kicked the line into its present position.

Sergeant Wilson scanned the area. "Look Barry," he said, "there are only those behind the trough. If we can get those I think we've won. You and Roy keep their heads down whilst I clear the line." Without waiting for any possible argument he fired a burst that raked the top of the stone trough and throwing open the door launched himself forward. Barry and Roy were firing rapidly, not stopping to aim, their FNs jerking in their hands as an almost continuous stream of rounds poured out. It seemed as if the sergeant would make it comfortably, not one of the terrs behind the trough dared show himself. Then with horrified shock they realised that somebody was firing from a hidden spot amongst the trees and Barry suddenly remembered the small group that had kept well away from the others. He turned frantically to cover the sergeant, screaming out a warning, but even as he did so he saw the sergeant spin as a bullet hit the side of his head, he saw the splatter of blood as the sergeant crashed to the ground.

Barry would never have known his actions from that moment. Bob Wilson, the man he respected and admired more than any other man in the world was down, probably dead. His face gorged with angry blood and an animal roar escaped his lips as he flung himself through the door. He had only taken a few paces when the first bullet hit him in the chest almost stopping him in his tracks, but he ploughed on. John, hearing Barry's cry and thinking that the enemy had managed to make it into the house, dashed through from the back. Sizing up the situation he joined Roy in covering the two outside.

Barry was now standing over the sergeant. He was hit a second time and then a third bullet caught him in the thigh forcing him to the ground. Still he reached out to Bob trying to draw him back. Finally a forth bullet jerked his head back and Barry McEvoy died, his body falling across his friend, seemingly to protect him even in death.

Roy changed magazines and kept firing, tears streaming down

his face. He was screaming continuously. "You bastards! You bastards!"

John, firing carefully and accurately, drove the group back further into the trees and the firing from that quarter stopped. He changed his aim to the trough. A stalemate was in evidence. They could not leave the house to get behind the terrs and unless they showed themselves they could not be killed. John was pondering the problem as he fired. How could they get to the line that was tied to the pin of the grenade? His eyes followed the line to where it crossed the stoep and on to where Barry and the sergeant lay and it was he who first saw a movement as the sergeant's hand moved to his head.

"Keep firing, Roy. Keep their heads down. The sergeant's not dead. I just saw him move!" John called.

"I'll go and get him!" Shouted Roy, rising to his feet.

"Stay where you are, we don't want to lose anyone else!" Snapped John. "Just keep firing!"

Reluctantly, Roy went back to his position.

The sergeant started to sit up, but at John's shout he lay back again, obviously endeavouring to collect his thoughts. John saw the added pain on Bob's face as his gaze took in Barry's body lying partly over his own. He eased himself out from under without exposing himself too much. His senses seemed to be returning.

"The line, Bob! Pull the line!" John shouted. The sergeant looked around blankly. John made pulling signs and continued firing.

"The grenade, Bob! Pull the line!" John called again.

John groaned with relief as the sergeant's hand inched towards the line where it came out of the far side of the rock. Pausing to gather strength he pulled the line towards him and then with a supreme effort, jerked hard. The explosion, when it came, threw all three bodies into view where they were an easy target for Roy and John. With the death of the three terrorists the firing ceased and all waited quietly. Greg came through from the rear of the house to report that he had seen the last remaining terrorist running towards the trees. He thought the man was wounded judging by the awkward way he ran.

They cautiously edged out onto the stoep.

"You two scout around!" said John. "Keep together and cover each other. I'll see to the sergeant."

As John turned to the wounded man Jane and Peter came hurrying over. "Let Jane look after your sergeant," he said. "She's a trained nurse."

Jane knelt in the dust beside Bob, her fingers probing the area around the wound. Checking his eyes, after a while she looked up and said "It's not too serious. I don't think the bone is cracked but he does have concussion. The bullet scraped the bone and has taken the flesh away but he'll be all right."

As she talked her hands were busy cutting away hair and sterilising the wound. John left Bob in her capable hands and walked over to where Barry lay. He stood looking down on his friend and comrade of many battles and his throat constricted and his eyes prickled with unshed tears. Peter's hand touched his shoulder in silent sympathy.

Sergeant Wilson looked up slowly, finding difficulty in focusing his eyes, his speech was slurred as he asked. "Is he dead?" John nodded. The sergeant sank back, and Jane could see the naked anguish on his face. Her heart bled for these strong silent men who could find no release in tears but who choked back their sorrow and turned it inwards to strengthen their resolve and feed their hatred of their cruel enemy.

"Greater love hath no man..," she began, quietly. "..than that he lay down his life for a friend," continued the sergeant wearily. "So many friends, so many lives. The job is not yet finished and the end not yet in sight, what a crazy world we live in, Jane!"

Roy and Greg returned to report that there were no signs of the surviving terrorists and that there were twenty four dead. John sent Greg to fetch the villagers who had huddled behind the store throughout the entire action, too terrified even to run. "Get them collecting the dead and piling them under those trees," he pointed. "You collect all the weapons and put them on the stoep."

Roy had walked over to where Barry lay and dropping to his knees started straightening out the twisted limbs. His shoulders shook with the effort to withhold his tears. John rested his hand on the boy's head. "Let it come, Roy, it's no disgrace. We all owe him tears for what he has meant to each of us. He was a man amongst men, but even he could cry for injustice or another's pain. It was his tears that kept him human. So cry for me too, Roy because my heart is dead. After years of this I feel no love, only hate. Cry and hope to stay human until this damned war is over."

The others watched with compassion as he walked away.

Whilst the Gunnings helped the sergeant into the house the dead terrorists were collected by the villagers and laid out under the trees. The final total was twenty-five, another body having been found a few metres back from the edge of the trees.

As Greg and John collected the weapons they removed the grisly objects tied to the barrels. For the most part the 'charms' consisted of parts of human bodies, mainly genitalia cut from luckless captives, a hand, a bunch of ears or a scalp. One scalp had long fair hair and was tied to the gun with a pale blue ribbon. John's heart bled as he removed it. Barry's body was laid gently on the stoep and covered with a blanket. His ammunition was shared between the rest of the patrol. Jane Gunning tried vainly to get the sergeant to go to bed but he stubbornly refused. He did however take the pain killers she offered him and sank gratefully into an armchair.

"We can't afford to waste too much time," he muttered. "We must get after them before they cross the border."

"What should we do with all this equipment and the bodies?" asked Peter when he returned from tidying up the store.

"When we move out we will be moving up onto the high ground half way up the mountain and we should be able to use the radio. I'll call my base and get somebody here to collect the weapons and arrange for the burial of the dead. I suggest you clear a spot so that the helicopter can land and mark it so that it can be seen from the air."

"I'll get the villagers on to it right away," he said and hurried out.

"Do you have to go after these men, sergeant?" asked Jane. "Don't you think you've done enough?"

"Jane, you sound like my fiancé," he said with a smile. "Our main task is to get their leader. There are lots of reasons which I won't go into. Suffice it to say that me and my men have several very good reasons, four of which concerns a father, mother and two young girls.."

"Sergeant!" Jane paused. "I can't even begin to thank you and your men for what you did for us. We must have sounded very naive to you but the fact is we have hardly heard about this war let alone come into contact with it."

"What will you do now? You must know you are no longer safe here!"

"We have already decided to pack up here and go back to England. We will hate to leave all this. We really love this country but we can't exist under these conditions."

"I can't say that I blame you. It's a great pity that you didn't know the country a few years ago when the various races lived happily in harmony. It's strange to reflect that we never knew that we had a racial problem until the world press told us we did. When you get back to England think kindly of us and put in a good word now and again, we could use a few friends." The sergeant hesitated.

"Do you know that your country gave fifty two million pounds in aid to countries around our borders, which is mainly spent on the arms used against us?"

"I never knew that!" Said Jane, "and I don't suppose many British do either!"

"Oh! They were very pleased when the early pioneers carved out another jewel for the crown of the empire, but the winds of change plus a guilty conscience has changed all that. We are now an embarrassment and expendable. In spite of all our efforts we all know that we can't win in the end"

"Sergeant," said Jane, "British politics have always been devious. You'll probably find in years to come that there is some sordid reason behind their actions. Now you lie back there and rest whilst I get you all some food. It's surprising that it's only midday and all this has happened."

The sergeant leaned back and closed his eyes. Within seconds he was fast asleep. It seemed only moments later that he awoke with someone shaking his shoulder. In the background he could hear Jane saying. "You should let him sleep, with a head wound like that he should be in hospital."

John's voice cut her off. "If I let him sleep and we missed those terrs he would probably shoot me, Mrs Gunning. Anyway, some hot food will do him a world of good. He's had a lot worse than this."

Sergeant Wilson opened his eyes and was pleased that they focused immediately. The delightful aroma of steak, eggs and chips set his saliva glands working overtime and he realised how hungry he was. As he stood up his gaze took in the blanket-covered shape on the stoep. A sharp pang caused him to falter and a low groan escaped his compressed lips. Roy, mistaking the cause reached forward and grabbed his arm.

"I'm all right, Roy, thanks," he said as he gently shook him off and strode resolutely into the dining room.

After the meal Jane insisted on making sandwiches for each of them and loaded odd corners of their light packs with homemade pasties and cakes. They filled their water bottles, shared out their ammunition and checked magazines. Then shouldering their packs they bade the Gunnings goodbye and set off northwards after the fleeing terrorists.

John, scouting ahead, soon picked up the trail and as the sergeant came up he reported. "There seems to be five of them. Three came from behind the trees to the right of the house and another two joined them here," he pointed. He stuck his finger into a damp spot and raised it to his eye. "One of them is injured he's bleeding pretty badly."

They moved on carefully knowing that the wounded man would slow the terrorists down. The trail was easy to follow and once Greg thought he saw movements about a kilometre ahead on the crest of a rise.

The heat was now intense, the high rocks to one side throwing the sun's rays down onto the men below and excluding any breeze that there may have been. Their footsteps were muffled by the thick dust that spurted up with each step and settled into red streaks on their sweaty backs and brows. Even the cicadas seemed muted in the oven-like environment and the geckos sprawled listlessly on the rocks, panting, only their eyes moving.

The sergeant plodded on, his head throbbing with the heat and the exertion. John up ahead took the brunt of the extra work that tracking entailed, criss-crossing the ground, following false leads, moving ahead then falling back, all the time keyed up to a high pitch anticipating a possible ambush.

They had gone about five kilometres, climbing slowly, and John was moving carefully about one hundred metres ahead when

Greg saw him fling himself sideways into cover. Immediately they moved into the cover of the dense bush waiting, poised. Sergeant Wilson moved forward silently and was soon swallowed up by the tall dry grass and shrub. Five minutes later he slid in behind them and motioned them forward. They found John squatting beside a terrorist. He looked dead but as they watched his head moved slightly.

"Take his water bottle out Roy and give him a drink." Roy, remembering Barry, looked slightly rebellious. "He may be able to tell us something," the sergeant added. "It looks to me as if his own crowd have bayoneted him. Probably slowing them down too much. They wouldn't want him to talk."

Roy unclipped the man's water bottle and raising his head allowed a trickle of water to run into his mouth. The wounded terr choked for a while and blood and water ran mixed down his chin. His eyes opened. Bob spoke to him in Swahili, the language of the tribes to the north.

"Did your own friends try to kill you?"

The man tried to speak but no sound came. The sergeant could see at least three wounds in his chest apart from the massive tear in his thigh where Greg's bullet had hit. Roy lifted the man up and gave him more water. The sergeant repeated the question. Finally one word was uttered like a grunt. "Yes!"

"How many are left?" Again he made a big effort.

"Three!"

"There were five of you, where did the other one go?"

There was a long pause this time, then faintly he murmured. "One man, he scared, he run away."

"Your leader is Chaka, is that right?" The man's eyes showed surprise but he did not answer.

"He is the one who ordered you killed. He was the one lied about the '*muti*' to stop our bullets. He is the one who is safe. Is his name Chaka?" The sergeant persisted.

Finally the man opened his eyes. "Yes, Bwana, he Chaka, the 'Hammer,' he lie to me!" His eyes closed and his body relaxed as death overtook him.

They left him and again took up the trail which led always upward into the wild desolation of the Mavuradonha wastelands.

As the shadows lengthened they topped yet another rise and

looking back could see down the valley and in the far distance the lazy curl of smoke rising from the cooking fires of the villagers. The sergeant called a halt. "Don't you think we should press on while there is light?" asked Greg.

"No, Greg, for several reasons. Firstly I don't think Chaka realises that he is being followed. He probably thinks we will rest on our laurels after wiping out most of his gang. If he were aware of us being so close he would have made sure that character back there was dead before he left him. Secondly, it will be dark in fifteen minutes, and the light is already bad for tracking. We could easily miss something on this rock or even overshoot and walk into a trap. Finally, Chaka stands just as much chance as we do of breaking a leg in this terrain so he must stop soon. We'll get away at first light and probably steal an hour on them."

They settled down in a hollow amongst the rocks, Roy standing guard whilst the rest ate their pasties and cakes, washing them down with water. Having eaten the sergeant drew out his map and code sheets and worked busily for a while coding a radio message. Completing his message he withdrew the tape aerial to its fullest extent and crossing his fingers turned the set on and tuned it.

"Echo Charlie One! Echo Charlie One! This is Sierra Papa One Five! Do you read me? Over!" The reply came back instantly. The sergeant smiled, obviously a very special watch was being kept.

"Sierra Papa One Five! Receiving you fours. Go!"

"Echo Charlie One, I have a message, are you ready to copy? Over!"

"Sierra Papa One Five! Go!"

"Shackles on. Contact with bandits at Mavuradonha Game Park. Twenty-five killed, four escaped, including leader. Action continues northward. Request stop line on Zambezi at coordinates … "

Here followed a list of figures. "Also request evacuation of two whites at Game Park and clean-up force." A slight pause, then the sergeant continued. "Regret the death in action of Corporal McEvoy. Over!"

There was a break of nearly a minute then Captain White's voice came through clearly over the static.

"Sierra Papa One Five! Message received and understood.

Wilco." There was a slight break as he struggled for words, uncoded, that would not compromise the sergeant. "You know my feelings. Good hunting! Out!"

Sergeant Wilson appreciated Captain White's way of sympathising over Barry's death without letting the ever-watchful enemy know they had lost a man. He switched off and replaced the aerial.

Turning to John, he said, "I've asked for a stop line on the Zambezi. If they can drop off a couple of sticks of Scouts to stop the terrs crossing we should be able to wipe them out. It's just a precaution. I'm hoping we will get them tomorrow but in case they give us the slip the Scouts should get them."

"What if they change course."

"Then we'll have to contact the Scouts by radio and give them a new position. Base will give us their call sign tomorrow when I report in."

Each man found a spot that suited him amongst the rocks and settled down to sleep in the cold air of night on the mountain slope. Always one pair of eyes watched, and one pair of ears listened for anything untoward. In that game only the dead relaxed completely.

The first crimson fingers of dawn were reaching out for the towering summit of Mavuradonha as the patrol chewed their biltong and prepared themselves for the day ahead. As soon as it was sufficiently light the sergeant ranged ahead and found the tracks, the rest followed two hundred metres behind. They had been on the move almost two hours when the sergeant up ahead signalled, his arm moving in a wide arc. The three men swung into a short skirmish line and taking advantage of every possible cover moved forward to where Sergeant Wilson crouched. He pointed.

Just behind a circle of rocks was evidence of a camp-site, mango pips, well chewed and fibrous lay around together with guava skins. A small fire had been covered with dirt but a thin wisp of smoke hovered over the pile.

"They couldn't have left more than half an hour ago," Sergeant Wilson said quietly, "they won't be far ahead." They gazed up at the rocky slope ahead of them, wondering if any of the hundreds of likely ambush spots hid a man hunched over the sights of his AK waiting for them to wander into a killing zone. The sergeant motioned them forward and moved ahead of them once more. John, still looking at the slope ahead fancied he saw a movement out of the corner of his eye. He studied the area for a long minute but saw nothing to alarm him he dismissed it as a figment of his imagination and followed the others.

Bob Wilson up ahead could follow the trail easily in the soft dirt, three sets of footprints, all about the same size in boots. He noticed that one set of imprints showed heavy wear on the outsides of the heels and the edge of the soles. 'Probably bow legged' he thought. The terrs seemed to be making no effort at concealment obviously totally unaware of their pursuers. The track climbed over a hill and down the far side, almost disappearing when they crossed bare rock. But they headed steadily north and the sergeant just kept walking and soon picked them up again. They plodded on for several hours in this fashion, never catching sight of their quarry, but getting occasional indications that slowly but surely they were overtaking them.

It was just after midday that a dry river bed, or donga, appeared off to the right and as expected the three terrs had altered course to take advantage of the easier going. It was an obvious move and did not strike the sergeant as untoward. The tracks were quite clear and from time to time sharply etched into patches of damp earth that had not quite dried since the last fitful rain.

The three were now walking side by side and Sergeant Wilson could picture them laughing and talking as they moved along. He listened carefully in the hope that the twisting sides of the donga might amplify any sound of voices, but he heard nothing. The three sets of tracks passed over a rocky shelf that lined the river bed and rose up the side to a towering cliff. About thirty metres on the tracks continued. He had gone about another thirty metres when something nagged at his mind, calling it to attention. He paused and scanned the tracks again and his eyes raked the rocky sides. But he saw nothing. He moved forward another twenty metres and a sharp warning buzzer sounded in his head. He stared at the tracks again and suddenly he knew. He threw himself sideways towards the meagre cover of a small river polished boulder, his FN swinging towards the rocks above him as an AK opened up. As the dust and chips of rock splattered into his face he could hear other guns opening up further back and knew that the rest of the patrol was also under attack. His position was untenable. The rock behind which he lay barely shielded his head and shoulders, the rest of him lay fully exposed in the dust. His hasty shots were keeping his assailant's head down but as soon as his magazine was empty the terr had all the time in the world to pick him off.

He could see where the shots were coming from. A rocky ledge rose from the river bed to a large boulder about four metres up. About three metres above the terr's head was a small sloping ledge on which, over the years, a pile of rocks had collected, balanced precariously, the largest being no more than twenty centimetres across.

The sergeant changed his aim and placed three shots at the base of the pile. The whole lot lifted as the high velocity bullets cut away the flimsy props beneath them, then they fell back and rolled and slithered over the edge. As the first stones hit the terr he threw himself sideways, away from cover and the sergeant's first shot drove him back against the wall and the second spun him around and threw him over the edge to the river bed below.

Sergeant Wilson was up and running before the body landed, changing magazines as he went. Fifty metres back down the donga the bank fell to a point where he could clamber up and he launched himself at it, scrambling up the first slope, tearing his hands on the rocks at the top as he hauled himself over. From his elevated position he could see around a bend in the river bed where the rest of his patrol were pinned down. One, he thought it was Greg, lay in the open doubled up in an unnatural position, either dead or badly wounded. Roy was wedged behind a flat slab of rock barely thirty centimetres deep. He had wormed his way down into the soft sand and was in such a precarious position that any movement would have exposed some part of himself. Sergeant Wilson could see his head twisting around trying to find some alternative cover, but there was none. The ambushers had chosen their site well. John had managed to get to a position below the terrorists, screened by the rock above on which they lay. But he could not get a clear view of them in order to attack, nor could he escape.

The sergeant moved quickly before Roy or John tried some desperate move to break the stalemate. Whatever they tried it was doomed to failure.

He worked his way along the rim of the donga towards the terrorist's position. Roy was gathering himself for a suicidal dash hoping that by doing so John might escape. He had heard the firing up ahead and was convinced in his own mind that the sergeant was either dead or pinned down. Then his gaze was attracted by a movement above the position where the terrorists lay and with a sense of overwhelming joy recognised the sergeant's stocky figure as he wormed his way forward. He sank back again holding himself ready to support the sergeant's move.

John, standing helplessly at the foot of the rock cursed himself for picking the cover he had, but in the heat of the moment when the AKs opened up it had been the nearest and safest place. His headlong dash had been instinctive. Now he considered his position. The sergeant up ahead must be dead, he would have been an easy target. Roy was in an invidious position wounded and with his cover being chipped away piece by piece. He was bound to make a dash for cover soon and he wouldn't stand a chance. Greg was dead, hit in the first onslaught. If he tried to make a break for a large rock about forty metres away he would draw the fire and if Roy were quick he could, with luck, withdraw to a better position. He drew himself up, put his head down and dashed out from under cover, his legs pumping furiously.

It was the worst thing he could have done. The two ambushers turning to fire at the plunging figure caught sight of the sergeant as he lowered himself over the edge of the donga to a position where he could attack. Roy groaned as he swung his rifle into position. A bullet hit John before he had covered twenty metres, breaking his right arm and sending his F.N. flying. Roy's hurried shots threw the second terr off balance, causing him to miss Sergeant Wilson who snapped a shot from the hip as he dived for cover. The shot hit Chaka, for it was he, on the thigh. It was not a dangerous wound but one that would play a significant part in the days ahead. Before the sergeant stopped rolling, Chaka's companion loosened off a shot that cut a groove across Wilson's shoulder and passed through the calf of his left leg. Roy made no mistake with the target offered and the terr was dead before he could fire another shot. Chaka, sizing up the extent of the reversal withdrew between the rocks and made his escape, limping badly and bleeding profusely.

Sergeant Wilson pulled himself forward to the terrorist's position and was just in time to see Chaka disappearing behind a rise one hundred metres away but was unable to get a shot at him. He lowered himself down gingerly to where Roy and John sat under cover of the rock.

With the sergeant assisting, Roy, regardless of his own agony, stripped away John's shirt and inspected his arm. It was a nasty wound, ragged and bleeding badly. Bone protruded making it very difficult to bandage. They packed dressings around the break and arranged a sling to support the arm. By the time they had done, John's face was white and sweat streaked. Then the sergeant pulled up his trousers and began to wipe away the blood. Again Roy took over. The wound was clean but painful. The bullet, having passed through the lower part of the calf muscle, had hit no bones and the exit hole was no larger than where the bullet had entered. Roy spread ointment onto the bandage and tied it tightly. The wound across the shoulders was superficial and had stopped bleeding but Roy insisted on cleaning it and taping it up. It was only then that the sergeant noticed the boy's distress and realised that Roy himself was badly wounded.

Damning the boy's stubbornness he slowly and carefully removed Roy's shirt, the back of which was heavy with blood. A bullet had scraped across his ribs, breaking several and passing under the scapula. The pain must have been enormous, the sergeant marvelled at the lad's guts. There was not a lot he could do with their scanty medical supplies but he cleaned it and laid strips of ointment soaked bandage over the wounds. Then he bound the whole lot with strip after strip of plaster.

"Well, that looks like it then, Bob!" said John. "That accounts for the lot."

"Not quite, John, we missed one and I'm sure it's Chaka. He was wounded and bleeding badly, so I don't think he will get far. I'm duty bound to follow it through to the end."

He looked at John and Roy. I'm sorry I got you into that scrape lads, bad tracking I'm afraid." They both started to protest.

"What happened, Bob?" asked John.

"They obviously spotted us following them and lead us into a trap",

John interrupted. "I thought I saw movements on the hill

above their camp but dismissed it. I should have known better."

The sergeant continued, "I was following three sets of prints. They were quite clear, as you know, John, in fact I should have been warned by that alone. Anyway they passed over rock from time to time and as the tracks always headed in the same direction I got into the bad habit of walking on and picking them up on the other side, very clever of Chaka. Then the trail led into this donga which seemed quite a natural thing to do. All the time there were three sets of prints. They even stepped into damp sand occasionally to emphasise them. Anyway, at a point up ahead the tracks crossed about thirty metres of rock and again I walked on, picking them up on the other side." Here he paused whilst he gathered his thoughts. "I knew there was something wrong but just couldn't place it. There were still three sets of tracks, but something was different."

"I know the feeling, Bob," said John.

"I followed for a few more metres and then my warning system went into operation. I knew I was walking into something, then I got it. I knew what was different. John, you know what happens when someone walks backwards?"

"Yes," John replied, "the toes dig in deeper normally."

"That's right!" Said Bob. "That's what it was. They had crossed the rocky patch and one of them had jumped sideways and climbed up the side of the bank, the other two had kept on walking. Then about fifty metres further on the second man had stepped sideways, walked backwards to the rock, and joined his companion. They had brushed away any slight signs on the rock as they went. The third terr moved up to his ambush position. His job was to get me. The other two moved back to ambush the rest of you."

"He must be a lot smarter than I thought," said Roy.

"Make no mistake about it, lad, he's a notch or two above the common herd. That's why I have to finish him off."

John smiled ruefully. "I'm afraid I'm not going to be much help, Bob."

Bob looked at his two friends, a hand on each shoulder. "You two are going back."

He held up his hand as they both started to protest. "John, you are going to be in agony in an hour or so, you can't shoot too well with your left hand and you would only be a handicap. You know it and so do I."

"I'm Ok, sarge!" Began Roy. Sergeant Wilson stopped him.

"Roy that wound in your back needs proper care. You, too, are going to suffer and suffer badly. I want you and John to stick together and make for the Gunnings' place. If you push on as fast as possible you should be in time to contact our chaps and the helicopter. They would not have arrived until this morning and it will take some time to tidy up and several trips to clear away the debris." He stood up, tested his leg, and limped over to where Greg lay. The terrorist's bullet had caught him just above the left ear. He stood looking down at the crumpled body with deep regret. He heard Roy come up behind him.

"He was a good man, sergeant," he said quietly.

"Yes, Roy, we hardly had time to get to know him but he was one of us and as God's my witness Chaka will pay dearly for his death."

The sergeant reached down and turning the body over removed the pack and the radio. One glance told him that the radio was useless. At least one bullet had shattered the casing and as he undid the canvas cover pieces fell out like confetti. He tossed it onto the ground in disgust. "So much for our special radio," he muttered. "Captain White will never believe me," he grinned ruefully.

They walked back to where John sat nursing his arm. The sergeant was limping badly. "How do you think you are going to catch up with Chaka with that gammy leg?" asked John.

"It'll ease off," he muttered hopefully. "Anyway, Chaka is no better off."

"I still think I should come with you, sarge," said Roy doggedly.

Sergeant Wilson ruffled his hair. "A right bulldog you are, always trying to muscle in on the action!" But behind his words he could hear Roy's father saying, 'He's all I've got, without him there's nothing,' and his resolve strengthened. "No! Roy, it will be me against Chaka and I think we are fairly evenly matched. I want it this way. I owe it to a farmer and his wife and daughters. I owe it to a poor insane woman and I owe it to Greg, Barry and Frank. One way or another that bastard is going to die."

"Is there anything we can do, Bob?" asked John.

"Yes John! Get yourselves back to base camp and make your report. I reckon we have smashed their belief in their invincibility and their charms. That terr that deserted will soon spread the word. I'll follow up after Chaka and when that job is finished I'll try to contact the Scouts and get a lift back with them. Failing that, I'll make my own way back. You and Roy are going to have a rough time. You will have to push yourselves to the limit of your endurance. Good luck!"

They shook hands solemnly and the sergeant picked up his pack, throwing out the spare ammunition and keeping only two magazines.

"If I can't kill him with forty rounds," he explained, "I deserve to lose!" He hefted his FN and turned to leave. He took a couple of paces then turned back. "When you get back give my love to Sally, will you?" he said gruffly. He limped away towards the bank and clambered up. They watched him as he disappeared from their view, on his way to intercept Chaka's trail.

Roy, moving painfully, made up one pack which he hung over John's good shoulder. Picking up both rifles they started retracing their steps. As the day wore on their stops became more frequent as John became light headed with pain.

Roy's wounds had opened up and blood seeped slowly soaking his shirt. Neither of them felt any desire for food as they stumbled onwards. The way was downhill and they were grateful for that. Towards evening John tripped and fell, wrenching his injured arm. He fainted with the pain and Roy dragged him to a rock and propped him up, gagging with the effort as waves of nausea threatened to overwhelm him. They rested for half an hour and tried to force down some food but their stomachs rebelled. So they drank water and dragged themselves up. Roy picked up the pack then discarded it. If they did not reach help soon the ammunition and the food would be of no value anyway.

Roy led the way carrying both FNs, they would have felt naked without them and the thought of abandoning their rifles would not enter their minds. John followed, swaying from side to side in a semi-conscious daze. They forced themselves onward in the darkness until exhaustion and the roughness of the terrain beat them and they collapsed into the soft dirt and slept where they lay.

Roy was the first to become aware as the first rays of the sun touched his face. His mind groped with the problem of trying to identify his surroundings. Gradually memory returned and with it a fiery pain across his chest where broken ribs and tortured wounds made breathing an agony. He turned his head to discover John lying a few metres away. His blood soaked arm and side were caked with dirt. Although he could not see it, Roy's back, from neck to waist, even below his belt, was also black with blood and caked with a rusty mud. They were a battle scarred and fearsome looking pair.

Roy inched his way over to John, not trusting himself to stand and shook him. John mumbled fitfully and his eyes opened. Roy could see they were bright with fever and it took a long time before recognition came.

"We'll have to press on, John. We can't have far to go now."

John nodded and struggled to rise. Roy pulled himself to his feet and helped his friend. Picking up the rifles they moved slowly on. John held on to the barrel of one of the rifles and was led by Roy. They fell several times and each time it took a little longer to rise.

Towards midday Roy fancied he heard the jabber of native voices but such was his exhaustion that he saw nothing. The ground drifted past under and behind him. Oft-times they would stop and then lurch ahead, balance themselves and stagger on. Time and distance faded into painful, semiconscious effort.

At the Mavuradonha Game Park Jane and Peter had watched as the job of removing the bodies began. It was fortunate that only one helicopter could be spared for the task or they would have done everything necessary and left long ago. As it was, this was their last trip to pick up the two whites to take them to Katari. They moved towards the smiling pilot who waited beside his chopper, a tall slim Captain of Commandos at his side.

"Your turn now," he said. "You'll be glad to get away from here after all you've been through." The Gunning's looked back towards the house and onward to the towering mountain backdrop where for two years they had revelled in their closeness to nature. Where they had gazed at the magnificent African sunset whilst they sat and sipped the traditional 'sundowners' and where they had watched the occasional kudu or zebra stepping daintily down to the distant waterhole, surrounded by the ticking cicadas, the sound of Africa.

"Not really, it will be quite a wrench," said Jane sadly.

The pilot introduced them to the tall Captain.

"Mr and Mrs Gunning, I would like you to meet Captain White, Sergeant Wilson and his men are part of his unit. He would like to hear any information you may have."

In their eagerness to laud the sergeant and his men, Jane and Peter held up the departure for about fifteen minutes. They were winding up their tale when from over the hill, beyond the store, three villagers appeared running strongly, shouting and waving. The pilot made a move towards his precious helicopter saying, "let's get out of here, it looks like more trouble!" But the captain waited until the breathless villagers arrived.

"Ah, baas!" They cried. "One, two soldiers, *maningi indaba*! Big troubles!" Captain White spoke to them quickly in Shona and they pointed back the way they had come.

He turned to the pilot and said. "Two wounded soldiers are just over that ridge, they are in bad trouble. You wait here!" He was off at a fast trot. Jane scrambled for her first aid kit and with Peter at her side carrying a captured AK they made off after the captain. The captain slowed down as he reached the turn of the track at the top of the hill realising that he could be running into an ambush, that this might be a trick. But he was convinced of the native's sincerity. Indeed, they were ahead of him showing the way. So it was that the three of them rounded the bend together and throwing caution to the winds dashed headlong to engulf the two shattered, semi-conscious men into their care. Roy, seeing the captain reaching out for him and not recognising the man, struggled to raise his rifle, which the captain gently pulled from his grasp. His hand reached for his knife, which he drew halfway from its sheath, then slowly he collapsed into the dirt.

CHAPTER TEN

Sergeant Wilson moved quickly and silently, in spite of his wound, and was soon at the spot where he had seen Chaka disappear. The trail was easy to follow because of the blood-stained leaves that had been brushed in passing and the considerable number of droplets sitting, oily, on the dry dust.

Chaka had made no effort to hide his passage and the trail led upwards into the dry rocky maze of defiles and gullies cut by wind and water over countless centuries. About a mile further on at a high ridge that afforded a clear view back down the trail, he came to a place where Chaka had obviously rested and spent some time attending his wound. Blood-soaked bandages and pieces of cut away cloth were scattered around and a small puddle covered with buzzing flies bore witness to the severity of the injury.

Sergeant Wilson's leg was by now throbbing incessantly, every step becoming progressively more painful and he marvelled, with grudging admiration, at Chaka's tenacity. He knew that soon Chaka would have to make a stand and the advantage was with him. He could choose his own ground and his own time and possible ambush sites were without limit. If he kept on following Chaka's tracks it was inevitable that he must walk into a trap. There was no possible way he could guard against it. He crouched for a long while in the shadow of the rocks, so motionless that a lizard crawled out of a crack between a pile of stones and ran across his foot to disappear in short dashes into the roots of a dry cactus plant six feet away. Finally the sergeant picked up his rifle and crossing to the other side of the gully he climbed up to the rim.

He worked his way between the jumble of eroded rock and brush with some difficulty. Soon he could see down into the next defile. It was as he suspected, very similar to the one he had just left. He knew that if he crossed that one there would be another, and another, kilometre after kilometre. Radiating outward from the centre of the mountain like a fan, each one with its tumble of rocks, in between which clumps of desert brush battled for existence and short dry grass, shrivelled in the heat of day, holding tenaciously to life awaiting the mercy of infrequent rain.

He watched as a small dung beetle not more than two centimetres long struggled with enviable determination to roll a ball of dried dung up an incline towards its nest. Standing on its front legs it pushed with its back legs, juggling like a circus performer to keep it balanced. But the ball proved intractable and overriding the beetle rolled back about a metre and a half. This never daunted the beetle and it scurried back and started again.

Ten out of ten for perseverance, thought the sergeant, but what a prize. He dropped down about twenty feet from the crest and made his way along the sloping side, the slope unfortunately putting extra strain on his injured leg. He consoled himself with the thought that Chaka was worse off than he. Although the thought cheered him somewhat it did nothing to alleviate the pain and he gritted his teeth as he drove himself forward.

About two kilometres further on he climbed once again to the ridge where he had a good view of the gully he had left, and standing behind a screen of rocks he carefully scrutinised every inch of the valley. He spent a good ten minutes waiting for any telltale signs of movement, there were none. Withdrawing carefully below the ridge he plodded on.

The slight rest, surprisingly, had not eased his wounded leg and he gritted his teeth as he limped along doggedly. Loose stones partly hidden in the stunted yellow grass caused him to slide sideways, twisting his leg cruelly. Soon his head began to thump in rhythm to his pulsating leg and his whole body ached with the effort of favouring his injuries.

The sun was now low in the sky, the shadows drawn out like long grasping fingers that seemed to flow over the rocks and undulating ground as they elongated. His need for rest was becoming an obsession but the thought of his quarry ahead drew him onwards like a magnet.

Again he carefully worked his way up to the crest of the ridge to where he could see into the other valley. Nothing! He considered going down to check the ground for tracks or any sign of Chaka's passing but decided to carry on for another hour, when darkness would descend making further progress impossible. Edging his way down from the crest where he would be visible to his adversary, he stood for a moment looking ahead into the wild trackless vastness and a sigh escaped his tautly compressed lips.

He was about to move on when a sparkle of light caught his eye. He gazed in the direction for a full minute before he caught it again, just above the bank of a gully where it twisted before climbing into the mountain proper. He continued his painful journey along the lower ridge.

Half an hour later he rounded the bend and saw, about a kilometre away, a small waterfall no more than two metres across where the water, captured in some mountain lake, overflowed and drained away into the arid lowland. During the rainy season it probably formed part of a considerable flow that would run on until it reached the Zambezi, by way of a series of normally dried out riverbeds. Now however, it meandered barely a kilometre or so before it was sucked into oblivion by the thirsty veldt.

He dropped down to a point amongst the rocks about a half a kilometre from the falls, where small pools of water hesitated before their suicidal dash to nowhere. He carefully studied the bush-studded sides of the hills on either side as he plodded on. He saw a herd of wild goats standing on a rocky promontory in the distance and heard baboons barking on the rocky peaks. Once there was a clatter of stones and loose earth behind him causing him to spin around in alarm, but it was only part of the natural process of levelling off the high places and filling in the low. He could see where it had broken loose, the scar fresh upon the face of the cliff.

Reaching one of the lower pools he sat down, removed his socks and shoes, and sliding himself to the edge of a flat mossy rock immersed his feet gratefully into the icy water. Rolling up his camouflaged trousers he slowly lowered his leg until the wound was covered. The hot skin cooled immediately and within five minutes, the pain had numbed sufficiently for him to start easing off the bandage, which had stuck fast. Gripping his leg with both hands on either side of the wound he pressed hard, twisting from side to side until it opened and puss oozed thickly from both sides. He kept it up until the blood flowed freely, letting the running water wash it thoroughly. Unwrapping a sterilised pad and bandage that all security forces were obliged to carry, he cut the pad into two pieces, applying half to each wound and bandaged them tightly.

Ten minutes later, his water bottle full, he started up the valley.

He had only taken a couple of paces when he saw a lumbering shape limp out of a side gully making for the pool at the foot of the waterfall. It was Chaka. He was in obvious pain and seeking the same relief as the sergeant. Caught by surprise he watched as the man disappeared behind a cluster of rocks about four hundred metres away. The ground between them was bereft of cover and to have attempted to outflank him by climbing the side would have courted disaster.

He braced himself against a large boulder and lined up his FN. A few minutes later he watched as Chaka limped towards the pool. Twice he nearly pulled the trigger but his line of sight was through a gap in the rocks and a clear shot never offered itself. He realised that the point to which Chaka headed was completely screened from him and cursed long and bitterly. As a clear shot was impossible he decided the second best objective, to stop Chaka getting the relief he needed. So the next time he caught a flash of movement he loosed off a shot that zipped between the rocks, buzzing angrily as it spent itself in the distance.

The shot sounded deafening in the enclosed valley, echoing time and time again being thrown back off the mountain sides, making the air itself vibrate. The effect on Chaka was startling. He hurled himself backwards into thicker cover, his scrabbling hands and legs flailing, oblivious to the pain on his wounded thigh. Birds lifted off hidden ledges and soared into the air shrieking their protests at this invasion of their sanctuary.

Wilson smiled grimly to himself as he loosened off another shot, seeking to find a gap, hoping that a ricocheting bullet would find its target. He held his fire and waited. Chaka would have no idea where his attacker was hidden; possibly thinking his enemy was working his way towards him. Ten minutes passed before he saw any sign of life, then he noticed movement about a hundred metres further up the valley and smiled again as he fired after the retreating figure, keeping him away from the water and hastening his flight.

Forsaking his cover he hurried across the open ground, keeping the outcrop that Chaka had recently vacated between them. Reaching his objective he discovered that the black man had disappeared once more into the vast rock strewn jumble of the foothills.

Darkness had now descended and the sergeant decided to hole up near the water, ensuring that Chaka would be denied its comfort. It was a long, cold night. The sergeant pressed himself into a slight hollow at the base of a large rock, the weathered stone overhanging about a metre above his head. Having had no chance to check it out before darkness fell he hoped that other inhabitants of this bleak land had not sought the same sanctuary. The area abounded in scorpions, poisonous spiders, cobra and mamba, to name a few. Even the lowly Matabele ants that emitted a powerful stench when crushed or tormented could soon render the most promising haven untenable. He raked a ridge of sand, dry leaves, and grass to partially cover himself and lay on his side, his back to the still warm rock, facing the waterfall.

For some time he lay motionless letting the tension drain slowly from his body. His leg was throbbing dully and his head ached. After a while a rumble in his stomach and the pangs of hunger reminded him that he had eaten little since leaving the game camp. Reaching behind his head, his hand burrowed into his pack and withdrew a large stick of biltong. Before being dried this would represent about five hundred grams of meat, now it had shrunk to half its size but still contained all the concentrated nutrients of the original. Without bothering to slice it he chewed slowly, tearing pieces off with his teeth and savouring the rich spicy flavour.

He woke several times during the night. Once the soft scuff of a hoof on rock caused his grip to tighten on his rifle, but he relaxed again as the weak glow of moonlight reflected off the twisted horns of a small herd of kudu drinking daintily at the pool.

Just before daybreak he eased himself out of hiding and flexed his muscles, very much like a leopard, stretching arms and legs whilst tensing the muscles to their fullest. Then under cover of darkness he walked quietly down to the pool where he splashed his face with the cold water and drank deeply.

Retrieving his pack he moved up the gully about half a kilometre, taking extreme care not to trip or dislodge any stones on the way. Each foot paused slightly before full weight was placed on it. Finding cover amongst some stunted bushes he sat and waited patiently for the sun to rise.

As the sky lightened he moved deeper into the cover of the

sparse bush; all the time his eyes raked up and down the length of the stream, from where the cascading water had carved a shallow basin in the soft rocks, along to where it tumbled its way down the twisting length of its course. Chaka must get water soon and to do so he would have to expose himself. The sun rose and its warmth chased the chill from his body. He watched as game, oblivious to his presence, stepped hesitantly down to the water to slake their thirst, seemingly poised and ready for instant flight. He watched as a chameleon on a branch above his head snaked out its heavy tongue and lassoed an unwary butterfly that fluttered pitifully as it was coiled down to the gaping maw.

Several hours passed with no sign of any other human life. But still he sat, motionless. Only his eyes moved, roving continuously up and down the river scanning the rocky sides of the ravine, watching and listening for birds lifting off the trees alarmed by the lumbering passage of an injured man. Nothing.

By midday he was beginning to despair and his attention began to wander. He watched a buzzard high in the air soaring in great circles. Its wings hardly moving as it rose in some thermal current, or perhaps in a standing wave off one of the mountain sides. As he followed its course it moved over his right shoulder and hovered high over where the waterfall broke through the cliff edge, two hundred metres above his head.

Suddenly he was intensely alert and he cursed himself. Chaka, for it could be none other, was outlined against the sky making his way towards the water. Picking his way painfully between the rocks and shrub, his agony was obvious even at that distance.

Sergeant Wilson clambered to his feet, a tearing pain shooting up his groin as the bandage tore away from the dried blood on his leg. He considered a hasty shot in spite of the range, but even as he raised his FN his target moved out of sight. He studied the towering cliff behind him and could see something which had escaped his attention in the poor light of the previous evening. To the left about a kilometre away, a track started from the ravine floor and twisted its way with many turns and convolutions, up the cliff face. It was obviously a game track, ill formed and tenuous, often precarious, and he marvelled at the tenacity and strength of his quarry, obviously a worthy opponent.

He cursed himself again for his oversight in not checking more carefully. He had been so sure that Chaka, in his condition, would not attempt to escape but would make a stand and fight for the right to the water that he had blinded himself to any other possibility.

Once again he set himself to clear his mind of self-condemnation and anger, to overlook his pain and hunger, and to make a hurried reappraisal of the changed situation. Chaka now had several hours start on him. All the ground made up over the previous days had now been lost. But worst of all the advantage of controlling the vital water had slipped through his fingers. He now had to follow Chaka up an exposed track where all the advantages lay with his quarry. In addition to that he had to leave the comfort of his proximity to the life-giving water and hope to be able to wrest the right to water from an enemy well entrenched. Their positions were now completely reversed.

He squinted his eyes against the sun's dazzle and slowly, very carefully checked every foot of the cliff. Dismissing the game trail as obviously suicidal, he concentrated his attention to the right of the waterfall. After ten minutes or so his area of possibility had been whittled down to a spot about four hundred metres away on the other side of the stream, where a heavy rock fall had created a steeply jumbled slope, difficult to ascend but not impossible. He wished, not for the first time, that he had brought his binoculars. Above the slope a large fissure in the rock angled upwards at approximately sixty degrees to a point about twenty metres from the top. From where he stood the crack appeared to be about a metre wide and a minimum of half a metre deep. He thanked his father, a keen mountaineer, for the many excursions into the Nyanga and Chimani Mountains on rock climbing outings. Heights had never bothered him, but the thought of a two hundred metre climb up that slope with a leg that threatened to collapse at any second was far from pleasant.

He shouldered his pack and crossing the stream picked his way to the foot of the slope. He soon ascertained that he would need both hands free to stand any chance of reaching the top of the tumbled mass of talus at the base, to the point where the oblique cleft originated. His rifle, like all the security forces' weapons, had long ago had the sling removed. Even the metal fastenings had been dispensed with. This was to ensure the least chance of entanglement when patrolling in dense bush and also guaranteed that the weapon would be carried at the 'ready' position and not slung casually over the shoulder.

He removed the pack from his shoulders and taking his knife cut a slot through the canvas flap. Through this he jammed the barrel. Then ensuring that the round was removed from the breach, he tied the trigger guard tightly to the strap of the pack with several thicknesses of bandage. Replacing the pack he began to climb.

The rocky parts were the easiest, but in several places earth alone formed the face of the slope, studded in a desultory way with shallow rooted shrubs that provided little in the way of substantial handholds. Several times he slipped back a metre or so, only to be brought up short by a rocky projection centimetres from disaster.

By the time he had reached the relative security of the fissure he was bathed in sweat and the wounds in his leg were bleeding steadily where the bandage had been torn aside. He jammed himself into the gap and drank deeply from his water bottle whilst the fitful breeze cooled his perspiring body.

Rested, he began his ascent up the tortuous fracture.

The first forty metres proved to be fairly easy going for a reasonably able rock climber. Twice he had to swing himself out over the abyss, fingers and toes searching unerringly for holds, as he worked his way around a rock fall to press himself back into the fissure on the other side with grateful relief. Once when climbing almost vertically up a short chimney he came face to face with a snake. He did not recognise the species but it was not unlike a black mamba. It was poised, motionless, in between the rock strata at the back of the slot. Its glistening forked tongue flicked in and out as it sensed the degree of danger. The sergeant froze to instant immobility and the two of them gazed across the half-metre space, each awaiting the other's move. The snake was the first to break, sliding sideways deeper into cover where it observed the sergeant's slow passage with coldly watchful eyes. As he pulled himself out of the chimney and back into the fault he let go his pent up breath in a rush of relief. He doubted if the snake was deadly, but it paid to show all snakes a good deal of respect. It must have been a male he thought, he smiled to himself as he recalled Rudyard Kipling's 'Female of the species' …

When Nag the basking cobra hears the careless foot of man,
He will sometimes wriggle sideways and avoid it if he can.
But his mate makes no such motion where she camps beside the trail.
For the female of the species is more deadly than the male.

Before long the rough rock had worn away the material from both knees and the constantly abraded skin began to leave bloody blotches to mark his progress. He tried using the tips of his toes whilst bracing his knees away from the gritty surface, but the strain on his stomach muscles became too great. In addition his rifle knocked continuously against projections and the pack scraped the roof of the slot. He returned to his original system and gritted his teeth against the pain.

He had progressed roughly eighty metres, resting every twenty metres or so when he came to a place where the roof of the fault narrowed down to such an extent that he had to drag himself forward flat on his stomach. His pack and rifle jamming occasionally forced him to slide back a little and try again.

Eventually the gap became so narrow that he decided to remove the pack and push it ahead of him. He pushed the straps out of their buckles and leaning out of the slot shrugged the pack to his left shoulder where he could grip it. He glanced down at the yawning gulf below him, the sheer wall seemed to shimmer in the heat and he felt the beginnings of panic. Closing his eyes he grasped the pack and swung it ahead of him, and thus missed the only chance he may have had of saving his FN as it arced out into space. He stared at it in dismay as it plunged down to finally bounce, smashed and twisted, between the jumbled rocks three hundred metres from the pool.

He rested his aching head on his torn and bleeding hands. The throbbing pain of his poisoned leg pulsed in his groin and his scraped knees added their protest. He groaned as waves of black despair swamped him. It was five minutes or more before his brain started to function again. But even after that terrible blow the thought of abandoning his objective never crossed his mind and he continued to climb as his brain raced.

He finally reached the end of the fault, but a line of action had still not presented itself and he drew himself up the last twenty metres whilst his mind grappled with the problem. The crumbled rim of the cliff provided easy foot and hand holds and he raised his head warily over the edge.

Slowly and carefully he scanned the rock and tree strewn plateau ahead of him. He could see the point where the waterfall began its long cascade to the valley below, a light spray hovered on the wind that surged fitfully over the rim. He could follow the river's twisting course by the patches of greener shrub and trees that drew sustenance from it. The deeper green contrasted sharply with the yellowed bush and seared grass that waited patiently for the first rains of the season.

To his left he could just make out the point where the game trail broke through the rim to fan out into a dozen tracks that lost themselves to view amongst the rocks. In order to watch the trail Chaka would, of necessity, have to be close to the cliff face. The game trail was so narrow that to try to bring his AK to bear from above Chaka would have been forced to lean far out from the edge, a most precarious position. With his injury that would not be possible. It therefore followed that he would probably position himself a couple of hundred metres to the right of the point where the trail crossed the rim. This would be approximately two hundred metres to the left of where the sergeant crouched. He concentrated his attention on that area.

An hour passed; another half an hour. Then a small buck stepped hesitantly up the trail and moved warily towards the stream. As it approached a cluster of rocks half way between the trail and the water it paused, its head questing from side to side, ears pointing inquisitively; indecision showed in its every movement. Then with a flash of its white tuft of a tail it leaped sideways into cover and disappeared from view.

'So that's where you are Chaka,' thought the sergeant. Crawling forward on his stomach he pulled himself into the shelter of a clump of thorn trees and shrub.

Removing his knife he cut a young sapling off about one and a half metres above the ground. Then working the knife into the ground around the root, whilst he pulled and twisted, he managed to remove the bulbous clump from which the sapling sprouted. He now had a stick just over one and a half metres long and about three centimetres in diameter, with a sizeable knobkerrie on the end. Checking that Chaka had not moved his position he set about fashioning a reasonable facsimile of an FN that, with luck, would fool Chaka from a distance and provide him with a practical weapon. Finishing at last he gave a low grunt of satisfaction as he hefted it, trying a tentative swing. It would do.

He began to move out of cover then recoiled swiftly. Moving towards the stream was Chaka, his limp very pronounced, his dragging gait a picture of extreme misery; he watched as he lowered himself to the ground and thrusting his head towards the water drank deeply. The distance was less than sixty metres and the sergeant cursed again the bad luck that had deprived him of his rifle. The target offered was so large and so close that given his FN the chase would have ended right there.

Easing himself out of cover he stood up and slowly walked across Chaka's line of vision towards the rocky hillock. He watched carefully from the corner of his eye as he deliberately exposed himself to the attack that he knew would come. His intention was to draw Chaka's fire; hoping that by so doing he would force Chaka to use up his vital ammunition.

In his hurried retreat from the ambush area Chaka had abandoned his pack and spare rounds and the sergeant reckoned that his quarry was unlikely to have more than half a magazine left. He realised that the large 'banana' mag of the AK held more than the FN and banked upon Chaka having between ten and fifteen rounds.

He was halfway towards his objective before Chaka saw him. He watched from the corner of his eye as the black man stiffened, his hand grabbing for his rifle lying in the grass behind him. The rifle swung up and the sergeant felt the sweat breaking out as he held his plodding step a few seconds longer. With nerves screaming he flung himself forward towards cover. Chaka's first shot passed close behind his shoulder, so close that he felt the disturbed air pluck at his shirt. Chaka's second shot went surprisingly wild as the sergeant leaped behind the rocks. 'Obviously not at his best,' mused the sergeant. 'He could have fired three or four rounds in that time!'

He moved towards a gap in the rocks where he was again

exposed. Chaka's AK was pointing straight at him, obviously anticipating his passage. This time his reaction was instantaneous and frenzied. Knowing that he had pushed his luck too far, his body stiffened in protest at the expected slamming pain, as he threw himself into a bone-cracking dive. Surprisingly no bullet came and he lay in the dirt collecting his thoughts and thanking his maker for the reprieve.

Either Chaka's reactions had been slowed to a remarkable degree or, alternatively, he also was out of ammunition. The thought was a comforting one. On the other hand, it was not beyond the realms of possibility that Chaka had not been fooled by the dummy gun and was playing a cat and mouse game.

The afternoon was drawing out and the sergeant decided to find somewhere to hole up for the night and hope that some brilliant plan would formulate. He withdrew about a hundred metres, keeping himself screened from his adversary and worked his way back towards the river. Chaka would be doing no more retreating. His only hope lay in an early conclusion to this private battle before his strength ebbed to a point where he could no longer defend himself. The sergeant's position was better but not noticeably so. His leg was now swollen to twice its size, and long red fingers of poison traced their way into his groin where the glands were bunched and angry.

He ached all over and shivered continually from the sepsis that had invaded his whole body. A green boomslang, the African tree snake, undulated across the ground ahead of him making for the leafy cover of its natural habitat. With a quick leap Sergeant Wilson planted his veltskoen just behind the head, pinning it in the dust where it spat and thrashed in its frenzy. Taking his knife he severed the writhing body about six centimetres behind the head, which he kicked away from him. Slitting the still twisting body down its entire length he pared the skin back about ten centimetres. Supporting it on a rock he trapped the skinned part with his veltskoen and gripping the skin with both hands he tugged away until it sloughed off. He placed the still twisting body on the trunk of a fallen tree and sliced it into thin pieces which he tossed to the back of his throat and swallowed. What he did not eat he stowed into a pocket to eat later.

Before darkness fell he had slaked his thirst and filled his

154

bottle. Finding a good hideaway amongst the rocks he curled up and tried to sleep. His body, shaking violently with the ague, kept him awake most of the night.

He awoke as sunlight touched his face and gazed around him in consternation. For a few seconds his fevered brain failed to register his surroundings and he groped desperately to focus his mind. It bothered him to an enormous degree that his wits should fail him in that manner. His relief as memory flooded back to him was immense and he determined to conclude his business that day.

He knew he was nearing the limits of his endurance. Sickness and pain were sapping his strength to such a degree, that even his iron will would not be enough to pull him through should this contest drag into another day.

As he sat up he disturbed a whole army of ants that had infested his pocket and surrounding clothes, attracted by the snake meat that had spread its juices over a large area of his jacket. He brushed them off with a casual flick and taking out the ant-covered meat repeated his previous evening's meal. The ten centimetres or so remaining he tossed to the ants still milling around in bewilderment in the dust.

Picking up his rifle-cum-club, he began his final attack, trusting his hunch that Chaka's rifle was no better than his own. If he was wrong he would know it in a few minutes.

He moved painfully, dragging his injured leg trying to nurse it along, willing it to move. But control was sadly lacking and he progressed by tipping it sideways and swinging his body to throw the leg forward.

Reaching the spot where he had last seen Chaka he stood there reeling.

"Chaka!" He called. His voice echoed amongst the still rocks. "Chaka, you bastard. Get your fat arse down here. You can't go any further, neither can I. It's got to be here and now!"

Silence still, but he heard a rock tumble somewhere to his left. He turned in that direction.

"Chaka!" He roared again. Spittle sprayed from his lips.

From amongst the rocks emerged a swaying shape. His eyes were sunk deeply into the grey putty face. Dried blood and puss caked his trousers from waist to ankle and the sergeant could see the bloated flesh through many tears. Chaka's eyes moved to the sergeant's 'gun' and a twisted smile fluttered across the thick, bloodless lips. He reversed his AK gripping it by the barrel and lurched forward to face the sergeant in the clearing.

They moved slowly into the last act. Both were giants amongst their own people. Both were prepared to die for what they believed in. Both were superb specimens in intelligence and physique. Each had qualities that in another place at a different time might have made them friends.

Both were where they were by the exercise of courage and endurance difficult to comprehend, made possible only by a lifetime of steady indoctrination from the crooning lips of a mother as she nursed them, to the acquisition of their own peculiar values through the years. Each was sure of the right of his cause. They faced each other, clubs raised, swaying in their fatigue. They were fighting not only the opponent ahead but the raging fevers within. Neither suggested a truce, neither asked nor expected mercy. They circled slowly, each feeling for a weakness.

Physically Chaka had a slight advantage in height and weight. Their injuries were on a par now that the poison had suffused their bodies. But whereas Chaka accepted the necessity of killing the sergeant in order to escape, he did not particularly hate him.

He had cursed his single-minded adversary over the months as he had watched his gangs being whittled away and his plans and hopes ruined. But the African mind respected and appreciated strength above all else, and his admiration had tempered his hate. The sergeant, on the other hand, hated his opponent. Whilst understanding the black man's indifference to the pain of another being, mainly he admitted as a result of vast cultural differences and disparate backgrounds, he still hated. He hated him because of his dead wife and son, his mother and father, dozens of tortured villagers. He hated him for the agony of the Chesterfields and the deaths of his friends. He hated him for what he stood for, the attempted overthrow of a legitimate government by force and terror, the stirring up of racial hatred and above all for his cruelty.

As he felt his hatred welling up his strength rose with it and with an animal growl he moved in for the kill. Neither man wasted breath on screams or imprecations. The only sounds that broke the cloistered silence between the towering rocks were the clashing of weapons and the occasional primeval grunt as evolution backtracked a million years.

The sergeant's first wild swing stopped short of Chaka's injured thigh as his opponent blocked it with his AK. His second swing missed the black man's head as he swayed with a fluid motion, back from the waist. The club continuing its murderous arc threw the sergeant off balance and Chaka, recovering quickly, smashed his rifle into the sergeant's ribs. His breath exploded as several ribs cracked under the savage blow and pain engulfed him.

Moving in quickly Chaka raised his rifle, again clubbing at the sergeant's head. The blow failed to connect as the sergeant, dropping his club, moved inside the arc, his hands reaching for the thick, corded neck, his knee slicing upwards into Chaka's groin.

They both fell to the ground, dust rising all around them. Chaka's thumbs probed for the sergeant's eyes, as the sergeant twisted his head violently trying to evade them. Chaka's face began to congest with blood as his fist hammered at the sergeant's broken ribs. The sergeant pulled himself closer to his opponent shielding himself against Chaka's body. Chaka, in a desperate effort, grasped the hands that choked him and strained to break the hold. Grasping the sergeant's little fingers he wrenched outwards and drew in gasping breaths as the fingers snapped and the strangle-hold loosened. The sergeant, lying on top of Chaka, his legs splayed and locked in the dirt, sunk his teeth into the black throat and worried it. The blood filled his mouth and splattered his chin, but the jugular vein was too deep and too tough and try as he might he could not sever it.

Chaka's powerful arms encircled the sergeant's chest, his hands locked across his back and waves of nausea washed over him as his broken ribs were forced into his lungs. Reaching down he withdrew his knife and as blackness threatened to engulf him he struck deep into Chaka's side and the hold loosened. He rolled sideways drawing the razor sharp blade through the black man's intestines. Blood welled up in the sergeant's mouth and mingled with Chaka's and there was nothing to distinguish the one from the other as they both sunk into that half world between the living and the dead.

CHAPTER ELEVEN

Chaka was the first to move some ten minutes later. He had never completely lost consciousness. He strained mightily to push the dead weight of the sergeant from him. Sweat from the effort, and the pain of his wounds, collected in his eye sockets blurring his vision. He shook his head with tired anger and the sweat splattered the dust around him. With one hand gripping the spilled mass of intestines that spewed from his gaping gut, he edged himself backwards into the shade of a stunted thorn tree and propped himself against the trunk. He never felt the cruel raking of the five centimetre long spikes as blackness engulfed him and he slipped into the merciful release of unconsciousness.

The sun was high in the heavens when once again Chaka's eyes fluttered open, clearing as they rested on the sprawled body of his adversary lying in the dust a few feet away from him. He felt a vague irritation that the sergeant was not conscious.

He could hear his rasping, bubbling breathing and the occasional minor explosive cough as the sergeant's survival mechanism fought to sustain life in its unfeeling vehicle.

Flies buzzed around angrily in the still air and crawled over the blackened blood in heaving masses. Ants darted frantically from one bloody pool to another, marvelling at their good fortune. A dry heavy rattle heralded the arrival of yet another of nature's scavengers as the vultures summoned by that mysterious telepathy straddled the already overloaded branches and spilled onto the rocks around. Already they were drawing closer, their obscene shuffling hop and dragging wings tracing chaotic patterns in the heavy dust.

Chaka wondered vaguely whether the sergeant would feel that first tearing wrench as his eyes were pecked from their sockets, or if he was too far gone to feel further pain. Why did these revolting albeit necessary creatures always go for the eyes? Were they a special delicacy to be snatched before another got at them first, or was if a defensive reaction? Remove the eyes and render a not quite dead prey harmless? He made no effort to frighten them away. Their presence was inevitable. This was Africa and the vultures were the veldt's equivalent of the city's municipal cleaners. Nothing was wasted and nothing was permitted to lie long enough to rot and spread disease. Lower down, the hyenas and jackals would start the process, but up here in the mountains, the pickings were too frugal and the lesser cleaners fed without fear.

He watched with detached interest as one of the more venturesome birds lurched forward, its scraggy neck outstretched, its wicked curved beak working like scissors in anticipation. It had almost reached the sergeant when one of the more violent coughing fits racked his body, shaking his shoulders. Bright red blood spewed from his mouth where it darkened quickly as the hot sun dried it. The sudden movement scared the hovering ring of birds and sent the closest of them stumbling backwards, hideous wings lifted to clear the ground, squawking their anger.

Sergeant Wilson raised his head slowly, a clot of blood-soaked earth hung for a while to the side of his face, then tearing loose, dropped soggily back, leaving a residue clinging to the stubble of beard that covered his chin.

"Ah! Sergeant Bob Wilson!" called Chaka softly, between clenched teeth. "So pleased you can at last join me and suffer the pain that I feel. I have envied your painless oblivion. Welcome to the land of the 'just living'."

The sergeant made no reply as he hunched his shoulders, his forearms pressing into the ground to ease the pressure on his shattered chest. He swung his head slowly from side to side, much as an animal does when mortally wounded. The motion seemed to epitomise hopelessness, pain, bewilderment and an acknowledgment of the ultimate submission to the inevitable. Chaka watched with detached interest, feeling neither joy nor compassion as he felt his own life ebbing.

The sergeant slowly inched himself forward into the shade of a large rock and with careful deliberation eased himself into a sitting position, his back supported. The movement caused him to choke again and he fought against an overpowering desire to slip into blissful oblivion. He gritted his teeth and waited once again for his head to clear. The pain in his chest was almost beyond endurance, but at least he could now breath. He could see Chaka sitting opposite him, his blood soaked hands buried in his intestines, holding them in place.

"So! Chaka, you lose!"

"I think we both lose, Sergeant Wilson," he rasped. "and whereas few will mourn my passing you will leave behind a lot of heartache. Especially I should imagine, for the beautiful Miss Ferguson."

The taunt dragged a low growl from the sergeant.

"You seem to be well informed on my personal life, Chaka. Would it be imprudent at this stage of the game to ask you where you get your information?" The words were clipped and uttered between short gasping breaths.

Chaka considered the question for a moment as he seemed to drift in and out of consciousness, then said. "I don't think either of us is likely to be in a position to use any information, sergeant, so I will try to satisfy your curiosity." He paused, as a ripple of pain reflected in his fevered eyes.

"You whites amaze me," he continued, "so clever in some ways, so stupid in others. You will take on impossible odds, … forsake your comforts and live like animals when you have to. Nothing is too … difficult for you to tackle when your backs are to the wall. You have fortitude and will go to extremes of discomfort and pain in defence … of your way of life. But the moment you return to so-called civilisation, you expect … all the trappings of self indulgence. Servants to wait on you, cook for you, clean for you. You have a misplaced idea that when you buy the services of my people you buy their allegiance, their devotion. … You should know by now sergeant that money has seldom surpassed or replaced the ties of blood, especially in Africa. A black man's loyalty is always to his tribe … "

There was a break for almost a minute as Chaka fought for control.

"You deride tribalism, the scourge of Africa that prevents unity and causes wars. Yet you know as well as I that the whites are as tribally orientated as we are. Why do you think the British, the French, the Germans … are always at loggerheads. Tribalism! On a larger scale, but still tribalism … and history proves without doubt that wars in Europe have accounted for vastly greater numbers of dead in this century than all the tribal wars throughout our history … "

160

The sergeant interjected.

"I asked a simple question, Chaka ... Do you think you could give me a simple answer?" He murmured through clenched teeth. "Time is short!"

"My apologies, sergeant, I digress. To come back to your question. You may recall Joshua, the barman in your sergeants' mess?"

"Yes I know him well ... He has been with the army for years.."

"You know him well ... do you, sergeant?.. You call him 'Shorty' and make jokes about the 'little man' ... "

"He is a little man, Chaka!"

"No, sergeant, ... he is a big man with short legs, there is a difference. He is also my tribal brother ... who risks his life to supply me with invaluable snippets of information that your NCOs drop when in their cups. ... Even the fact that you feel safe discussing confidential matters in front of him is an insult ... You are saying, in effect, that he doesn't exist, that he is not there ... Your own intelligence should tell you that most people would rather have active, tangible antipathy than suffer the degrading experience of a complete nonentity."

"So he's the one is he ... "

"Yes, and the assistants in your armoury ... and stores and officers' mess too. Your whole lifestyle is ... against you, sergeant, and you will never learn. You cry out when a 'trusted' servant of twenty years opens the door to his tribal brothers. But blood is thicker than water. You never understand that the easiest way to make an enemy is to give him something ... thus making him feel indebted. Nobody likes to feel inferior, even when the action is done with kindly intent." Chaka stopped talking and gritted his teeth as he fought against his pain, he settled back. His once ebony face a strange grey, as if the black was leaching out. Then he seemed to feel less pain as a relieving numbness invaded his body.

"Even so, Chaka ... even allowing for your legions of informers, you're finished ... your invincibility destroyed ... and your gangs dispersed and you are dying!" The effort sent the sergeant into a paroxysm of coughing and Chaka waited for him to recover.

Chaka shook his head slowly.

"No, sergeant!" He said finally. "For the first time I feel sorry for you, for your naivety and ignorance ... I hate to disillusion you at this time, but in spite of this little setback the struggle will continue. Others will take my place because our struggle is born of desperation. Do you want me to continue?"

"You have the floor, Chaka, and I see no profit in lies now. I would appreciate it ... But don't take too long."

"I will be as brief as possible, but of necessity I have to go back a few years, bear with me.." He paused for a while and the sergeant watched in amazement as he fought to contain his spilling guts. He watched a glow of fanaticism appear in his eyes and his voice strengthened. ...

"I was born in a small village in Mozambique ... close to the Tanzania border. My father was the village headman and much admired. One day Portuguese soldiers came, both black and white, and after accusing my father of helping terrorists groups from the north, they shot him. ... I ran as fast as my legs would carry me and hid in the bush, the soldiers went crazy, shooting and raping ... Things have not changed much have they, sergeant?"

Sergeant Wilson did not answer, so Chaka continued.

"About three days later, very hungry and frightened, I crept back to my home, but everyone was dead. My father ... my mother and two brothers. Bodies of the people of the village lay everywhere, some partly eaten by scavengers, all fly blown and rotting. I sat amongst all that death and horror ... nearly out of my mind with grief and hunger. Two white hunters found me and took me to a mission station near Beira.

I was sent to a mission school. A guilty conscience is a mighty force, sergeant. They could not do enough for me ... Once the newspapers got hold of the story I was inundated with gifts, money, clothes and offers ranging from education to adoption."

He was quiet for a while and the sergeant thought he had fainted, but he slowly raised his head and the sergeant saw that the zeal had gone, obliterated by his pain. He made a great effort and slowly continued; his words hesitant and disjointed.

"A trust fund ... I was sent overseas on funds supplied by the World Council of Churches. My religious training was liberally laced with communistic dogma ... Later, I realised that I was

162

being brain washed but was not inclined to resist it. In all honesty, I had nothing better to take its place ... I studied at the London School of Economics. Then I went on to Oxford to study Law and Political Science ... I joined a left wing group who spent a lot of time on 'Ban the Bomb' demonstrations, yelling against police brutality, inciting strikes. Anything to undermine law and order ... " He spoke slower now as if his batteries were running down.

"You'd be surprised, sergeant, how easy it is to get people incensed with moral issues, especially if you're black. ... All whites have got a guilt complex ... students in particular are prime targets. Arouse their righteous indignation by a slight distortion of the facts, throw in a little racism ... toss in a catchy slogan or two, they soon turn into fanatics. They never considered the good that came out of colonialism. No, sergeant, they don't want to hear about that. It's not the material that glorifies the 'angry young man' image ... our cause is not fought by our own people, who tend towards slothfulness and indifference, content with their own limited betterment. It is the whites, stirred up by a few well chosen words who ... fight our battles against their own kind on our behalf, and whilst we use them gladly, we despise them for their weakness and perfidiousness ...

White women in particular, sergeant, are the easiest to con. It almost became a religion with them ... to prove their liberal mindedness, by dragging a black man into bed on every possible occasion. It reached the point of becoming an embarrassment to us ... " Chaka stopped as the sergeant cut in angrily.

"I don't want to hear your rabid sexual fantasies, Chaka ... Get to the point!" The sergeant struggled for breath, his face contorted. Chaka continued hurriedly.

"Relax! I am nearly through. After graduating from Oxford I was one of a select few sent to Moscow and Cuba for further training ... special grooming for a political posting in Africa for the final solution of the white problem.

"My role was to organise the various terrorists groups with the intention of overthrowing the white governments and installing black communistic ones ... At the same time, in the political arena, agitators all over the world would demand sanctions, the World Council of Churches would add their weight, also Amnesty

International and the Anti Apartheid League, and so on. We had many strings to our bow, sergeant ... We fought hard politically and in the field, a lot of it before my time ... we cracked the Belgian Congo, Rhodesia and Angola. We infiltrated Zambia ... and our efforts in South Africa broke Apartheid and with it white domination ... "

"Don't try to tell me that you did that for altruistic reasons, Chaka, and communism ... is as dead as the dodo."

"Again you are right, sergeant ... but over the past year or so our aims have changed. We, the owners of this continent want all the whites out, or at least subservient to us. I want us to make the decisions in our own countries."

"But you won't be there to see it, Chaka ... and with you gone the drive will go."

"My death will not even slow the tide. So.. you ... lose after all."

The sergeant started to speak but fell silent as he watched a convulsive shudder rack Chaka's body and his hands fall away from his stomach, allowing the long lines of bloody entrails to spill on to the hot sand.

"We both lose, Chaka."

He watched as the sun started its frantic dash for the horizon. He watched as the first vulture edged forward to take a tentative peck. He watched as they crowded in only metres from him, fighting over the long lines of intestines that seemed to unwind for ever. He listened to the tearing flesh and the raucous cries of the scavengers and felt the chill of night. And as darkness crowded in upon him he felt the hot rush of blood into his mouth. He seemed to hear voices as he struggled for air. Then he felt nothing.

CHAPTER TWELVE

Captain White opened the door of the debriefing room and slowly stepped inside. He gestured vaguely to those inside to remain seated and walked to the head of the room. He stood for a while deep in thought then absently picked up the cleaner and cleaned the jumble of writing from the blackboard that covered half the wall. Having given himself sufficient time to collect his thoughts, he stepped behind the lectern and gazed around at the dozen or so people seated before him.

"Good morning, Sally! Good morning, gentlemen! We'll just wait a few moments for Colonel Jameson to arrive and then we'll get started, please feel free to smoke."

He produced several pages of type-written notes from his briefcase and glanced casually through them until the door burst open and Colonel Jameson arrived, together with his own personal smoke screen, thrown up by a particularly dilapidated favourite pipe. Everyone rose to their feet and responded to his gruff "Good morning!" then settled themselves once more into their seats.

"Carry on please, Captain," he muttered and occupied himself by adjusting the angle of his pipe stem to suit his taste.

Captain White cleared his throat. "Most of you know each other, however I'll read out your names. Kindly identify yourselves to these two gentlemen from Special Branch."

He read out the names then paused and looked at each face raised expectantly in front of him. Sergeant McGrath sat huge and dominating in the centre front row. Beside him sat Sally Ferguson and the dark shadows under her eyes bore mute witness to weeks of tears and agony as hope of Bob Wilson's return faded into improbability. Her father's hospitalisation after a stroke added to the intolerable burden she carried.

Next to her sat Roy van Houston, officially still on sick leave, as was John Kelso, who sat beside him. Both were recovering slowly from their cruel injuries and had been brought back for a few hours especially for this meeting.

Behind Sally sat Sergeant Ngombe, equalling McGrath in

height and breadth of shoulder, but narrower in the hip and darker than the average African. His ebony face seemed to reflect red and blue hues. When he smiled, which, was often, his large teeth seemed starkly white against the black backdrop.

Captain White consulted his notes to refresh his memory.

Ngombe was born in Zambia but moved to Nyanga in his early teens to work on the mines. He had joined the NLI (Nyanga Light Infantry) at the age of nineteen and rose to the rank of corporal. He was a special friend of McGrath's, and the two had seen action together for many years. Two years ago he had transferred to the elite Scouts, where his exploits behind enemy lines had earned him a fearful reputation and promotion to sergeant. His knowledge of African languages was extensive and would prove invaluable.

Alongside Ngombe sat Harry King, twice a corporal but once again busted back to sapper. At a mere one hundred and seventy-five centimetres, he looked diminutive beside the black man. Having dealt with him on many disciplinary issues Captain White knew him quite well and had no need of his notes. Born in London within the sound of Bow Bells, King had followed his father's errant footsteps as a confidence trickster, burglar, forger, and would be procurer. Since his rapid and unscheduled flight from underworld gangs who appeared intent on uniting him with his two-weeks dead father his visits to various European countries had been brief and hectic. In an attempt to avoid irate police forces he had eventually joined a mercenary army being recruited to fight in what was then the Belgian Congo. His delight in licensed murder, mayhem, and pillage was total and lasting and he had proved invaluable as a mercenary in blasting open bank vaults. He had eventually arrived in Nyanga where the constraint and discipline rested heavy on his shoulders. His expertise with explosives was unequalled.

During the sorties into Mozambique and Zambia he took great delight in blowing up bridges, arms dumps, and anything else authorised by the army, yet his ready wit and constant cheerfulness ensured his popularity with his companions. His inclusion in the team, in spite of Captain White's protestations, was mainly to keep him occupied and out of the way.

Max Schroeder, sitting in the second row, was something of an enigma. He seemed to have appeared from nowhere. He had entered Nyanga from Colombia, South America, and that was as far as his background went. He never talked about himself and had no friends. In battle he was coldly efficient and showed no emotion. On special commando raids his favourite weapon, apart from his knife, was a six hundred millimetre length of wire with a handle on both ends. He had been known to creep up on a dozing sentry, slip the wire over his head, and with one sharp tug, virtually decapitate the unfortunate guard before he could move. He was almost as broad as he was tall and well muscled. An expert in close quarter combat he had soon established himself as untouchable and was generally given a wide berth. No great loss if he failed to return, thought the captain. His Sandhurst trained mind, tempered on classical battles, shrunk from the murderous host that necessity had drawn to the Nyangan cause.

Next in the line was George Bolton, solid, thickset and strong, likeable and cheerful. His large round face was sun-tanned and frequently creased in a broad grin. He carried his MAG machine gun and looped ammunition belts as easily as his companions carried their FNs. His stamina was legendary.

To one side sat two helicopter pilots and their gunners and behind them, seemingly ever watchful, were the two men from Special Branch.

"Thank you, gentlemen," said Captain White as the roll call came to an abrupt end.

"How are you two feeling now?" He nodded towards van Houston and Kelso.

"Fine, thank you sir!" They replied, almost in unison.

"So sorry to hear of your additional troubles, Miss Ferguson." Sally nodded mutely.

"Now, gentlemen!" He continued. "You all have a good idea as to why you are here. You all know of Sergeant Wilson's mission, or at least have some knowledge of it. Miss Ferguson is here because of her own very personal interest. I trust it does not prove too painful to you. You may of course leave, if and when, you so desire." The last was directed at Sally.

"Two weeks have passed since Kelso and van Houston were picked up, and up to now we have had no word from Sergeant Wilson. Several patrols of Scouts have scoured the whole area northwards of the Mavuradonha Mountains to the Zambesi and have discovered no trace of either Chaka or Wilson. However we have good cause to believe that Chaka is dead," he paused to look at Sally for a long moment, "and as much as I would like to believe otherwise, I am convinced that Sergeant Wilson perished also." He paused a second time as a deep growl escaped from Andy McGrath's throat and shifted his feet in sympathetic embarrassment as McGrath's arm went around Sally's shoulders, hugging her to him.

"I will now give you a precise account of all that transpired up to the time that we picked up Kelso and van Houston. ... and the last sight of Sergeant Wilson, as reported by van Houston, was as he disappeared into the rocky slopes of the Mavuradonha Mountains after Chaka. At that time Chaka was known to have sustained a fairly serious wound in his thigh and was losing a great deal of blood. Sergeant Wilson had a wound through his calf and a slight wound across his shoulders, he was possibly in better shape!

Now, before I go into the details of your mission, I will hand you over to these gentlemen from Special Branch who have something to tell us."

He nodded towards the S.B. men, one of whom rose and walked to the front. He unfolded a map of the relevant area and pinned it to the board.

"Miss Ferguson! Gentlemen! I would like to congratulate Sergeant Wilson and his men on what we believe to have been a totally successful job. I am sure Colonel Jameson has more to say on that subject. As you are aware we have our men planted in various camps in Zambia and Mozambique, and we are extremely pleased to report the total demoralisation of Chaka's super elite group. Survivors, and there were precious few, spread the word of their total defeats and those who haven't defected are no longer a threat to us. Our information is that not only the special camp personnel," he pointed to the map, "here, have been affected but other camps have been split up also! I may add that our group did a good job spreading the word." He smiled briefly. "So far there is absolutely no sign of Chaka and as far as we are concerned he is dead. Your job will be to confirm this, if at all possible. Captain White will brief you on that." He looked at Sally. "The sacrifice of men like Sergeant Wilson is intolerable, but believe me when I say that in successfully completing that mission he and his men have saved the lives of hundreds of white and black families scattered all over the country, possibly thousands. I can only hope that future events make it all worthwhile."

His companion rose and the two S.B. men left the meeting. Once again Captain White took over.

"Sergeant McGrath and Sergeant Ngombe, you both have very much the same record and seniority. However, as you, Sergeant Ngombe, have been seconded from the Scouts to the Commandos for this mission you will be second in command. Sergeant McGrath will have overall charge and will take full responsibility for the success or failure of the mission, is that understood?"

Sergeant Ngombe spoke. "Sir! McGrath and myself have served together for many years. There will be no problems!" McGrath nodded his assent.

"Good. With you will be Lance Corporal Bolton, Sapper King and Trooper Schroeder. Everyone of you is an expert in his own field and specially chosen for this job. Your mission is to find out what happened in those final days, to confirm Chaka's death and to find out what became of Sergeant Wilson. Should you find either of these men alive you are to do everything," he paused, "everything possible within your power to get them back to us alive."

He turned to Sally.

"Sally! As the rest of the meeting only concerns the men perhaps you would rather leave us?"

He waited a while as McGrath walked with Sally to the door. Amos Ngombe watched McGrath's face as Sally walked away. He saw clearly that his friend's feelings were not only of sympathy and he wondered anew at the strange complexities of life.

Two hours later all possible arrangements had been made and likely snags discussed. They would leave the next day at first light, in the two choppers, for the Mavuradonha Game Park, and Roy van Houston would guide them to the ambush site and Chaka's last known position before returning to base in the helicopter.

CHAPTER THIRTEEN

The lead helicopter cleared the ridge by a few feet and swept down towards what had once been the Gunning's home. The pilot checked the sideways drift and straightening up, hovered just clear of the ground. Roy van Houston, sitting beside him noted the broken doors and windows and the hordes of native villagers erupting from the building and dashing in all directions. So much for locks he thought. He pointed up behind the house where the trail disappeared into the bush and the chopper tilted and swung around with that seemingly uncontrolled motion peculiar to them.

They followed the trail for nearly half and hour, picking out its tortuous passage through breaks in the trees at first, then moving more easily across the rocky slopes and defiles that led forever upwards. Roy could identify quite clearly where the terrorist camp had been and his throat ached as he re-enacted the earlier scenes. He saw again the vigorous bulk of Bob Wilson striding out ahead and he fought against his misery, pointing mutely the direction to take. Coming at last upon the scene of the ambush in the dry river bed Roy signalled the pilot to land.

Andy McGrath was out of the chopper before the rotors had stopped, closely followed by George Bolton, both bent double as they ran to the edge of the donga. Bolton hefted the heavy MAG effortlessly, the looped bands of ammunition bouncing on his shoulders as he ran.

McGrath, without appearing to do so, watched carefully as the second machine swung in to make its landing. He had carefully studied the terrain from the air and was sure that there were no lurking bands of terrs in the vicinity. His men were reputedly the elite of their profession, although mostly unknown quantities to him, and he was still evaluating their behaviour.

George Bolton moved smartly into the jumble of rocks and set up his machine gun. One belt was laid neatly to one side, the other was in the ready position, cool and efficient, no worries there.

The second chopper touched down and Sergeant Amos

Ngombe stepped out, his rifle ahead of him. He paused to say something to the men behind him and dragging his pack moved quickly to the opposite side of the machine. Schroeder passed him at an easy jog and climbing the bank disappeared into the heavy fringe of bush. Harry King was busy stacking the rest of the packs. McGrath noticed that his FN never left his hand.

He called van Houston over and together they walked a short distance to where Roy could point to the spot where Chaka had last been sighted.

They stood for a while deep in conversation. Finally Roy returned to the helicopter and at a signal from the sergeant the two machines lifted off barely clearing the bush as they turned onto a bearing that would take them back to camp.

Silence descended once more and for the first time the men could feel the heat reflected off the stark rocks and sense the utter desolation that surrounded them. Far away in the distance the echoing bark of a baboon warned an unseen troop of the presence of the predatory leopard and a lone cicada opened a chorus from a nearby thorn tree.

They hefted their packs and set off in the general direction taken by Chaka and Sergeant Wilson. Within the rock confines of the gully the way was obvious and the patrol fanned out to cover as much ground as possible. McGrath cursed the two week delay that made their chances of picking up tracks remote, but they quested back and forth continuously like a jackal after guinea fowl, searching for any minute sign to prove them on the right track. Ahead, Sergeant Ngombe moved up amongst the rocks with a fluid motion that made light of his huge size and weight.

The tops of the rocks that edged the gully still caught the last rays of the sun, although where the men were all was in ever darkening shadows when at last McGrath called a halt and ordered camp. A site was carefully chosen amongst the rocks but no fires were lit and nobody spoke above a whisper. They settled down to await the dawn.

Sergeant Ngombe moved over to sit beside McGrath, his sleeping bag draped around his shoulders to ward off the cold mountain air of early morning.

"Andy! I think we are going about this the wrong way." He paused.

"Go on man! If you have an idea that might help spit it out. I'd be grateful."

"Ok, Andy! The way I see it we could search for weeks trying to follow a two-week old trail, it's cold Andy. We may find a broken twig or a piece of torn cotton but we'd have to be very lucky. Tracks have been washed away, or blown away, or even smeared over by game. What I suggest is that we two take Chaka and Wilson's place. Leave the others to follow up as they were yesterday. I must be able to think pretty much as Chaka did and you knew how Bob Wilson operated."

"Great idea!" Andy McGrath's spirits rose. "I'll give you half an hour start and come after you. Remember, you have a bad wound in the thigh ... "

"And you have one in your leg," continued the other. "Try to make it real, Andy. Really hunt me, and I'll do everything I can to get away."

They made their preparations carefully, ridding themselves of all extraneous equipment, bringing themselves to the same state as the two they hoped to emulate. The rest of the patrol were ordered to stay at least a kilometre behind.

"I'll give you a half hour's start, Amos," said McGrath. "Good luck! It's a good plan, I hope it works."

Ngombe picked up his rifle and moved off. McGrath smiled faintly in appreciation as he watched the tall figure, limping badly, disappear behind a rock. He glanced at his watch.

McGrath spent the next half hour 'thinking' Bob Wilson. Concentrating on the 'feel' of his wounds and how he would favour them, thinking of his tiredness and pain, his thirst and his burning hatred of Chaka. When at last he arose and picked up his FN he set off in pursuit of Chaka and only Chaka.

He had progressed barely a kilometre when, like Wilson, he realised the futility of directly following his quarry, and from the cover of a rocky outcrop he surveyed the gully walls for a place where he could climb out. He could not know that within a few hours he would see the same sparkle of light on water that had caught Bob Wilson's attention and see Sergeant Ngombe busy slaking his thirst. Such was his state of mind that he had almost raised his FN to his shoulder before full realisation came to him and he hurried down to join his friend. Amos, hearing his approach, waved him on excitedly. He pointed to the base of a stubby thorn bush where, caught amongst the thorns was a blackened field dressing partly covered by leaves and dirt. McGrath scooped it up eagerly.

"That's an army dressing. So Bob Wilson must have changed it here. Great work, Amos. We're on the right track so far." They carefully scouted the area and inevitably found the cartridge cases.

"It looks as if they had a stand up battle!" Ngombe muttered.

"I don't think so, Amos. There would have been a whole heap of cases, so far we have only found two. It's more likely he was trying to keep Chaka away from the water."

"Hell, Andy, what a nasty mind you have!" Amos grinned to his friend.

"We'll wait for the others to catch up and fan out, see if we can find out where he went from here. If we can find where Chaka was when Bob shot at him it may help you to decide his next move."

Half an hour later the rest arrived and sank down gratefully beside the water, drinking deeply and splashing necks and faces.

It was Harry King who discovered the bullet creased rocks whilst relieving his bladder. He looked up and there they were. For a few seconds their importance failed to register on his heat-numbed mind, then his excited call brought the rest running. Taking a line from Wilson's last known position they soon found the tatty shreds of cloth left by Chaka and carefully scanned the forbidding terrain ahead.

"What do you reckon, Amos?" McGrath spoke at last.

Ngombe stared at a point on the seemingly unscaleable cliffs that stretched from left to right as far as the eye could see. For a long moment he was silent.

"There is a track up the face, over there," he pointed. "I can see 'bokkies' coming down. It's pretty rough, more so for Chaka with his problems. He couldn't have done it in daylight because Wilson would have him cold. To do it at night is the next best thing to suicide. But I guess he didn't have much choice."

McGrath punched his friend lightly on the arm.

"Hell! I didn't even see it! But if Wilson followed him up there Chaka would have an easy job picking him off!"

"That's right, so there must be another way up, probably this side of the falls. Let's scout from the falls downwards a couple of kilometres. If we don't find anything, we'll try the other side."

McGrath and Bolton saw the shattered rifle simultaneously. It lay on a rocky slope, its stock split but still intact, the magazine twisted to one side. McGrath took a run at the slope and his momentum carried him near enough to make a frantic grab before he started to slip back.

"That's Bob's!" He said quietly, after a brief look. He recognised the staining on the butt. It was crescent shaped like a moon on its side with a rough star in the centre, probably an old oil stain. Bob called it his good luck sign.

"So from here on he was unarmed! That's tough, Sarge. He didn't have much chance against an armed man." George Bolton's face showed his sympathy.

"But how did it shatter like that, Andy? It must have fallen a long way." They stood and gazed upward.

"I see it but I don't believe it," muttered Sergeant Ngombe. "He couldn't have crawled up that crack, its worse that the game track."

"He was a good rock climber, he used to climb with his father!"

"He'd have to be mad too!"

Harry King was looking up at the fissure that angled brokenly upwards towards the rim way above them. "He climbed up that?" he muttered disbelievingly. "You're having me on. What sort of bloke was he?"

"A man, Harry, all man!" Muttered McGrath.

They camped close to the waterfall, sheltered from prying eyes by a jumble of rocks. McGrath looked across at Amos. He could see his eyes were wide open and he stared fixedly at the stars above. He seemed to feel Andy's eyes upon him.

"What a shame, Andy," he murmured quietly. "Men like Wilson and Chaka are hard to find these days. What a pity their guts and energies were not directed to some other enterprise." McGrath didn't answer, he couldn't.

They scaled the cliff by way of the game track, Sergeant McGrath, Bolton, and King going first whilst Sergeant Mgombe and Schroeder covered them. When they had recovered McGrath led them along the rim, easily jumping the small stream at the head of the fall and headed to a spot above the fissure. It was only a few moments before Ngombe saw the chips and shavings scattered around the severed sapling.

"Cut himself a club by the looks of it."

"More than that I think. By the pile of shavings I'd say he was shaping it, probably to look like a rifle," replied McGrath. "Spread out, see if you can find anything. We are fairly sure Chaka came up the game trail and that Bob Wilson came up over there," he pointed. "Chaka was hardly likely to move far from the water. They were both in a desperate state so the site of the final outcome has to be close. Amos and Schroeder take the other side of the stream! We'll check out this side."

They moved out. The sun was high in the heavens when McGrath heard his name being called. They crossed the stream and jogged back to where the black man and Schroeder stood.

Ngombe waved his hand to encompass the bleached and scattered bones.

"That was Chaka!" He stated flatly.

"Almost like an amphitheatre," muttered Sergeant McGrath, "how appropriate." He shivered briefly in the overpowering heat reflected from the glowing rock. "No sign of the sergeant?"

"None so far."

"Scatter out and keep looking. Check everywhere where a badly injured man could have crawled to die out of the sun. Under bushes, gaps between rocks. Don't go further than half a kilometre, he wouldn't have made it."

McGrath paused a while, his jaw muscles working.

"Don't worry, Andy. If he's anywhere around we'll find him. Let's go!" Ngombe moved away, the rest of the patrol scattering in all directions.

Andy McGrath was left alone with his personal misery. He stared at the remains of Chaka with mounting anger. The bones were scattered over a large area, already bleached by the harsh African sun and hollowed by ants and bugs. They conveyed little idea of the giant frame they had once supported. He kicked the skull hard and watched as it bounced unevenly over the hard ground, coming to rest against a rock. "Bastard!" he swore, "bastard! Bastard!"

He turned and joined the search.

For three days they searched every possible and impossible hiding place. They moved outwards in concentric circles covering and recovering the same ground until at last McGrath called a halt.

"What do you reckon, Amos? Any of you? Any bright ideas?" There was a pause, then Schroeder spoke. There were surprised glances and McGrath tried to remember if he had ever heard him speak before.

"Dar iss no sign of your frient, Sergeant, so vee must assume he got avay or vass carreet avay. Ve haff seen a few tracks vere people haff valked." His accent was strong and difficult to follow. "If he vass carreet avay the local natives veel know aff eet, so vhy done ve look for da local fillage?"

"A good idea, Schroeder, but I can't imagine there will be villages up here!"

"No, but diss mountain slobes downvarts to da Zambeesi. Da riffer can only be about seex or seffen miles avay, und dere are bount to be tribes dere. At least it is und place to start."

"What do you think, Amos?"

"Well, I don't think we can do any more up here and we have seen tracks, very old ones it's true. They head generally north-west. I'm in favour. We're already close to Mozambique."

They started down from the mountain at first light hoping to cover most of the distance to the river before the ferocious midday heat sapped their energies. However, so difficult was the terrain, that it was mid afternoon before they saw the green track of the mighty Zambesi as it cut its life giving swathe from Lake Kariba to Chinde in Mozambique, where it stains the Mozambique Channel for over a hundred square miles with its rich mud. At the same time they spotted the kraal.

The village rested its back against the rocks, and bush-covered ground filled the three-quarter of a kilometre gap between it and the river. From where they stood they watched a woman, bent double, come through the dark doorway of a pole and mud kia. The grass thatch on the roof was protected in places by old polythene bags and pieces of chicken wire. She ambled slowly over to the fire and bending from the waist pushed the sticks inward to radiate outwards like the spokes of a wheel. Smoke spiralled upward and enveloped her pendulous breasts that hung like strips of well-tanned leather. She picked up a soot-covered pot and settled it firmly in the flames. Then, picking her nose she walked off into the bush.

They sat for a while watching. There were two men sitting on logs talking, a young girl hacked half heartedly at a mealie patch with a budsa and a small boy spun around on his stomach in the thick dust. Otherwise the place seemed deserted. They picked their way carefully downwards and entered the village without incident. They approached the two men, who now sat quietly, eyeing them warily.

McGrath spoke to them in the Shona language.

"Kanjan!"

"Kanjan! Baas."

They settled down to the necessary polite questions and answers before coming to the point.

"We are looking for a white man, a soldier like us. He was badly wounded. Did you see him?"

The black man's eyes flicked momentarily to his companion then focused on the dirt between his feet.

"No! Baas."

McGrath knew he was lying.

As McGrath pondered his next move. Schroeder walked behind the man. He seemed to pause a while then lunged for the man's wrist, which had been resting on the ground behind him. With a powerful jerk he pulled the man's arm up high behind his back and then pressed forward until the black slipped off the log and buried his face in the dirt. He cried out in pain and the boy sitting in the dust began to cry, the tears mixing with the slime from his nose and trickling down his chin.

McGrath reached forward, a reprimand on his lips, and then saw what had incited Schroeder's action. He grabbed the man's wrist and eased off the watch, it still had the camouflaged strip around it and it was Bob Wilson's. He changed his grip to the man's shirt and dragged him to his feet. Putting his face close to the other's, he gritted.

"Now tell us what happened to the white man!"

The villager's eyes opened with fear but he said nothing. Schroeder moved in again. There was a flash and the black man screamed as the knife cut a shallow groove down his stomach, severing his belt and allowing his voluminous shorts to cascade to his ankles. Almost in the same motion Schroeder's hand collected the man's testicles and his muscles bunched as he ground them together. The black man screamed and retched. His eyes rolled to his companion, still seated on the log unmoving. "Ah! Baas, he works for the terrorists, he will tell them I help you and all die!"

Once more it was Schroeder who moved, his arm swept in a vicious arc and the seated man was thrown backwards, his mouth worked but no sound came as the blood spurted from the severed throat.

The sergeant again started forward involuntarily but once more stopped. Their job was to kill terrorists and that was what Schroeder was doing. He turned his attention back to his prisoner, who now seemed prepared to talk all night.

It appeared that a band of terrorists had happened upon the final scene of the battle on the mountain. They had been attracted by the hordes of vultures. Their leader realised immediately the value of a Nyangan army sergeant and did all in his power to keep him alive in order to get him to a terrorist base near Lusaka in Zambia.

Arriving in the village the man had spoken for a long time into a radio and later that evening a white doctor had arrived. He did not speak good English or any native tongues. They had stayed two days and then crossed the river, taking the soldier with them. He knew nothing else. The white doctor had told one of the terrorists to give him the sergeant's watch in appreciation of the villager's help; that was how he came to have it.

The two sergeants conferred quietly for some time, then the patrol left the village and keeping under cover made their way down to the river.

They were well into Mozambique territory now and the longer they stayed there the greater were the chances of running into Mozambique army patrols, so they decided to head directly south-west and cross back into Nyanga, then move west above Supolilo. McGrath had many friends amongst the farming community in the area and the plan he had formulated necessitated some assistance. He also needed to send a report back to base and he wanted to be well on his way before the army could stop him. His intention was to get to Lusaka in the hope of rescuing Bob Wilson.

Strictly speaking within the parameters of his orders, 'You are to do everything possible to bring them back alive,' he had a free hand, but he was well aware that the colonel would baulk at a direct raid into a neighbouring country. He pondered his decision a long time, trying to decide whether or not he had the right to risk the lives of the whole patrol on what he knew was a very personal issue. However, when he put the suggestion to them their enthusiasm decided the matter.

For three days they ploughed on, the terrain becoming progressively flatter and less broken. They crossed back into Nyangan territory and headed westward north of Supolilo and came at last to the farm of Johannes van der Groen, a long time friend of Andy McGrath.

They approached the security fence warily. Johannes was the type who shot first and checked afterwards. His farm had been attacked no less than seven times, but his wife and seven sons had so far proved more than a match for the terrorists.

McGrath moved into the glare of the floodlights whilst the rest kept out of sight amongst the darkened trees. The house was in darkness, the lights being directed outward, and McGrath could not see even a chink of light. Their blackout arrangements were obviously a product of necessity perfected over the years. He placed his rifle on the ground, spread his arms wide on the wire fence and called loudly. His voice carried easily over the fifty metres to the house. A voice answered almost immediately, proof of their vigilance.

"You had better have a good story man, or you're dead!"

"It's me, Andy McGrath, is Johannes there?"

There was a short pause.

"Who did you say you were?"

"Andy McGrath!"

"Prove it!"

"I took two hundred bucks off you, you old bastard, up at Karina casino and your wife's name is Milly. You've got seven kids, you randy old bugger, and if you don't let me in I shall yell out what else you did up at Karina that weekend!"

"Hold it, Andy, I'm coming!"

McGrath grinned to himself in the darkness.

He saw the huge South African emerge into the light and caught a fleeting movement in the darkness on either side. Johannes was taking no chances, at least two of his boys were covering him and he knew that Milly would have her FN ready to come to his assistance were it required. The rest would be at windows at the rear and sides. For this and other families in the area, caution was the keynote of survival.

"I'll unlock the gate, Andy. Lock it behind you and come on up to the house."

"Fine, Johannes, but I've got a patrol with me. Three whites and a black, he's a personal friend of mine. Ok?"

"You're all welcome, Andy. Any friend of yours is acceptable here."

He unlocked the gate and moved back until the darkness swallowed him up.

The sergeant called the rest to him and they moved into the yard and waited until he had relocked the gate. With McGrath leading they moved up to the house.

They entered the darkened farmhouse and heard the door close behind them and the curtain rustle. There was a slight pause and the lights were switched on flooding the room with a warm orange glow.

The farmer grabbed McGrath's hand and McGrath marvelled yet again at the size of the man. He was well over two metres tall and weighed over a hundred and fifty kilos. His sons seemed to fill the large room and appeared destined to outgrow their father, even the twelve year old was close to one hundred and eighty centimetres. Milly barged him aside using her ample hips and he leaped aside in mock fright.

"Give me a kiss, man, it's nice to be able to do so without breaking my neck!" She threw her arms around Andy.

"I've given her seven sons and now she complains!"

The sergeant introduced them to the patrol and noticed the slight hesitation before Johannes took Ngombe's hand. His South African heritage was still strongly ingrained.

After they had washed and eaten McGrath outlined his plans and enlisted his friend's help in gathering the things they would need.

"Ag! Man! The clothes are no problem, except for the picca-ninny here." He nodded at Harry King, the smallest man in the room. "But the rubber dinghy poses a bit of a problem. Keith Lambert over the way had one that he collected from under a crowd of terrs but I don't know if it's still there. Are you in a hurry? You can stay here as long as you like. We could drive over to see Keith tomorrow."

"We want to get away as soon as we can but another day isn't going to make much difference. I have to report back to base, but I'll leave that until the last minute. By the time they find out where we are we'll be gone."

"Ag! man! I wish I were coming with you. I have the greatest regard for Bob Wilson, make sure you bring him back, mind!"

Johannes signalled to one of the boys who disappeared to return a few minutes later with mugs of beer and the conversation became more general.

Andy noticed that there were always at least two of the boys missing.

The following morning McGrath and van der Groen left the others in the barn, trying on a miscellaneous collection of shirts, trousers and shoes and set off through the security gates to the Lambert's farm.

"Keep your eyes open for freshly disturbed earth, Andy. The terrs sneak in at night and plant a couple of landmines in the track, lost some good friends that way!" Johannes gave a short laugh. "One of my pals was driving his Landrover along a track on the outskirts of his farm and as he rounded a corner he saw a piccaninny to one side with his fingers stuck in his ears. He jammed on the brakes and checked the ground ahead. Sure enough there were two mines right in the wheel ruts. The kid had seen the terrs plant them and was waiting for the big bang. The daft little bastard didn't realise that he was so close that he would have been blown to bits!" He laughed again.

"They sure can be funny sometimes, Johannes. Whenever I used to leave the farm to go on patrol I used to call Sabina, you remember her, Johannes, my cook?" Johannes nodded.

"Ja! I remember her cooking better!"

"Well," Andy continued, "I used to call her over and tell her that if everything was *mushe sterik*, very good, when I returned she would get a *bonsala*, a present. Then I went out and collared Kingston the gardener. I don't think you ever met him, the skellum. I told him the same thing. I had gone into the house to collect my rifle and ammo and was just getting into the car when he came running up. 'Baas! Can I have my *bonsala* now?' I said, no you can't you get it when I get back.' He said, 'Baas! What if you don't come back?' I said, 'Kingston, you take your chances the same as me!'" Johannes' laughter drowned out the sound of the engine. He was still chuckling as they pulled up at the Lambert's front stoep.

Andy had not met the Lamberts before. They were fairly new to the area. Keith and Judy were a charming couple and as soon as they heard what was required and why it was required, Keith dragged the dinghy out of the shed and pumped it up, repaired the leak and threw in a foot pump. They had a beer and were on their way back within an hour.

As they pulled up outside the van der Groen's house Johannes surveyed the men of the patrol strutting around in their 'civvies.'

"Geez! Andy, what a bunch of cut throats. They look worse in civvies than they did in uniform. Where the hell did you rake up that lot?"

"Don't be fooled, Johannes, everyone is an expert in his field and I need all the expertise I can get. But we will have to separate once we get over the border, as a bunch we'll be far too conspicuous."

"Ag! That's no lie, man."

During the afternoon, McGrath composed a message to base.

'Confirmed Chaka dead. Wilson badly wounded, prisoner in Lusaka. Following up.'

He transposed it into Shackle code and gave it to Johannes who would deliver it to the nearest army post in the morning.

They made their preparations carefully, practising stripping their FNs into concealable pieces and then reassembling them. George Bolton reluctantly handed over his machine gun to the van der Groen's for safe keeping, much to their delight, and in return borrowed a .38 special. He hefted it a few times self-consciously, muttered, "hell! I feel naked!" He spent the next two hours getting the 'feel' of it.

As soon as it became dark they all piled into the Landrover and headed down twisted game trails towards the Zambezi River. They were packed tight and Andy prayed that they would not run into any terrorist ambush. In addition to the patrol and Johannes, there was the eight man dinghy lashed on the roof and two of Johannes' boys who had come along to accompany their father on the way back, overriding his protestations. There was a very strong family tie under the banter and nothing would dissuade them.

About a kilometre from the river they reluctantly said farewell to the van der Groens and carrying the dinghy between them picked their way down the game track. Crossing the Zambesi proved easier than expected. They chose a spot where the river widened and where the current was subsequently slower. As they grounded on the Zambian side McGrath breathed a sigh of relief. The thought of being a sitting target for Nyangan security forces and terrorist alike had not been a particularly appealing one. They deflated the dinghy and hid it amongst a particularly thick screen of brush. They had a final briefing and headed westward towards Lusaka. When daylight came they would strip their weapons, pack them into carryalls and separating into two groups, would make their way independently to the Zambian capital.

They arranged to rendezvous in the bar of the Ridgeway Hotel in two days' time and to wait a further day for stragglers. McGrath had shared out the Zambian money he'd acquired from the van der Groens into five piles of *kwatcha* and *ngwee*. It was precious little, but once in the capital he knew where he could get more. The sergeant breathed a sigh of relief. They were now totally committed.

CHAPTER FOURTEEN

When Andy McGrath arranged to have his report relayed to base camp he could not possibly have realised the consequences of his actions. Whilst he was relaxing over a cold beer with the Lamberts, elsewhere a certain Julie Parker had finally succumbed to an irritating and highly embarrassing itch and reported to the duty doctor. She was given three days off from duty and a whole pack of pills and ointment, much to her relief. McGrath had never met her and indeed never would. Her release from duty coincided with both Colonel Jameson's absence in Katari and Sally Ferguson not being required for secretarial work. Julie Parker's duties were in the radio section of the camp which was, unfortunately, already short handed. Having little else to do Sally was detailed to help out the section and by chance it was she who recorded the relayed message from a sergeant in the Scouts, stationed just north of Supolilo.

Sally, white lipped and shaking visibly, continued her three hour shift, but her mind was on other things. Whilst she automatically recorded messages and passed on the information her mind was racing ahead. Bob was not dead, he was badly wounded and a prisoner. One moment her heart sang, the next she was gripped by deep despair. She must do something positive. Andy was risking his life and she knew instinctively that he was doing it for her as well as for Bob. She must help. When her shift finished Sally Ferguson disappeared. Nobody actually saw her leave but her suitcase was gone and she did not turn up for lunch with her friends. The guard on the gate saw a car pass but failed to recognise the occupant. Sally Ferguson was AWOL, absent without leave.

Because of the winds of change sweeping the international political scene Nyangan passport holders had become 'persona non grata' in most countries of the world. One of the very few countries which accepted the Nyangan passport was South Africa.

Mr Ferguson's appointment with the Ministry of Agriculture had involved a certain amount of foreign travel, exchanging ideas, and keeping up with the latest developments around the world.

Even his British passport became unacceptable because it stated that he was a resident of Nyanga and his passport was duly endorsed. The restrictions on his movements were irksome and harmful to the country's progress. In desperation he had taken a month's holiday and moved to Gaborone in Botswana and installed himself in a flat. A few days later he applied for residency. Whenever he travelled overseas he was seen as a visitor merely passing through Nyanga. The subterfuge, born of necessity, worked admirably. Having the foresight to appreciate that his daughter might one day be in a similar situation he had persuaded Sally to follow his example. As a consequence they both held a Nyangan passport as well a British passport depicting them as Botswana residents. With the advent of Botswana hostility towards Nyanga this outlet was choked off, but not before several Nyangans had availed themselves of the opportunity.

Sally laid her plans carefully, telling her mother that she was going to Durban for three weeks to stay with friends. Her mother was delighted, having tried unsuccessfully to talk her daughter into going away for a while in the hope that it might ease the pain of Bob's disappearance. Sally collected her passport and applied for her holiday allowance, then without further ado she caught a plane to Johannesburg where she drew money from a South African account and caught the next plane to Kenya's Entebbe airport. She booked into a local hotel for the night and early the following morning she was winging over the endless bushlands en route to Lusaka. It was not beyond the realms of possibility that Andy McGrath and his two companions trundling along on an overcrowded bus on the outskirts of the city could have seen the aeroplane as it circled over the airport awaiting clearance to land. If they had the event could have held no particular significance.

She cleared customs and immigration without incident and was soon on her way to Luanshya on the Copper Belt in a hired car. Darkness settled in north of Kapiri Mposhi, and it was after ten-o'clock at night before she turned off the Ndola-to-Kitwe road and eventually passed under the 'Welcome' archway and up the beautiful tree lined and be-flowered approach road to the town.

She vaguely remembered from previous visits, the hard work of the successive horticulturists employed by the old Roan Antelope Mines and wondered who kept it neat and tidy now. She reached the shopping centre and turned left between what had been Solanki's super store and Bovek's place and went on over the railway bridge to the private houses scattered beyond.

Once she lost her way and had to backtrack, but she eventually found the house she was looking for and drove up to the front door which opened as she picked up her bag and closed the boot of the car. A large man with a beard stood on the doorstep, a look of utter surprise battling for existence against mounting pleasure.

"Molly!" he yelled over his shoulder. "Look who's here!" He swept Sally to him in a fierce hug. Sally pushed her head into the front of his shirt and burst into racking sobs.

"Oh, Alex! I'm so miserable!"

An hour later having downed two gin and tonics, had a bath, changed and eaten a light meal on Molly's insistence, Sally was now seated in the Benson's comfortable lounge. Alex walked over to the small bar that decorated one corner of the room and mixed more drinks. "Now, Sally, tell us all about it. We won't interrupt. It must be important or you wouldn't have come all this way," he smiled. "Tell your Uncle Alex."

He was not really her uncle, in fact Molly was only distantly related, being Mrs. Ferguson's niece. Alex had been a dashing young paratrooper in the British Army when they met and married. On his discharge he had chased various apparent opportunities that had not matured and six months later was talking about rejoining the 'paras,' much against Molly's wishes. In desperation Molly's mother had written to her sister in Nyanga, and Molly and Alex had subsequently appeared on the Ferguson's doorstep and stayed with them for six months. Sally had only been a schoolgirl then and a very enduring friendship blossomed with Alex and Molly loving her like a daughter. They had no children of their own.

In Africa, Alex revelled in the space and freedom and was soon in business for himself. A year later he was offered the job as manager of a sheet metal company in Luanshya, and three years later he owned it. Ninety percent of his work was for the various mines scattered along the Copper Belt, which extended almost up to the Zaire border. Sally sipped her drink and began her story.

CHAPTER FIFTEEN

In a large timber panelled room in Milton Buildings in Katari, under a cloak of intense security, sat most of the top brass of the Nyangan army, air force, police, and Special Branch, together with many aides and a sprinkling of cabinet ministers. Amongst this illustrious gathering sat Colonel Jameson, which was the reason why he was absent when Sally went AWOL.

For two days the arguments had been fierce and vitriolic, but now all seemed in agreement and the meeting had settled down to considered discussion. The case put forward by Internal Security and Special Branch regarding terrorist concentrations along the Zambian border and the prospect of imminent massive incursions had been overwhelming. The arguments of the politicians concerned with escalation of the war, world opinion, reprisals, and so on had all been overridden and punitive strikes against various camps were in the final stages of detailed planning.

It was decided that Nyangan Air Force DC3s would drop airborne troops to secure strategic positions, the Hunters would provide air cover, Allouette helicopters would ferry in backup troops, mostly NLI. The Scouts would be taken across Lake Kariba to mop up and secure the route for returning ground forces. The army and police marine divisions would be fully employed on the Lake, transporting and guarding the troops whilst on the water. Already the necessary supplying and equipping was well advanced and all forces were on stand-by. Every man in the room realised the necessity for speed before rumours began to circulate and the enemy became alerted. The strike would be against three well-known camps and the operation would be launched in just two days' time.

Early on that morning people in towns and isolated farms on the route would gaze skywards and listen. Hearts would flutter for loved ones and fingers would be crossed for the small band of men who would be pitting themselves against overwhelming odds to secure Nyanga for its people, both black and white. Tears would be shed for husbands, fathers, and sweethearts. Old men would speak again about past battles and the younger men would plead with their parents to allow them to volunteer a year before they officially needed to. The whole country would seem to hold its collective breath and wait impatiently for the news bulletins, and finally would come the unintentionally selfish sigh of relief when the list of casualties failed to include their man.

The chosen man would crack false sounding jokes, laugh too much or sit tight lipped accordingly to his nature. On the last night he would copulate with unusual fierceness or be extra considerate and lay awake drawing strength from his woman, and his woman would feel his tension, know its reason, and cry inside.

CHAPTER SIXTEEN

Andy McGrath pushed open the lounge door of the Ridgeway Hotel. The inside was refreshingly cool. He gazed around but recognised nobody in the room. The subdued lighting failed to carry to the farthest corners. He started towards the bar, George Bolton and Harry King followed a few paces behind.

"First here by the look of it," he began. Then King jerked a thumb towards the corner and gave the sergeant a nudge.

"Over there, sarge!" McGrath gave him a withering look.

"Andy! You bloody peasant!" He ordered drinks and walked casually over to where Amos and Schroeder sat.

"Hi there! How long have you been here?"

"Just one drink's worth; take a pew!"

The three squeezed in around the table. McGrath noticed that Amos had chosen a fairly isolated spot but he cautioned the two with him to warn him if anyone came too near.

"Well, Amos, you two made it I see. I knew if I made the rendezvous a pub you would go all out to get there!" He grinned. "You didn't waste much time!"

McGrath took a sip of his beer. "Now listen, this is what I have in mind for our next move... " Amos raised his hands.

"Hold on a minute, Andy. We've already got the jump on you. We arrived here early this morning having got a lift right into town on a lorry and I thought we'd make a start. In Zambia it's an advantage to be black, there can't be many places left!" He smiled and his large white teeth caught the light and seemed to shatter the gloom of the room.

"Keep your mouth shut, Amos, you'll draw attention to us!"

"Balls! As I was saying, we had a coffee and sat and watched the police headquarters for an hour or so. Then I went in and applied to be a policeman."

"You've got to be joking!"

"No, Andy! It's true. Dat's just vat he dit!"

Andy nodded to Schroeder. "Ye gods! What happened?"

"Well they thought I'd make a first class policeman," said Amos modestly, "but I was too old to go through training school. I spoke to them for a while and one of them suggested that there might be a place in the prison service, they need big guys. Whilst I was talking to them another mean looking bastard came and joined in."

"I told them a few good yarns. They didn't seem to have much to do. After a while one of the constables pointed to the mean looking bastard and said. 'You want to join his mob. Interrogation!' Well naturally I got immediately interested and flattered him a bit; he didn't seem to have many friends. After about another half an hour I invited him to join us for a drink after he knocks off work at eight o'clock. He should be here soon."

"He'll be suspicious if he sees all of us here!"

"No! He'll be in his element telling a crowd of whites how important he is. All we have to do is get him pissed and flatter him a bit. I told him we were all working on the mines up at Mufilira and had come down here to spend some money. He's all for helping you do it."

"Hell! That's great, Amos. Beats my idea!" He turned to the rest. "Not too much to drink and watch what you say! Leave most of the talking to Amos."

"Yeah!" Muttered Harry King, "and if he doesn't come across with the goods Amos can use his voodoo on him, turn him into a frog!"

Amos grinned. "There's not much of that about now in Africa, most of it has died out, I'm glad to say."

"Don't you believe it, Amos, it's there still, below the surface and it's powerful too," said McGrath. "You take my gardener for instance. I started losing meat and beers out of the fridge, well you get used to a bit of pilfering, but it was getting beyond a joke. I called him over and accused him of stealing my meat and stuff. Naturally he denied all knowledge. I threatened to fire him if he didn't own up. I must have threatened to fire him twice a month for fifteen years. He waved his arms, '*Icona* Baas! *azeco*!' I never touched them! The next day was the same. 'No Baas! No Baas!' Well as most of you know there's a pill sold in Katari called Dr. McKenzies's Veinoids, you take them for your kidneys. About an hour after you swallow them it turns your urine a bright green. Well I took his scoff, his dinner, off the cook and told her I would give it to him myself. When she wasn't looking I stuffed about four of these pills into his dinner and covered them up with his mealie meal. When I gave it to him I again accused him and he again denied it. I said, 'Kingston, you are lying, and the next time you have a piss it will be bright green and you'll die.' He just laughed and walked away. Well, about an hour later he came dashing up. 'Baas! Baas! I stole your beers and your meat, and your sugar, and your tea. Am I going to die?' I said, 'I bloody well hope so, you bastard.'" They were still laughing when Amos stood up waving his arm.

"Hey, Patrice! Over here!"

The man who turned and headed towards them wore a light grey safari suit. His nose was high in the air and a sneer that passed as a smile deformed his mouth. Both hands were jammed into his pockets, reminiscent of some long past movie dandy. Even in the dim light his whole demeanour suggested self-conscious importance. He was a gross caricature of the self made man!

As Patrice stopped beside the table McGrath could see that his eyes were dead, which made him a mean looking man indeed.

"Patrice, meet my friends. This is Andy, George, Harry, he's English but we don't hold that against him, and Max!" He shook hands all round as they moved their chairs to make room for him. Amos beckoned the waiter and ordered drinks.

"Well, Patrice, that's a long day for you, from eight in the morning until eight at night."

"Oh! I wasn't on duty all that time. I was off from twelve to four. If we have a lot of work we carry on all night. When there's little to do we can take time off."

"What sort of work do you do?" asked McGrath casually as he handed around the drinks.

"A lot of our work is too confidential to talk about here. We evaluate intelligence reports, collect information, advise the government on reactionaries, and so on... " He tailed off giving the impression that he was the 'power behind the throne' a man with far reaching control and influence.

"Geez! That sounds like a lot of work for one man," said Amos.

"Not one man, Amos. My department is quite extensive. I merely control it. I could have you all deported tomorrow with a

191

snap of the finger." He tried unsuccessfully to snap his fingers but failed miserably and reached for his glass. McGrath laughed. "Don't do that, Patrice, have another drink instead!"

They refused to allow him to buy a drink. He did not insist too much, he merely jingled his money in his pocket but it never found its way onto the table. He failed to notice that as the rounds of drinks arrived there were always two or three glasses short. By this means Patrice was drinking two drinks to everyone else's one.

McGrath was constantly on edge, alert for the slip of the tongue that might give them away, waiting for the first searching questions that might leave them exposed. He need not have worried. Patrice was not really interested in anyone but himself and he dominated the conversation with one boring anecdote after another, all depicting his own brilliant handling of an impossible situation. They tried several times to bring the conversation around to the political situation or the interrogation of prisoners, but each time he would pause for a while and then take off at a tangent and they would have to suffer another egotistical diatribe.

The waiters had started to clear away glasses and mop up tables when George Bolton looked up and addressed what was probably only his second remark all night.

"Was you father a policeman before you, Patrice? Or are you the first in that line of business?"

"My father started off as a constable and after twelve years he graduated to plain clothes duties. He was a very clever man but promotion was not easy under a white government. It is much better now, and is your father also in mining?" he enquired.

"Oh no!" Said George innocently. "He's farming down near Undali."

It is possible that the black man would have overlooked the remark, egocentric as he was, but the stunned silence that ensued focused his befuddled attention and George's stammering attempt to cover up made things infinitely worse.

Undali? That's in Nyanga isn't it? So you are a Nyangan. How is it that you are in Zambia?" He rose to his feet and peered at them closely. "There's something odd about the lot of you," he grated thickly. "Your hair is shorter than most and not one of you have talked about mining. All you've talked about all night is my job!" "Couldn't get a word in edgeways, mate!" Harry King tried to joke, but the official was not to be sidetracked. The drink had made him even more pedantic and single minded than usual and the offered opportunity to exert his authority was overwhelming. He leaned forward over the table and stretched out his hand. "Let me see your passport, Mr. George!" He emphasised the 'mister'.

"I don't carry it around with me. It's up at the mine."

The policeman was now becoming excited and it was obvious that he was not going to let the subject drop. McGrath looked across at Amos and gave a surreptitious nod. He looked casually around the near empty room. All the staff seemed fully occupied. Nobody had noticed anything. Amos stuck his knife under the officer's rib cage and pushed gently upwards. The man started up.

"Sit! And keep your mouth shut, or you're dead!" The man sat heavily, his mouth working but no sound came. McGrath rose over him and chopped hard to the back of his neck. He caught him as he slumped forward.

"He's drunk, make it look good!"

McGrath laughed loudly as he hoisted the unconscious man to his feet. "I told you, Amos, that a white man could drink a black man under the table," he laughed loudly. Several of the waiters looked up from their work and grinned. Harry King started singing, "There's an old mill by the stream, Nellie Deeean ... " and they all stood up laughing and talking loudly.

McGrath and Ngombe supported the official between them and weaved their way to the door. A waiter hurried over entreating them to please be quiet. He grinned in reply to their shouted "good-nights" and held the door open for them.

They barged out into the night.

There was hardly anyone around and those who were took no notice. The occurrence of drunkenness was too common to make an impression. McGrath hurried them around the side of the hotel into the darker shadows.

"Harry, we need transport, a Landrover if possible. Can you arrange it?"

"No trouble at all, sarge!" McGrath overlooked the 'sarge'.

Harry King, late of London, had been on probation at the early age of fourteen for stealing cars. Amongst the gang he had mixed with, starting a car without the aid of keys was considered part of your normal education. Harry disappeared around the corner. The rest waited. Ten minutes later he still hadn't returned and their prisoner was beginning to show signs of returning consciousness.

"I wish he'd hurry up," muttered the sergeant. "This character will be awake in another couple of minutes."

"Dat's Ok, Andy, he can be put back to sleeb again!" Schroeder moved forward.

Five minutes later a vehicle drove slowly around the corner and pulled up beside them. Harry King stepped out.

"Your wish is my command sir!"

"Ye gods, Harry! Did you have to pinch a police wagon!"

"Well, sarge, I found one just around the corner, but there was only a quarter tank of juice so I ditched it. This one was parked outside the police station. They'd even left the keys in. It's full. Anyway what's wrong with giving a copper a ride in a fuzz truck?"

"Ok! Everyone in. Dump him on the floor and let's get out of here. I'll drive around the back streets until we get out of town. Tell me where your bags are stashed and we'll collect them on the way."

They drove off and half an hour later, having collected the bags, pulled off the road onto a side-track to the north of the town.

McGrath switched off the engine. "Right! Drag him out; let's get some information out of him."

They dragged the prisoner out and dumped him onto the ground. He was conscious and his superior air had been abandoned. Like most bullies he could give pain but not take it. His eyes had at last come alive and fear outstripped any other emotion.

"Now, Patrice!" began the sergeant. "We want to know all about a Nyangan sergeant who was brought here about two weeks ago. We don't have much time so if I were you I'd talk fast and save yourself a lot of agony."

"I don't know anything about a Nyangan sergeant. It's not my department!" His voice was high pitched and quavering.

Amos's boot landed in his mouth about the same time as Schroeder's landed in his groin. He screamed and doubled up spitting out four or five teeth, his hands clutched his battered testicles.

"I don't know anything!" He blubbered.

Schroeder pulled the man's hand away from his groin twisting the arm upwards and outwards. The black man was forced onto his stomach. Casually, with no emotion at all he held the arm stiff and dropped his knee onto the back of the elbow joint. There was a sickening crunch as the joint snapped. He twisted the arm.

They waited ten minutes for the man to regain consciousness.

"Now, Patrice, talk!" McGrath's voice was thick with bile. He hated torture of any kind but recognised the necessity.

"Alright, no more!" He retched into his lap. "The sergeant was delivered to us from hospital. He had been badly injured and a Cuban doctor had been treating him." He paused to cry out in pain, sweat beading his bloody face. Schroeder took a pace forward.

"I'm talking!" He shrieked. "Give me time! They hoped to gain a lot of information from him but he was *panga*, mad!"

"What do you mean, he was mad?" growled McGrath.

"He had no mind, couldn't remember anything, something to do with his injuries. So they passed him to us to do what we liked."

"And just what did you do to him?" asked the sergeant quietly.

"It wasn't me! I was only there. It was Detective Inspector Nyregona, he thought he could do what the Cubans failed to do but the Nyangan just kept going unconscious. They tried for four or five days, but it was no good. He was *panga!*"

"Where is he now, you bastard!" Snarled McGrath

"We passed him over to one of Ngomo's training camps."

"Is he still alive?"

"I don't know," he mumbled.

"Which camp and where is it?"

"He was sent to Victory Camp, about ten miles from Kapiri Mposhi. You go west along the Lukanga River. It's on the south bank."

"How many in the camp?"

"About eight hundred!"

"Any Cubans?"

"Two!"

"Is there anything else you can tell us?"

"Nothing, that's all I know." He tried to pull his shattered arm to him but the pain was too much and once again he fainted. He never regained consciousness. Schroeder saw to that.

"What now, Andy?" asked Amos quietly.

"Well you know what they would do Amos. They'd keep him around as long as they could to humiliate him. Show the terrs what a weak crowd we are. All the time they could make propaganda out of it they would keep him alive. There's one consolation. The poor bastard won't feel too much. When they get fed up with the sport they'll use him for bayonet practice."

They left the body where it lay, got into the Landrover and ran back onto the road. Whilst the rest slept McGrath drove through the night towards Kapiri Mposhi, the big railroad junction on the way to the Copper Belt. His thoughts were bitter.

Reaching the railroad he drove off the road and down the gentle slope to the river. Parking amongst the trees he settled down to snatch a couple of hours sleep.

Before the sun had risen high enough to chase the darkness from the land, McGrath shook the rest of the band awake and grabbing their bags they followed the path down to the river. The air was still chilly and curls of mist spiralled up from the surface of the water. The river was low and sluggish. Dust and leaves covered the surface in places and filled the corners where the current failed to reach. For the first four miles they followed the many tracks that paralleled the river. They met several villagers on their way to collect water or making an early start on their mealie patch. Amos invariably made the same remark and just as invariably received the same laughing reply.

"Kanjan! How far do we have to go to find fish in this river?"

"Ah! fish! There are no fish in this river, all gone long time go!"

They would laugh, pass the time of day, and wander off still chuckling.

Eventually the tracks ran out, probably man and animals alike gave the training camp a wide berth. Skirting away from the river they climbed to higher ground, always keeping under cover and making the minimum amount of noise. Without conscious thought they had slipped into the patrolling box formation. Reaching the top of a hill they approached the summit carefully.

The training camp was easy to see. A large area had been devastated for firewood and cleared roughly for firing ranges, parade grounds, and a sprawling hutment camp surrounded by a two-metre high wire fence in a poor state of repair. They obviously felt completely secure this far from the border.

They lay in the shade of a msasa tree and studied the camp for over an hour, noting the various activities, identifying the armoury, the guard house, the officers' quarters, the men's billets.

"Get the layout fixed firmly in your minds. When we hit the place tonight I don't want anyone stumbling about getting lost!" McGrath turned to Amos. "Here's what I think we should do Amos. If you have any better ideas let me know!

They will eat fairly early, probably six o'clock. The guards, such as they are, are probably changing every four hours. We'll check that out during the afternoon. We want to get away with as much night cover as we can, so I suggest we make our entry over there," he pointed, "where the wire has been pushed down. It looks as if plenty of other people use it. Harry, you and George make straight for the armoury, that's the long tin shed on the far side of the parade ground and fix George up with something more useful than that pop gun he's got. Then wire the place up so that we can blow it when we leave. Any other place you can destroy at the same time is all-right with me. We'll stay here until after dark and then make our way down to the camp. I reckon to move in at oh-one hours and be away by oh-two hours. Amos! Max and I will try to find Bob. All of you keep an eye open and see if you can spot where they are keeping him. Any questions?"

"What the hell are we going to do if we do find Sergeant Wilson, sarge? They are not going to like us blowing up their bleedin' camp. How are we going to get back home?"

"Well Harry, the way I see it is that they won't have any idea which direction we've gone or where the attack came from. We'll try to get back to Kapiri Mposhi and get transport, by-pass Lusaka, take the game trails down to Siavonga, and pinch one of the boats there to cross the Lake!"

"They are going to set up roadblocks!"

"Well, Amos, if they do set up a roadblock we'll have to crash it and take to the bush. We'll have to play it by ear. I know it's not going to be easy."

They settled down in the shade to await darkness.

George Bolton awoke from a fitful sleep and gazed through the canopy of leaves and branches at a lone cloud hanging motionless in the still air. He could hear the steady quiet murmur of voices and the sounds of the African bush. He could hear somebody chopping wood far away and the crackle of rifle fire from the range across the valley. He rolled slowly onto his stomach and gazed with distaste at the unmilitary appearance of the camp below. For ten minutes or so he committed to memory the patchwork of buildings and the relative position of key targets, then his attention began to waver and he gazed towards the blue tinged mountains shimmering in the afternoon sun. His thoughts turned to Katari and his girlfriend as he had last seen her. Her yellow swimsuit had accentuated her tan as she lay on her stomach, her bra straps, untied, had allowed him an occasional glimpse of her firm rounded breast with just a hint of a nipple exposed in the fallen cup. He spread his legs and stretched sensuously in the hot dust. Remembering where he was he glanced quickly around but no one way watching.

He again focussed his eyes on the camp below, casually at first then with mounting interest. What he had first thought to be a light coloured dog tied to a tree seemed to be the focal point of general interest. As the various groups moved from the firing range to the armoury or to one of the scattered huts they would invariably pause to gather and gesticulate.

Bolton could hear the occasional burst of laughter even at that distance. He noticed one or two bend down and pick up something from the ground and throw it at the unfortunate animal that, seemingly impervious to the torment lay curled at the foot of a tree. A group moved off and Bolton's interest was beginning to flag once more when the creature rose from the ground onto its back legs and endeavoured to stretch. It seemed restricted in its movements.

"Sarge! Sarge! Over here quick!" McGrath frowned at the sudden noise, but he reacted to its urgency with a fluid speed that made light of his bulk.

"What is it, lad, and it had better be important!"

"Down there!" Bolton pointed. "Under that thorn tree, to the left of the parade ground, before you get to the armoury. Can you see it?"

"I can see something. What do you make of it?"

"Sarge! Hell I'm sorry, sarge, but I think it's your pal. They've got him chained to a tree, he's bollock naked. I watched them for some time. They keep taking the piss out of him. He looks done in!"

McGrath raised himself and shielding his eyes, gazed for a long while. Everyone was now wide-awake and looking towards the camp.

"I think you're right, George. The bastards, the stuffing bastards!" His huge fists clenched and the veins in his neck stood out like cords.

"Easy, Andy, another few hours won't make a lot of difference, cool it man. We'll make the bastards pay for it tonight." Amos gripped McGrath's arm and pulled him down beside him on the grass. "Keep down, Andy, they can see your fat arse ten miles off!"

Just before darkness they changed their crumpled 'civvies' for their camouflaged uniforms and spent some time assembling and cleaning weapons. Just after midnight, looking like a hump-backed multi-vertebrate, with the holdalls tied to shoulders, they moved out in single file and picked their way carefully across the sparsely covered ground, to the point where the fence sagged. With hardly a pause they pushed their way through and headed towards the armoury. The casual discipline which they had studied during their vigil practically guaranteed there would be no sentry, nor was there!

"Ok you two! Get in there, don't make too much noise. You know what you have to do. Make sure you get the guardhouse. They've still got their AKs, but the rest put theirs back into the armoury when they came off the firing range."

McGrath turned to Amos and Schroeder. "Let's find Bob Wilson!" They disappeared into the darkness. King and Bolton set to work on the locked door.

They had worked their way along the line of billets and were just about to cross behind the last in line when a short sharp squeal of metal on metal came from the direction of the armoury. They froze into stillness in the darkness close to the wall. McGrath cursed quietly as they waited for any reaction, but the chatter from within continued, punctuated occasionally by deep laughter. He expelled his pent up breath and started forward.

Schroeder gripped his arm restraining him and pointed. From the rear of the last hut appeared the glow of a cigarette. Schroeder reached for his knife, but McGrath stopped the movement. "Wait!" he hissed.

They watched for a few minutes and eventually the stub was flicked in a curving arc to land in a shower of sparks as it hit the dusty earth. They saw the shadowy form rise and heard the splash of urine as the man emptied his bladder up against the wall of the hut. Then the door opened spilling light and for a second the camouflaged figure was etched in gold. Then the door was slammed shut. They cleared the last billet and headed for the thorn tree at the side of the parade ground.

"They may have locked him up for the night, Andy," whispered Amos.

"Then we'll have to search the camp until we find him."

McGrath moved forward quickly, sure footed in the darkness.

They found the thorn tree and almost fell over the huddled body beneath it. McGrath swore. "They didn't even give the poor bastard a blanket!"

He reached down and covered the man's mouth. "Bob! Bob!" He said quietly.

But there was no reply. He slid his hand down to the carotid artery and after a moment felt the faint but regular beat. The skin was cold to the touch. He shook him harder and shrank back in horror as an arm rose hesitantly to shield his head and his body coiled into a tighter ball.

"Jesus Christ! What the hell have they done to him?"

He ran his hands down the shrinking body and could feel the filthy plaster strips that still covered the injured chest. He could feel puckered skin and suppurating sores and his throat constricted at the thought of the untold agonies his friend had suffered. The right leg was tied tightly with fencing wire to a chain that was padlocked to the trunk of the tree. His exploring hands could feel the cruel tears in the skin and the caked blood that covered the wire. The wire had been twisted with pliers and they removed it with difficulty. Their hands were wet with fresh blood before it was done. The tortured body lying in dirt, surrounded by rotting bones and scraps of decaying food, made no further protest.

"I think he's unconscious," whispered Amos. "It's probably a defensive reaction that has developed over the weeks, he's taken too much punishment. Some bastards need killing, Andy!"

"Yeah! We'll get him over to the fence then we'll do just that!"

With Schroeder ahead, the two sergeants carried their injured comrade between them. They moved close to the fence and followed it until they reached the place where they had entered. They passed him gently through the gap, carried him about two hundred metres away and laid him gently on the soft earth screened by shrub. McGrath used the rope that retained his holdall to tie the injured man's legs together below the knees, then he pulled a shirt over the man's shoulders.

"Sorry about the hobble, Bob," he muttered, "but we don't want you wandering off. We've got work to do!" He turned to the others. "It's hardly likely but you never know. Let's go!" They retraced their steps to the camp.

Radios were still blaring out from at least three of the huts. They neared the armoury and approached the door. George Bolton stepped out behind them a loaded AK rifle in his hands.

"Christ, sarge! I nearly blasted you! I was expecting you to come the way you went. I thought it was a crowd of terrs coming in through the fence!"

Inside, Harry King was in his element. He had covered the single window with sacking, masked the light bulb with insulating tape and in the resulting dim glow was busy concocting his own lethal brew.

"How's it going, Harry?"

"Ok, sarge! In that can there is a 'special' for the officers' quarters!" He pointed to where an ammunition box stood. "I emptied the ammo out of it and packed it with high explosives. The H.E. is activated by that wire which is connected to a grenade wired to the top. Plant it underneath the place somewhere and run the wire out. There's only about fifty feet, so give it a hard pull and run like the clappers of hell. You've got about six seconds to get behind something. Over there is a case of grenades, good old British 'pineapples.' You can grab a fistful for the guardhouse and billets!"

"That's great, lad, what have you fixed for this place?"

"Well, I've removed the other bulb and wired it into the socket on a three metre extension. I've broken the glass without damaging the element so that it glows red hot when the switch is made and buried it in that other ammo box!"

"What's in the box?"

"Oh, all that garbage that I've emptied out of those rockets and landmines!" He grinned. "There'll be so much heat in this place everything will go up. It'll be like Guy Fawkes night. Just in case they don't switch on the light I've arranged a trip wire connected to a bunch of grenades, it will do the same job. I'll set it as we leave."

"Good work, Harry, we'll take the special and grenades and get out. Set your wire and duck out through the fence!"

"Ok, sarge, just make sure none of you come back here!"

Amos and Schroeder grabbed the special and loaded themselves up with grenades. McGrath and Bolton carried the box of grenades outside and selected about a dozen each.

They stood in a group in the deep shadow. McGrath was extremely surprised at the ease with which the operation had gone so far. The last radio was turned off and apart from the odd voice the camp had settled down for the night. The time was twenty past one in the morning and they were well ahead of the schedule he had set.

"Ok, Amos! Set your watch to mine." He held out his wrist. "You've got fifteen minutes to get set up. Is that enough time?"

"That should be plenty, Andy. We'll start the ball rolling!" They moved away, carrying the box between them.

At twenty-five to two, exactly, all hell broke loose. It started with a shattering explosion under the officer's quarters. McGrath, crouching by the wall of the guardhouse one hundred metres away was knocked off his feet by the blast and he covered his head as pieces of corrugated iron and masonry struck the ground around him. He pulled himself to his feet. His ears were ringing and felt as if they were stuffed with cotton wool. He pulled the pin from the first grenade and lobbed it through the open window above him and he could see George Bolton do the same thirty metres away. Running to the next window he tossed in another and headed towards the sleeping quarters as the multiple burst of four explosions tore the guardhouse apart. He did not look around but dragged open the nearest door and rolled another grenade along the floor.

He could hear the mounting uproar as the startled occupants, bemused by sleep, shouted frightened questions at each other. Slamming the door he headed for the next block with hardly a pause. He knew Bolton would be doing the same along the other end of the blocks. As he ran he wondered vaguely what King had packed into that special of his. He hoped Amos and Schroeder had managed to get under cover before it went off.

He reached for the next door just as it burst open and men began to pour out. He swung his FN and kept pulling the trigger. He seldom used the automatic lever considering it a complete waste of ammunition.

Several of the terrs spun to the ground and the rest fought each other to get inside again. A grenade followed them in and McGrath jumped the dead and dying and kept running. A burst of AK fire started up in the vicinity of the wrecked guardhouse and was answered somewhere off to his left. Then two FNs opened up. He could differentiate between the two rifles quite easily. He shouted to Bolton to stop firing and get out. He did not want their fire to give the terrorists any indication of the direction of their flight.

Behind him he heard the authoritative voice of a NCO roaring at his men to get to the armoury to collect their guns. McGrath smiled in approval. He almost missed the gap because of the dark. His night vision had not returned after all the explosions. Then he heard King calling, "Over here, sarge!"

He spun around and narrowly missed colliding with Bolton as they flung themselves through the gap. The rest were already waiting. Amos had a deep cut across his cheek and Schroeder was limping badly, otherwise they were all intact.

They headed off into the bush and had gone a scant one hundred metres when the armoury disintegrated into a million unidentifiable pieces. They dived for cover as the whole country-side stood out in stark relief and the scream of tortured metal rent the air all around them. Ammunition popped off and the noise reached a fearful crescendo with tracer rounds criss-crossing the sky like a filigree of red hot wasps. The pattern changing constantly was at one time beautiful and awe inspiring. In a few seconds it was over and a fearful silence descended in which every man held his breath.

It was five minutes before their tortured eyes could begin to distinguish objects around them. McGrath dragged himself wearily to his feet and galvanised the rest into action. A few yards further on Bob Wilson lay where he had been dropped. He had not moved. Although his eyes were open and staring there was no life or recognition in them, as if the owner had gone away.

They dressed Sergeant Wilson in one of McGrath's shirts and an ill-fitting pair of civilian trousers and they pulled a pair of rubber soled shoes over his cut and blistered feet.

With Andy on one side and Sergeant Ngombe on the other they made their way back along the game trails to Kapiri Mposhi. Their progress was painfully slow and as pursuit seemed non existent, McGrath sent King and Bolton ahead to steal some sort of transport, arranging to meet them on the south side of the town in case the police wagon had been spotted and an ambush set. The sun was just breaking over the horizon as they reached the rendezvous, to find Harry King cock a hoop standing beside a lorry. It had a canvas covered back.

"He's a bloody marvel, sarge. Picked the lock on the gate of a roadworks depot as quickly as I could have opened it with a key, he even locked it after he'd driven the truck out! Somebody will be scratching his head this morning!"

"Well done, Harry! It should do us fine!"

They all looked up as low flying aircraft passed overhead with a shrieking roar.

"Hell, Andy! They're Hunters, ours, they must be hitting the camps!"

"It sure looks like it!" A few minutes later they could hear the distant thump of bombs ...

"Geesus! They're pasting that Victory Camp again!"

"Poor bastards. It just aint their day is it, sarge!" Harry King shook his head sadly.

They laid Bob Wilson gently on the floor of the lorry as speculation over the Nyangan raid continued.

"Harry, you come in the front with me. Amos, you look after that lot. If we hit a roadblock we'll probably have to shoot our way out. I'll try to get through Lusaka and down to the lake, be ready for anything."

He found two pairs of blue overalls jammed under the driver's seat. They were a tight fit but would look alright from a distance. He screwed his nose up at acrid combination of rancid sweat and tar and hoped he wouldn't catch anything. He drove onto the road and pushed his foot down on the accelerator.

CHAPTER SEVENTEEN

There was a slight pause when Sally came to the end of her story.

"Well," said Alex at last. "What a fantastic story, Sally. I can understand you wanting to get involved, but you can't take on the whole of the Zambian police force!" He walked over to the bar and began mixing more drinks. "Quite a problem! Quite a man, Sally. You must be very proud of him."

"I am."

"What are your plans? Have you anything in mind?"

"No, not really. I thought I'd call in at the police headquarters and find an excuse to make a few inquiries."

Alex turned to his wife. "Do you remember that girl, Celia Morteson?"

"The one that came up from Lusaka for the wedding?"

"That's her! She works at police headquarters. Apparently, she's about the only white girl left. She started in the records office when she was eighteen. She's twenty four now. Has some sort of photographic memory. They kept her on because of her tremendous capacity for remembering where everything was. Now she's your girl. She would probably know what happened to your Bob."

"Celia Morteson," repeated Sally slowly. "Now that could be a very useful contact, Alex. Thanks a ton. At least it's a starting point."

"Yes, Sally, it's a starting point, and tomorrow I'll sound out a couple of my pals. They work for me, both ex-paras, like myself. They're good blokes always ready for a bit of excitement. We'll come up with something never fear. But right now it's time for bed. We'll all sleep on it. It usually helps."

The next morning Sally awoke to the sound of voices and the rattle of cups. She looked at her watch, almost seven o'clock. She stretched luxuriously then lay back with her eyes closed trying to think of her next move in her efforts to get to Bob Wilson. She retraced her activities over the last few days. She had not accomplished much. She was in the same country as Bob but still had no idea where he was, or indeed, if he was alive. She bit her lip as a deep ache threatened to overwhelm her. Andy and his patrol must have crossed into Zambia several days ago. She wondered where they were and wished desperately that she could meet them. Had they discovered where Bob was? Was he still alive? Was he dead? Oh dear God, not that!

She heard the soft click as the bedroom door opened and glanced up.

"Oh! You're awake, dear. Would you like a cup of tea?"

"Good morning, Molly and yes please, but I'll get up for it."

"No! Just stay where you are. I'll be driving Alex to work in a few minutes. He thinks it's pointless leaving his car tied up at the office all day in the blazing sun. I shan't be long." She brought the tea and a few minutes later Sally heard the front door close and a car starting up.

Moving quickly she crossed to the Benson's bedroom. The bedclothes were turned back to air and an ashtray stood on the bedside table on the far side. Slipping around the bed she tried the top drawer. Cigarettes, a lighter, pens, pencils, the usual bric-a-brac. She closed the drawer and pulled out the one below, moved aside a pile of hankies and removed the fully loaded Beretta pistol that was hidden underneath. She had been certain that there would be a gun. Most whites in Africa felt the necessity of some protection once darkness covered the land to cloak the activities of the lawless. She took a pencil and wrote quickly, "Sorry, Alex, but I need it. I knew you would get yourself involved and get hurt and I don't want that. Thanks for everything. Sally."

She tucked the note under the hankies and closed the drawer. Moving quickly, she dressed and stowed her bag in the car. Then she ran into the kitchen and left a note for Molly. Three hours later she was in Lusaka. She parked her car in a side street a block away from the police headquarters and gripping her bag she set out.

She mounted the steps and found herself in the charge office, a particularly austere looking room with an atmosphere to match. The brown counter that divided the room was unattractive and so tall that Sally had the distinct childhood impression of standing in front of the teacher's desk which had stood on its own plinth and had towered above her.

A seemingly disjointed constable (her mother used the expression semi-detached) ambled over and tapped a pencil on the top of a blotting-paper-less blotting pad, whilst he looked her up and down with some disdain. Before she could speak he moved away to a filing cabinet, he seemed to move to some unheard music. He thumbed the racks aimlessly for a few minutes before deigning to inquire.

"You got a problem, madam?" He managed to make it sound insulting and his eyes seemed focused on her groin. She wondered vaguely if the light was behind her and he could see through her dress. She kept her knees tightly together just in case.

"Yes please, I would like to speak to Celia Morteson if it's not inconvenient."

"Who's she?"

"I believe she works in the Records Office."

"Are you a friend of hers?"

"No, a friend of a friend!"

The constable turned to the two others sitting either side of a very cluttered desk. "Wasn't that the one deported for Anti-Zambian activities?"

"Failing to cooperate with the police, more likely!"

He turned his head aside and made a low comment that caused general laughter. Sally just caught the words, 'Namely Detective Inspector Nyregona!'

He turned back to her and told her to wait then he ambled out of the office and down a long passage. He was gone nearly twenty minutes and Sally was on the verge of leaving when he stuck his head through the doorway and beckoned with his forefinger. He was in no hurry and stopped twice to talk to friends. His slow pace irritated her. It was not too bad to follow a person who moved quickly even if you had to stride out to keep up, but trying to match his slow pace made her feel ridiculous.

She was positive that it was all done deliberately and wondered what was the reason for it.

She was shown into a carpeted office that held a desk, three chairs, and nothing else. Sitting behind the desk was a man of average size. His hair was longer than the average African's and his colour several shades lighter. He could have been handsome if it was not for his tribal scar, which appeared to have been inflicted with some casualness and ran into the lower eyelid pulling it out of shape. He motioned her to sit.

"Do take a seat, Miss, ah …?" he paused.

"Ferguson!" Sally supplied.

"Ah! Miss Ferguson. I believe you wanted to see Miss Morteson?"

"Yes, that's right."

"Why?"

"Oh, nothing important, she's a friend of a friend of mine."

"What is the name of your friend?"

"Just friends that I'm staying with in Luanshya."

"You are not residing in Zambia then?"

Sally felt herself being drawn into a web that was becoming stickier and stickier by the moment.

"No! I'm here on holiday."

"Ah! Where from?"

"Ah … Botswana!" She could feel the perspiration on the palms of her hands. "Look, if Celia Morteson isn't here I'll be on my way, I want to get back to Luanshya before dark." She started to rise.

"Please sit down, Miss Ferguson, may I see your passport?" It was not a question.

Sally fumbled in her bag. She could feel the heavy weight of the automatic and her thoughts were racing. Should she say she had left it in Luanshya? No, that would involve the Bensons. They might even look through her bag and find the weapon. She handed her passport over.

He was a long time studying it.

"You have an exit stamp here dated several years ago. Where have you lived in the meantime?"

"Oh! I was in South Africa for a while." Her throat was dry and she very much wanted a drink.

"Yes, I see that but there is an entry permit and an exit permit dated several weeks later, so you weren't there long, Miss Ferguson. Where have you lived since then?"

"England!"

"But there are no official stamps to corroborate that!"

"As a returning Briton, I didn't need them."

"Oh?"

"Look!" She said as defiantly as she could. "If there is any problem with my passport let's contact the British Consul and sort it out!"

He looked at her for a long time, tapping her passport on the desk all the time. Finally he tossed it to her side of the desk.

"If I were you I'd sort that out first thing in the morning!" He nodded dismissal.

Sally, near panic, grabbed her passport and gripping her bag rose and made for the door. The police constable moved at the same time to open the door and the two collided. Sally's bag, overloaded with the weight of the gun, flew from her hand and spread its contents over the floor. The gun clattered its way to the feet of the Detective Inspector. She tried to retrieve it but his foot hooked it towards him and reaching down he picked it up and placed it on the desk. Near to sobbing Sally scooped the rest of her things back into her bag.

"So! Miss Ferguson, you carry a gun!" Where did you get it?"

Once again she sank into the chair, she felt sick.

"Botswana!"

"So you brought it through two airport checks?"

"Yes!"

"You have a licence of course?"

"It's at home!"

"Which home?"

"Botswana!"

"Where you haven't lived for several years; very convenient." He signalled the constable to leave. She watched his attitude change and his voice become silkier.

"Stand up, Miss Ferguson!" She rose to her feet, her legs felt too weak to hold her up. Slowly and deliberately he ran his eyes over her body, his tongue darted quickly in and out. Sally was reminded of a cobra. The colour flooded into her cheeks as she suffered the insulting scrutiny.

"You realise that carrying a gun in Zambia carries a very severe penalty, Miss Ferguson? With a stroke of my pen I could have you thrown into prison for a long time. You are not in England now!"

She nodded dumbly. She remembered the Englishman who had been caught carrying a gun in Lusaka several years earlier. There had been a meeting of the Organisation of African Unity at the time. He had been thrown into prison for two years before various organisations had managed to secure his release.

"Yes, I'm sorry. It was stupid of me. It was just for protection!"

"A woman's prison in Zambia is not the best place for a white woman, you understand? There are some very tough ladies in there and the newcomers are shared out. Lesbianism is rife. You would be very popular!"

He watched as the colour drained from Sally's face and she swayed.

"Sit down, my dear ... don't upset yourself. I'm sure something can be arranged."

The message came over loud and clear.

"I don't wish to cause you harm or spoil your holiday in Zambia, but you realise I shall have to complete my inquiries. My duty demands it!"

Play his game! Her mind screamed, go along with it, you may be able to escape later.

Sally nodded mutely.

"Well we can carry out the investigation here, in which case it becomes official, or ... " he paused to flick his tongue over his lips, "we can do it at my house, then nobody but you and I will know about it. Which would you prefer, Miss Ferguson, or may I call you Sally?"

She nodded again. "Please do ... and your house will be fine." She forced a smile to her lips. "You are so kind."

"Fine, I'll just clear up, you wait here until I return. I'll only be a few minutes." He walked around the desk to where Sally sat and cupped one of her breasts in his hand.

"Don't worry, Sally, I'm sure everything will be all right!" He walked out failing to notice the shudder of revulsion that shook her body.

CHAPTER EIGHTEEN

When Molly Benson returned the first thing she noticed was that Sally's car had gone. Puzzled, she entered the house calling her name as she wandered through the rooms. Sally had left. Female-like she immediately looked for a note, which she discovered on the kitchen table. It said simply. 'Dear Molly, you are so lucky having your man. I do not want either of you involved. I am driving down to Lusaka to talk to Celia Morteson. Hope to see you this evening. Love, Sally.' She phoned Alex straight away at his office and read the note to him. "I'm worried, Alex!"

"Oh! I shouldn't worry. Sally's not a fool and Celia is probably the only one who can help her."

It was not until fifteen minutes later when she went to make the bed that she discovered the note and realised the gun was missing. She opened the drawer to get a fresh handkerchief and immediately saw Sally's name on the note. She ran to the telephone and informed Alex.

"Hell! That's not so good. I'll ring Celia and get her to tell Sally the seriousness of carrying a gun in Zambia. She could get herself into real trouble!" he found the number in the directory.

A man's voice answered.

"I would like to speak to Celia Morteson please!"

"Oh? that's not possible."

"Why is that? Is she on leave?"

"No! She was deported about a month ago!"

"What the devil for?"

"That's none of your business! Who are you and where are you calling from?"

He replaced the phone.

"Damn and blast!" he muttered then reached for the internal phone.

"Get Frank and Bill in here quickly!" he snapped.

Within ten minutes they were speeding down to Lusaka. They were fortunate to make it in near record time because of the paucity of the traffic. Alex drove straight to the police headquarters and parked on the opposite side of the street about one hundred metres away.

"What are we going to do, Alex?"

"Damned if I know, Bill. I'll just walk in and look around."

"For God's sake, be careful!"

"I will!" He walked to the steps and entered the building. He was hanging around the corridor hoping to catch a glimpse of Sally when a tall gangly constable came out of the change room.

"Were you wanting something?"

"Just seeing if a friend of mine is here, she should have been here about an hour ago."

"Ah, Miss Ferguson?"

"Yes, that's right."

"She's in the Detective Inspector's office." He looked sharply at Alex. "Wait here a moment." He stepped into the charge office.

Alex saw the look and wasted no time retracing his steps. He joined his companions in the car.

"Did you find her?"

"She's in there with the Detective Inspector. I didn't like the look of the copper who told me, so I scarpered!"

"What do we do now?"

"We'll just wait. If she's not out by five o'clock we'll contact the British Consul."

They settled down for a long wait and were almost caught out when Sally was ushered down the steps some thirty minutes later.

"That's her! I wonder where they are off to?"

He started the car and followed. The car ahead passed through the centre of Lusaka and turned off into what had once been a very select white suburb. Alex kept a discreet distance and lost sight of the car as it turned a corner. When he reached the road the car had disappeared. They cruised slowly along and were just fortunate enough to see the inspector ushering Sally through the front door of a beautiful ivy-covered villa. Its previous owner, a white politician, had been given twenty-four hours notice to quit the country some eight years previously. Most of his belongings were still in the house. They drove a short distance along the tree-lined road to where they could see across the well kept lawn and waited.

— ✦ —

"A beautiful home you have here," said Sally nervously.

"Yes, we look after our government officials in Zambia. Would you like to look around?"

"Yes, I'd like to." Her mind was racing, searching for any avenue of escape. The Inspector watched her for a while.

"I should like to point out Miss Ferguson that there are two guards outside. We find it prudent to protect ourselves. Don't leave the house without telling me first." He seemed to read her mind.

"I've ordered dinner early," he continued, "so that we can have all evening to complete our business." Once again his eyes raped her body causing her to flush with embarrassment.

A servant entered the room quietly to pull the curtains against the increasing darkness. She switched on a standard lamp in the corner of the room.

'Well versed in seductive lighting!' Thought Sally grimly. 'I'm obviously not the first'.

"Would you like a traditional sundowner drink, Sally?"

She started, her thoughts had been elsewhere.

"Ah! Yes please! Gin and tonic." 'I wonder if I can get him drunk,' she mused, then remembering her own limited capacity, she discarded the idea.

At six-thirty the servant entered to tell the inspector that dinner was ready. Sally was pleasantly surprised at the meal. Roast beef, Yorkshire pudding and three vegetables, preceded by a good soup and followed by ice cream and fruit salad. He noticed her surprised look.

"In honour of your British heritage," he smiled. The servant came with the house. She was well trained." Wine was served with the meal and he drank copiously. He was a good talker and did not need or even encourage a reply. Sally surprised herself by eating well. She had eaten nothing since the light meal the night before. The meal dragged on for nearly two hours and Nyregona became progressively more drunk and expansive. It suddenly dawned on Sally that now was the time to get information out of him. That was what she was here for.

"You must have an interesting job," she interrupted. He looked surprised at the unexpectedly friendly tone and assumed his charm was having the desired effect.

"Oh, a lot of it is routine, but occasionally we get something out of the ordinary." For the next two hours she tried desperately to show appreciation as he rambled on about various cases. They had by now moved into the lounge where the inspector sat beside her on the couch. Sally steeled herself to accept his crude advances. He occasionally slipped his hand into the front of her dress to cup her breast; she smilingly moved his hand away and led the conversation back to his work.

After a while his hand rested on her knee and slowly, as he talked, he moved his hand up under her dress. She tried to move away a nervous laugh on her lips. He gripped her wrist and his hand moved quickly across her stomach and down into her panties. He gripped her pubic hair and pulled. She cried out in pain and tried to free his hand.

"Don't forget, Miss Ferguson, that we have not completed our business yet!" He snarled.

"I know that," she stammered, trying to smile, "but don't let's rush things. We have all night. There is no hurry!" She leaned forward and rested her head on his shoulder. He seemed to purr like a cat as he removed his hand.

"You're quite right, Sally, why rush?" He smiled and walked over to the bar to replenish their drinks.

She rose and walked over to the wall that held the fireplace. It was covered with primitive weapons of all shapes and sizes. She recognised the bark quiver and quill arrows of the Bushmen and the Zulu short stabbing spear. There was even a Masai spear beautifully carved and polished.

"You like them?"

"They are beautiful, and cruel!" she replied.

"The collection was started by the previous owner. I have added to it over the years." He talked about the collection for some time, his words were often slurred and as he walked he had to spread his legs occasionally to maintain his balance.

"It's a pity that such a collection has to have cruel connotations," she replied, in answer to a question.

"Ah, Sally! You whites worry too much about cruelty. Sometimes it is necessary. Sometimes you have no choice."

"I don't believe that. I can't see the necessity at all!"

He moved ahead of her. His drink slopped over the edge of his glass. Reaching forward he picked up a four-pronged tool something like a hooked hand-rake. The points were barbed. "Take this for instance, a tool for torture. You can make a man confess to anything by the correct application of this." He had trouble pronouncing 'application'. "I wanted to use this on a Nyangan sergeant we had here a few weeks ago."

Sally swayed and would have fallen. He reached out to steady her.

"Oh, Sally! You've had too much to drink. I think it's time to go to bed!" He moved towards her.

"Alright," she whispered, "we'll go in just a moment. First tell me more about this and the Nyangan."

He laughed shortly. "You women are always the most blood-thirsty when you get going." He continued with obvious relish. "Oh, the sergeant? We couldn't get anything out of him. He had been badly wounded. It had affected his mind. We tried for a while but it was no good. I wanted to use this on him but never got around to it." He bent to replace the implement.

Sally was shaking violently. Her mind seemed to explode. She pictured Bob, her Bob, stretched out on a table or hanging in desperate pain screaming in agony whilst the fiend in front of her, who staggered and slurred his speech, had tortured a man driven out of his mind. Without conscious thought she unhooked the Zulu spear and with a sobbing cry drove it deep into the bent back. The broad blade grated on bone and she recoiled, terrified and nauseated at what she had done. The man before her tried to straighten up but the weight of the spear twisted him sideways. He tried to scream but the blood gushing from his mouth just bubbled and frothed. He lay on his side still doubled up, jerking spasmodically as he died. Sally watched dumbfounded, a scream on her lips, her hands pressed to the sides of her head. As he finally stilled she leaned forward and was violently sick.

She ran to the bathroom. The servant had been dismissed several hours ago. Running the taps she scrubbed her hands until they were red and sore, then she washed the sticky sweat from her face. Sitting on the side of the bath she rested her face in her hands and shivered uncontrollably for a while. As the spasm passed she set her mind to think coherently about her desperate position. In the lounge lay a dead inspector of detectives. Outside were two guards. They could not have heard anything or they would have been in to check up. The question was how to get away? The gun, she knew, he had brought with him. She could collect that from the bureau in the lounge. Her passport was in his desk at police headquarters. When they discovered the body they would soon deduce who had killed him, even the guards could tell them that.

She walked into the lounge her eyes avoiding the dead body lying in a pool of her vomit by the fireplace. She moved quickly to the bureau and recovered Alex's gun, at least he wouldn't be involved. The thought of violence was anathema to her in her conscience stricken state. She moved to the window that was in virtual darkness, the lamp being on the opposite side of the room, and pulled back the edge of the curtain. She could see the guard etched in silver by the rising moon. He was leaning against a tree near the front door. She knew the other guard would be at the rear. She could not bear to stay in the lounge and the bedroom conjured up nauseating visions, so she walked through to the darkened kitchen and sat at the table. Waves of tiredness swept over her as reaction set it. She rested her head on her folded arms and tried to think. Within seconds she was sound asleep.

She awoke with a start and looked at the lightening sky through the window with mounting panic. Glancing at her watch she cried out in dismay. Instead of wrestling with the problem of escaping she had slept the night away and her chances were now considerably reduced. She could see the guard rising from a garden seat, he stretched slowly and spat on the ground. He had probably slept away most of the night also. She felt tears pricking her eyes as she hurried through to the front. She started back in embarrassment at the sight of the man urinating up against a tree. It was now light enough to see the bougainvillea arch above the gate and the cars parked in the driveways of the houses opposite. Soon the guards would change or the servant would arrive from her quarters at the rear of the house. It had to be now.

Gripping her bag she started for the front door but the guard was only a few metres away. She could see him through the small porthole-type window by the side of the door. She waited; he was bound to move away soon. The sun broke over the horizon and the darkness scattered before the darting rays. Too late! 'You stupid fool' she moaned to herself, 'you should have tried earlier.' She lowered her head resignedly, totally dejected.

A shrieking roar brought her tear stained face to the window. She saw the guard staring upward, his slack mouth open in dumb amazement. Then shouting, he ran around the back calling his colleague. "It's the Nyangans! They're going to bomb the town! Get under cover!"

Sally realised that by a fantastic turn of luck, totally undeserved, a chance to escape had been given her. She grabbed the opportunity and flinging open the door ran pell-mell for the gate, her feet flying over the dew-wet grass. She heard a shout behind her and the sharp crunching of running feet down the driveway. She sobbed as she ran, her breath rasping in her throat. As she reached the gate she knew she wouldn't make it. She threw the hooped catch back, dragged at the heavy gate and slipped through just as a hand grabbed roughly at her hair drawing her back. She cried out in pain and frustration and began to sink to the ground. Then swift shapes pushed passed her and closed on the surprised guards. There was rapid shuffling and sickening thuds. She looked around.

"Oh, Alex!" she cried. He caught her in his arms and swept her off the ground.

"Get the car started, Bill. She's fainted!"

When she came to they were racing through the western suburbs of Lusaka.

"Oh, Alex!" she wailed. "I killed him. He was bragging about the way he tortured Bob and I killed him. It was horrible!"

"Try to forget it, Sally. The bastard deserved it. Just calm down we'll soon be home."

"But they've got my passport, they know who I am, I shan't be able to get out!"

"We'll think of something, just relax."

Bill drove fast, heading back to Luanshya. Alex concentrated all his faculties on the problem of hiding Sally until they could find some way of spiriting her out of the country. The big problem was the fact that she had a British passport. If she could be smuggled into Nyanga she might get away with it, but South Africa or England could not condone murder no matter what the reason. His mind raced.

They had been driving for about three-quarters of an hour. The traffic was very scant; so infrequent indeed that the advent of something passing was an occasion to take notice. In addition, in her highly emotional state Sally was noting the occupants of every vehicle that passed in anticipation of hidden danger. That was why when a covered lorry approached she recognised Andy McGrath immediately.

"Turn around!" she screamed. "Quick! Turn around!"

"Take it easy, Sally!" Alex remonstrated kindly. His immediate thought was that she had taken leave of her senses. She grabbed Bill's shoulder.

"Turn around! That was Andy McGrath. He's the Nyangan sergeant I was telling you about!"

Bill looked at Alex questioningly.

"Are you sure, Sally? Really sure?"

"Positive!" Alex gave Bill the nod.

He braked quickly and spun the car around in a tyre squealing 'U' turn and headed back. He had a dubious look on his face.

It was nearly five kilometres before they came up behind the lorry.

"Overtake him!" She cried. "There's nothing coming!"

Andy McGrath saw the car coming up behind him but took no particular notice. When it failed to pass him and kept alongside he stared down from his higher elevation at the upturned face shouting something to him and his surprise was total. He swerved off the road onto the grassy edge, almost losing control. Braking hard he brought the lorry to a dirt scattering halt banging Harry King's head against the windscreen.

"Geezus C! Sarge, what are you trying to do? Kill us all?"

In the back there were muffled cries and the back flap raised slightly showing startled men scrabbling for weapons, mouthing imprecations.

McGrath hit the ground running fast towards the car pulled up ahead. He met Sally head on and gathered her into his arms.

"My God, Sally! I don't believe it. What are you doing here? I left you in Umdali!" His face showed a comical mixture of delight, amazement and consternation.

The next five minutes was a bubbling mixture of laughing, crying, explanations, introductions and bewilderment. Andy

McGrath tried hard to make sense of everything.

"Hold on, Sally," he said at last, holding up his hand. "We'll get the details later, have you any idea how you will get back to Nyanga?" He looked at her companions. Their attitude showed plainly that they had no ideas.

"We'll think of something," muttered Alex, repeating himself.

Sally took Andy's arm. "Have you any news of Bob, Andy?"

Andy McGrath showed his surprise. In the general excitement he had completely forgotten the object of the whole exercise.

"Hell, Sally! I'm sorry. He's in the back of the truck."

"Oh, Andy!" A mounting joy suffused her face and she turned quickly towards the lorry.

Andy restrained her and pulled her back.

"Before you go to him, Sally, there's something you should know."

Her face reflected her sudden agony. "He's all right, isn't he?" she pleaded.

"Physically he's in poor shape but as he has survived this long, miraculously, he's sure to make it." He winced at her immediate pleasurable reaction. "But!" He continued. "He's had a very rough time. His injuries were so bad that they have affected his mind."

"He's not mad, is he? not permanently. He'll recover. I'll help him...."

"No, Sally, he's not mad," he cut in, "but he is mentally disturbed. In fact his memory has gone. He probably won't even recognise you."

He carried on as Sally tried to interject. "Amos thinks it's some sort of defensive mechanism that his body has developed against pain. I think that a couple of months in a good hospital will sort him out ok. But, Sally, don't expect too much right now, ok? Right off you go." He released her arms that were straining to pull away and she fled to the back of the lorry and clambered in.

Willing hands helped her and there were greetings from all sides as she knelt down beside her man. Cradling his scarred head in her hands she pressed her face to his.

"Bob! Oh Bob darling! What has happened to you?" she sobbed, her hot tears falling on his face. The blank eyes gazed at her for a long while and a puzzled frown creased his forehead. His lips moved but for a while no sound came. Then a cloud seemed to drift away from his eyes and brokenly he murmured her name. He tried to raise himself but the clouds gathered again, the curtain drew across his eyes, and he fell back.

Sally rocked back and forward, her body racked with uncontrollable misery and she cried as if her heart would burst. Schroeder stared studiously at his locked hands as the long dead emotion of sympathy touched him briefly. George Bolton stood at the rear of the truck and gazed with unseeing eyes at the black macadam roadway that stretched behind them. Amos Ngombe put his hand on her head and stroked her hair, his big black face reflecting genuine pain on her account, as an African really can.

"Now, now, baby," he crooned softly. "He's going to be just fine, don't take on little girl. He'll be chasing you 'round in no time, already you have him talking. Come on baby, don't cry, you'll spoil that pretty face of yours ... " He just kept talking quietly and slowly her sobbing ceased and she sat up, mopping her face on her sleeve. She pressed her face against Amos's huge hand and smiled her thanks.

"Sally, I don't want to rush you at all but we will have to make a move soon. We're a bit pushed for time." Andy called gently from outside.

Sally walked to the rear and looked out. "Give me two minutes to change out of this dress Andy. I'm coming with you." She clambered over the tailboard and jumped to the ground.

McGrath was appalled. "Sally you can't do that, it's just not safe!"

"Andy, I'm safer with you than I am staying here with all the Zambian police searching for me and this way Alex and his friends need not get involved; so please don't argue, I'm coming!" She spoke for a while to Harry King who pulled off his overalls.

"Glad to get out of those," he muttered. "Just like a poor man's palace, no ballroom! Ah, no offence, Sally!" But Sally was heading for the cover of the bushes. She returned a few minutes later rolling up the sleeves and accepted a short length of rope from the grinning Harry to tie around her waist.

She said goodbye to Alex and his friends and turned to McGrath. "I'll get in the back with Bob Andy. Don't worry, I wouldn't want it any other way and I promise that I won't get in the way." She smiled at the suddenly confused sergeant and as far as Andy was concerned all was well.

They pushed on fast without incident. From time to time they saw Hunter aircraft sweeping low over the hills and once three helicopters in close formation bustled noisily away to the south.

"They must be hitting other camps south of Lusaka, sarge; seems a lot of activity that way."

"Good, Harry! It'll keep them too busy to bother us."

About sixty miles south-east of Lusaka they turned off the Chirundu road onto the dirt track that lead down to Siavonga on the north bank of Lake Kariba and immediately ran into trouble. Almost blocking the road ahead of them were two Zambian army trucks. About twenty soldiers were scattered around, some sitting in the meagre shade cast by the vehicles, others in groups talking. Nearly all of them were looking down the road towards Kariba whence could be heard the distant rattle of gunfire and the deadly roar of high explosives. They never noticed the truck roaring down upon them until it was within a hundred metres. McGrath hammered the metal panel behind his head to warn the men inside and then jammed his foot down hard on the accelerator.

The soldiers evidently expected no trouble from that direction and appeared totally surprised as Andy failed to react to the signal to stop.

As it became obvious that whoever was driving had no intention of obeying the order there was a mad scramble to get out of the way. Andy aimed for the gap between the trucks and prayed it was wide enough. It was not!

There was a tearing crunch as the vehicles scraped and the door on Harry King's side was ripped off, almost taking him with it. A burst of AK fire tore through the canvas hood and they were through. From the rear came a deafening crescendo as Sergeant Ngombe and the rest opened up, scattering the soldiers in all directions, then they were spinning around a bend in the track into safety.

"Well done, sarge. That's much cooler; should have thought of it before!"

"For Christ's sake don't fall out, Harry! Just stick your head around the corner and ask Amos if they're ok."

Amos' booming voice roared out. "We're all fine Andy but you should do something about your driving!"

About two kilometres from the lake they had a puncture. The

twisted metal over the wheel arch had pressed against the tyre every time the wheel was turned sharply and eventually it had gouged through the casing.

"Blast!" Growled the sergeant. "Harry, get the spare out!"

He returned a minute later. "No spare, sarge! We're going to have to hoof it from here!"

"Shit! A fine truck stealer you turned out to be. Next time I'll take a real thief with me!"

With McGrath leading and Amos following up the rear they pressed on. Schroeder and George Bolton hurried the exhausted man along with their arms around his shoulders. From at least three different directions they could hear automatic fire and grenades exploding.

Away to the right a pall of smoke mushroomed out in the still air and the Hunters switched their attention to a point left of the track. About a kilometre from the lake the firing intensified until the air around them seemed to crackle with violence. McGrath came running back.

"Off the track! Quickly! There are about sixty terrs coming up fast!"

They threw themselves into the dense bush, disregarding the tearing thorns and whipping branches that slashed their bodies and tore at their clothes. About forty metres from the track they went to ground and hid themselves as best they could.

The terrorist band that passed would hardly have been termed a danger. Only about a third of them had rifles, the rest having discarded them in flight. They ran fast with backward glances, fear rampant on their sweaty faces. They were all very young and were obviously new recruits.

"Poor bastards, they're only kids. Someone has a lot to answer for when this war's over."

"You're right, Andy! I'm sure they don't know what the hell they are letting themselves in for. It'll take years to wean them back to being normal, decent citizens."

"That probably applies to our lads too! Amos."

They dusted themselves down and headed towards the lake, only to dive for cover again as the sound of running feet and snapping branches heralded the arrival of more trouble.

They were about to open fire when McGrath called, "Hold it!

They're ours!" He rose to his feet, calling "Over here. Hey!"

The three men spun around at the call, their guns at the ready. The men had bloody faces and one was wounded in the shoulder, he was being helped by his pal. The face of the one nearest them split into a broad grin.

"What do you know? It's Sergeant McGrath! Hey, are we glad to see you! Didn't know you were on this lark, sarge!"

"We're not. We just got caught up in it!"

"We're lost, sarge, trying to get back to the lake."

"So are we. You're going the wrong way. Where the hell did you do your training?"

"Under you, sarge!" He replied with a grin.

"Well I ought to be shot, you'd better join us."

"Our pleasure, sarge, but there are about fifty terrs behind us and they're as mad as hell. There were six of us who were separated from the mob and ran right into them. They're pretty good, sarge."

McGrath didn't ask where the other three were.

"Ok! Let's go. Harry, Max, you push on ahead with Bob and Sally and this lad," he pointed to the wounded newcomer. "We'll cover you."

George Bolton handed Sally the pistol as she moved away. "And don't be scared to use it Sally. It's you or them."

They let them get ahead about fifty metres and fanned out to cover the rear. On the right George Bolton made contact first and the rest moved around in support. The terrorists seemed to be everywhere.

Sergeant Ngombe led the two latest arrivals in an attack on a rocky outcrop where a large group had taken cover and they lobbed a couple of grenades behind the terrs. The terrorists pulled back to regroup and reappraise the situation. McGrath and Bolton harried them as they retired to a position fifty metres away.

"Come on, George! Let's get out of here!" His voice trailed off. George Bolton was not going anywhere.

They could now see the lake glistening in the fierce midday sun. About a kilometre out he could see the Marine Division boats, their 20mm cannons pounding away at some hidden target. Close to the shore a small scattering of army and police vessels bobbed in the slight chop. As they filled the boats with retreating soldiers they moved out into the lake to discharge their human cargo onto the larger craft and hurry back for more.

Again the terrorists attacked. This time a group had circled to get ahead and Harry King and Schroeder were cutting them down with calm efficiency but were slowly being driven back. McGrath saw their danger and forsaking cover sprinted to their aid; Sally was uppermost in his mind.

Amos Ngombe saw his friend of many years and many battles fall. He saw the mob make for him, their rifles raised to smash down on the injured man and time backtracked. From his throat came a mighty roar out of antiquity and a blood haze clouded his eyes. He leaped forward, firing as he ran. When the last round was spent he gripped the burning hot barrel and ploughed on. He did not feel the burns or smell the singeing flesh; he only felt the jarring shocks that shot up his arm as he crushed his opponents before him. He heard the war cries of his ancestors and his blood sang through his veins. He died with exaltation in his heart and an unholy joy on his face, and he took a lot of his enemies with him.

The men waiting in the small boats could hear the rising and falling pace of battle approaching and readied themselves. They saw a beautiful young woman burst from the trees dragging a stumbling man behind her, but they had no time to wonder. The hill behind heaved with a black horde that leaped like demons and screamed high-pitched battle cries as they flung themselves at the survivors, only to be beaten back time after time. Sally and Bob made the beach-head, blood-soaked and tired beyond imagination.

Now all the machine guns and rifles of the little fleet joined in with the cannons of the larger boats and the hill erupted into an angry hell of shrieking metal. Eager hands reached out and dragged the two in. They had great difficulty getting the exhausted girl on board, being unable to prise her hands away from the man who looked near to death.

The boats moved out of hell onto the lake, the girl holding the man close to her. The noise was ear-shattering and the water erupted into chaotic flurries around them. In line astern they picked up speed and the helmsmen weaved their boats in a desperate attempt to dodge the enemy fire. All seemed well until a random shot struck the man in the side of the head killing him instantly. Sally screamed as Bob was torn from her grasp by the force of the impact and hurtled over the side to drift behind in the heaving wake.

"Go back!" She screamed. "Go back!" She hammered on the helmsman's shoulder.

"It's no good miss, he's dead!" He shouted, trying to steady the boat. A high pitched wail rose from her throat as she leaped to her feet, fighting the bucking craft. A burst from a machine gun blazing away on the shore tore across her chest almost cutting her in half. She plummeted over the side just thirty metres from where the body of her man floated. The boat behind ploughed into Bob's body, slewing the craft to one side; the helmsman cursed as he wrestled with the wheel.

The body broke free and spun around a few times until it hit the drifting shell that had been Sally. They seemed to rest for a while as if to gather strength and then they began a slow spiral through the clear water to the cool depths of the lake a hundred metres below.

ISBN 1-41205254-8

Made in the USA